"What will I do to protect myself?"

"You?" He looked at her in surprise. "You set out through a dark forest alone to escape me. A feat that could very well have earned you death, or worse."

Rhian felt the heat of embarrassment on her cheeks. "I fail to think when I am angry."

"No. Truly?" He rubbed his forearm, bringing more heat to her face. "I find that hard to believe."

"If your sarcasm was any thicker, you'd drown in it."

"And if your nails were any longer, I'd have bled to death."

"A strong warrior like you? I doubt that."

He tapped his hand against his chest. "Ah, she thinks I am a strong warrior. My heart will burst at your kind words. I could take that as a compliment."

"Take it as you wish." Rhian sat up. "You will release me?"

"Not while I draw breath...!"

FALCON'S HONOUR

Denise Lynn

MILLS & BOON®

All the characters in this book have no existence outside the imagination of the author, and have no relation whatsoever to anyone bearing the same name or names. They are not even distantly inspired by any individual known or unknown to the author, and all the incidents are pure invention.

First published in Great Britain 2007
Harlequin Mills & Boon Limited,
Eton House, 18-24 Paradise Road, Richmond, Surrey TW9 1SR

© Denise L. Koch 2005

ISBN-13: 978 0 263 85160 1
ISBN-10:   0 263 85160 5

Set in Times Roman 10½ on 12¼ pt.
04-0207-72009

Printed and bound in Spain
by Litografia Rosés S.A., Barcelona

Award-winning author **Denise Lynn** has been an avid reader of romance novels for many years. Between the pages of books she has travelled to lands and times filled with brave knights, courageous ladies and never-ending love. Now she can share with others her dream of telling tales of adventure and romance.

Denise lives with her real-life hero, Tom, and a slew of four-legged 'kids' in northwestern Ohio, USA. Their two-legged son, Ken, serves in the US Navy, and comes home on occasion to visit and fix the computers, VCRs or any other electronic device Mom can confuse in his absence. You can write to her at PO Box 17, Monclova, OH 43542, USA, or visit her website, www.denise-lynn.com

A recent novel by the same author:

FALCON'S DESIRE

With many thanks and love to:
Doc Eva and her wonderful sense of humour,
caring ear and love of romance novels,
The Harlequin Hussies, a fountain of information
and a steady port in a storm,
Melissa, for making the second-book syndrome
an easier hurdle,
My mom, for her ability to juggle schedules
and always be there,
Tom, my best friend, my heart,
the man who shares my dreams.
Bless you and love to you all —
this one's for you. Huzzah!

Prologue

~~~~~~~~~~

Spring, 1142
Northern England

Sir Edgar, the captain of Faucon's guard, watched thin wisps of smoke from the crackling campfire curl upward to disappear into the darkness of the night.

The howl of a lone wolf, the soft snorts of nervous horses and the familiar scrape of sharpening stones plied against sword edges interrupted the silence of the surrounding forest.

Edgar and the other men circled around the fire for safety, warmth and companionship paid little heed to the night's sounds. Their full attention remained riveted to the raised voices coming from their lord's hastily erected tent.

While each of them had been scorched by the heat of Faucon's tongue at one time or another, they had never heard him raise his voice to a female. Bets were placed between the men. Would their lord hold his temper on this occasion, or would his uncooperative charge push him too far? Edgar's gold was on Faucon.

"My God, save me!"

The lady's repeated cry for help went unanswered. While her shouts set their hearts to racing, Edgar knew that none of the men would assist the woman. Her steadfast determination to do her own will instead of King Stephen's landed her in this current role of captive.

Had she come peacefully as ordered, she'd not find herself in such dire straits now. Instead, she'd fought this journey to her mother's family every step of the way. For two solid days now she'd made their lives miserable.

Edgar couldn't decide whether he admired or pitied his lord's patience. If she were his charge, she'd have felt the back of his hand by now. None would blame Faucon for doing just that.

"Unhand me!"

The sharp crack of a resounding slap caused more than one soldier to flinch as they envisioned the smack on their own face. Others peered intently into the bottom of their ale mugs. Edgar wondered how much of the brew would be required before this night ended.

"You filthy swine!"

"Enough of this madness." With a heavy sigh, Edgar rose and headed toward his master's tent.

Before he could cross the clearing, Lord Gareth of Faucon backed hastily out of the tent inspecting his arm in the light emanating from the tent. "You black-haired wench, never try something like that again."

Edgar sucked in a breath at the menace evident in Faucon's low, emotionless tone. From the corner of his eye, he saw the others freeze. All knew that deadly tone meant Faucon had reached the limit of his patience. Edgar feared for his stash of gold; in his mind's eye he saw it shrink considerably.

Gareth glanced at his stinging forearm where she'd raked her nails in an attempt to further prove her displeasure. "By God, I am bleeding!"

Enraged, he swung away from the tent to tend his arm and collided with his man, nearly knocking the two of them to the dirt.

"Milord." Edgar caught his footing first and swiftly pulled Gareth upright. "Perhaps it would be best to explain the situation to her one more time?"

"*One* more time?" Gareth looked down at his man in surprise. "You think I have not tried?" His amazement was obviously not lost on his shamefaced captain. "Repeated discussion has brought me only an aching head, stinging cheek and bleeding arm."

He stomped toward the fire and accepted a proffered wineskin. The overly fermented grape coursed a bitter trail across his tongue, then down his throat. He swallowed hard, seeking to hold back his grimace as he returned the container to its owner.

Ack. Sour wine and sour women had one thing in common—they both sought to ruin his good nature.

"Milord Faucon!"

Gareth instinctively turned toward the man's shout, only to see his captive rush around the side of his tent and disappear into the blackness of the forest.

"By all the saints' bones!" he cursed aloud. If that crafty little wench who barely came up to his chest thought for one heartbeat she would escape, she needed to think again.

Gareth and his men reached the edge of the clearing as one. Long association made spoken orders unnecessary. When Gareth motioned with a quick jerk of his hand, the men fell into a line on either side of him. They would comb the dark forest with little more than an arm's length separating them.

Surely, ten and five men working as a single unit would be able to find one obstinate woman. Gareth cursed again.

He'd vowed to deliver this wench to her kinsmen and return to the king's service within a month. What had seemed nothing more than a brief respite from war, suddenly appeared to be a quest to retain his honor and life.

Honor. Gareth swore at the memory of honor lost. He'd already besmirched his honor and his family name at Lincoln.

Even though he had only followed his overlord's orders to retreat during the battle, Gareth's guilt weighed heavily on his soul. They'd left the king unprotected, enabling the enemy to capture and imprison Stephen for months.

Aye, he'd find the woman all right. It was not as if he had a choice. If he failed his sire this time he'd find his head adorning the battlements at Windsor—compliments of King Stephen.

Another, smaller gathering of men watched in silence. When the woman escaped, all glanced toward their leader. He waved them back with one hand. Their time would come. She would be theirs eventually.

It was best for now to remain hidden—unseen. Let

Faucon catch the wench. Much satisfaction would be gained in taking her from him.

Time and preordained fate was on their side.

Chapter One

"*Choose.*"

Rhian jumped. The hissed order seemed to come from the very air itself. She nearly dropped the ewers of ale she carried to the great hall.

Choose what?

After rebalancing her load, she swallowed her dread before heading toward the boisterous gathering.

She had not the leisure to contemplate the uneasy feeling that started as little more than a prickle at the nape of her neck and now swept through her limbs like a cold winter wind. She'd not been at Browan Keep more than a few days and had no intention of staying long enough to discover what caused her unease.

This was naught but a temporary haven—one that grew more unpleasant by the day.

And now a formless voice urged her to choose.

Choose what?

"Wench!" The shout came from one of the men in the hall. "Be quicker with that ale." An order that had been repeated many times this evening.

The act of serving those gathered in the great hall bothered her little, but the drunken louts yelling and pawing at her set her teeth on edge. There was no master at Browan. She'd heard that the lord here had died in a hunting accident and King Stephen had not yet replaced him.

The man who was temporarily in charge had no control over the others, so they ran wild. Their entertainment had risen to the level of a game this night. The more they drank, the more they sought to pull her down onto their laps or to fondle her as she walked by.

While some of the other girls welcomed these advances, she had no wish to be compromised in such a manner. She'd already compromised herself enough by coming here alone in the first place; she'd not make her lot worse.

After slamming one ewer down onto the table with a heavy thud she spun away, successfully avoiding a pair of reaching hands. Slurred curses met her maneuver.

No sooner had a smile of success twitched at her lips, when she plowed into a smelly, beefy wall of flesh. "Ah, my beauty, you show excellent taste." The man wrapped his arms about her waist, securing her as neatly as herring caught in a net.

Rhian mumbled her own curse. She'd spun too far— right into the snare of yet another lout.

When he sought to lean in for a kiss, the stench of his breath gagged her and fueled her need to escape. She nearly growled before rapping a pitcher of ale against his head.

The earthen jug shattered, leaving her holding naught but the handle. Either his skull was made of rock, or he was too far in his cups to notice, because he did not fall, nor did he release her. At least not at first.

In expectation of the worst, her heartbeat slowed and breathing ceased. The man's reaction appeared to happen in a manner slower than normal. He shook his head and smiled briefly before letting his arms drop to his sides as he sank like a leaf borne on a breeze to the floor.

Without pausing to see if he still breathed, Rhian ran from the hall into the smaller entry chamber. Boisterous hoots of laughter followed her hasty departure.

As more men entered through the great doors, she bolted past them with a prayer on her lips that the small footbridge connecting the keep to the partially finished inner wall would still be in place. Her prayer answered, she skirted quickly across the moveable planks to the wall.

A chilled wind buffeted her as she raced blindly along the torch-lit wallwalk seeking a way to reach the bailey below. Night had fallen and she was nothing more in this keep than a lowly serving wench who had no business on the wall. She wished to avoid being dragged back into the overcrowded hall. The men would only make sport of her and the other girls would torment her unceasingly.

The tromping of horses' hooves stopped directly below her. "Hail!"

Rhian froze midstep. Her breath and heart skipped over each other. She clenched her fists at her sides and closed her eyes. She'd no wish to see the danger heading her way.

"You, girl!"

The approaching danger didn't sound extremely threatening. She took a fortifying breath of air before peering over the walkway to look down at the man in the bailey.

Rhian shielded her eyes from the torch he held aloft. The light flickered across his face. His voice had belied his age. This *man* was little more than a boy. A squire perhaps? Since he was not demanding to know why she was on the wall, it was apparent he was not from Browan.

"Ah, she does hear."

When the men around him snickered, Rhian backed away from the edge of the walk. By himself he didn't appear threatening, but the men with him seemed a scurvy lot and they were many years beyond boyhood.

"I mean you no harm. Just a question if you please."

The pleading in his voice beckoned her to answer. "I've no time for idle chatter, be quick."

"Is your master in residence?"

"Now how would—" She caught herself. "Nay. There is no master of Browan."

"Surely someone is in charge."

"Sir Hector holds the keep until the new master arrives." Why was he asking her this question in the first place? Had he not inquired at the gates?

"Excellent. My lord will be pleased to hear that." He tugged on his horse's reins as if to leave, then turned back to her. "Tell me, are Browan's gates always unguarded?"

Rhian gasped softly. That explained why this lad questioned a serving wench. What type of imbecile was in charge of the haven she'd found? While it did explain why nobody had noticed her on the wall, it did not explain why during a time of unending battles a sane man left a keep open for conquest. She realized she was taking too long to answer and fumbled for a suitable response. "I...I know not. Perhaps the guards were occupied elsewhere."

If she valued her safety, she knew that her time at Browan was at an end. She'd leave at first light. Surely there was another keep nearby. One where a residing lord valued his property and those inside the walls.

The young man nodded. "Perhaps you are right. I will bid you good evening then and thank-you for your kind assistance."

Without waiting for him and his companions to leave, Rhian paced back and forth, resuming her search for a ladder down to the bailey.

The man cleared his throat. When she peered at him, he motioned toward her left with the torch. "If you are searching for a ladder, there is one a few feet that way." Without another word he turned and left. The men with him followed, their renewed snickers echoing off into the night.

To her great relief, she managed to descend the ladder without breaking her neck. The relative quiet of the inner bailey provided her a small semblance of peace as she crossed the nearly dark yard. The two guards she encountered paid her little heed other than asking her business at Browan. It amazed her that once she admitted to being a serving wench, they waved her on her way. Aye, she'd have no regrets about leaving in the morning. She had no intentions of being in residence when this keep fell to the next enemy who approached.

Rhian leaned against the wall of a shed to rest awhile before heading back to the kitchens. Hopefully, Hawise would not notice her absence until she found a measure of ease for her weary body and mind. While the tenseness left her body, her mind ran in circles. How could she have come here like this? Had she lost her sense of reason? Why did she not just stay with—?

"You! Girl!"

Why did everyone call her *girl?* Did the clothes she'd filched fit that poorly? She quickly realized her mistake—being seen as nothing more than a *girl* was a blessing, not a curse.

After banishing her unwarranted ire, she looked up at the man on horseback. In the near pitch blackness of the night, she could see little more than his silhouette. Since he was mounted and accompanied by a host of others, she assumed he was of some consequence.

"Aye, milord?"

"Where are the stable boys? Why has no one come to greet us?"

Disoriented by the night, Rhian looked toward what she hoped was the stable before replying, "There is a great celebration this night. Perhaps all are making merry in the hall."

"'Tis a poor excuse."

While she could not discern his features, something in his voice rang familiar, causing the hairs on the back of her neck to rise. *Nay, she'd been careful to hide her trail. He'd not have been able to find her so quickly.*

Confident of the abilities learned at her father's side, Rhian shook off her concern. All men of rank spoke with that same arrogant tone, making their names and faces blend into one indiscernible toad in her mind. Instead of replying with the barb that wanted to escape her lips, she said, "It is the only excuse I can offer, milord."

"Why are you out here alone on such a dark, moon-less night?"

A question she should have asked herself before seeking refuge in a dark, nearly deserted bailey. Still, her safety was none of his concern. "I just wished for a breath of air. The hall is overcrowded and airless."

"And have you had your air?"

"Aye."

"Then return to the keep where it's safer."

She jerked away from the shed at his order. Of all the arrogance she'd witnessed this night, he was by far the most…the worst…the—

He moved his horse closer until she could feel the beast's hot breath on her cheek. She shrank away from what felt like the fires of hell. "Unless you seek to dis-obey an order, go. Now."

The urge to argue with him was nigh on irresistible. His demeanor, his tone of voice, his haughty bearing all begged for a good tongue-lashing. Rhian knew that she was more than capable of performing the task. But it would raise suspicion if a serving wench addressed her *betters* in such a manner.

Suspicion she could not risk.

It took one deep breath to swallow her wayward urge. And another three to become as close to meek and sub-servient as she could.

"Oh, nay, milord, one such as I would never seek to disobey an order." She winced at the tone of her own voice.

He ignored her tone. And ordered again, "Go." In a voice so low, so sinister that it brooked no further argument.

* * *

"*Choose.*"

"Choose what?" Rhian knew her voice was tinged with anger, but cared not. She was tired of being told to choose, tired of being told to do anything. What was she to choose? She glanced around the smoke-filled kitchen in confusion. Outside of half a dozen serving girls, a cook and three helpers, she didn't see anything that warranted choosing.

"Ack." Hawise, an elderly servant, shook her head. "Girl, you could pick any man in the hall—"

Rhian's harsh laugh stopped the older woman's absurd comment. "And what, pray tell, would I do with him?" It was ludicrous to even consider choosing any of the louts gathered in this hall.

Hawise leaned closer, whispering, "Anything he wants. Anything you want. 'Twould do much to improve your lot in life."

Nothing short of a miracle would improve her life at this point. And the Dear Lord did not deem it necessary to bestow any grace or miracle on her. Perhaps in truth He didn't exist. Rhian silently prayed to be forgiven for her blasphemous thought. "My lot in life needs no improving, but I do thank you for your concern."

"It was not a request, you nit." One of the younger serving girls snarled as she huffed out of the kitchen.

Another one, a blonde, chimed in. "They are like dogs circling a bitch in heat."

Rhian gasped. "What are you saying?"

"Since you are neither blind nor dull witted, 'tis a sly game you play at our expense."

"I play no game."

"Then what would you call it if not a game? You flaunt yourself in front of our men, yet do not avail yourself of their pallet. They ignore those of us who have always freely made our charms available to pant after the one who gives harder chase."

Surely insanity had struck the entire keep. "I would never avail myself in such a manner."

"Oh?" The blonde lifted one eyebrow. "You are too high and mighty for a little dalliance?"

"High and mighty has naught to do with it. I will not compromise myself in such a way."

The girl motioned toward the others. "Did ye hear that? Milady here will not *compromise* herself with a man between her legs." She tossed an errant braid over her shoulder before picking up an ewer and stalking past Rhian. She paused long enough to add in Rhian's ear, "You know not what you are missing."

By the time Rhian found her voice, there was no one left in the kitchen except the cook and Hawise, and the woman cackled so loud that Rhian forgot what she'd been about to say.

"What, what…" Hawise finally managed to stop cackling long enough to ask, "What be wrong, little lady? Swallow your tongue?"

Rhian tried to think of a way to make the older woman see the absurdity of the situation. But she could find no excuse that would keep her identity safe from discovery.

Hawise frowned at her in a way that made Rhian nervous. The woman seemed to look through the coarse gown and snarled hair, to Rhian's soul. Finally, Hawise shook her head before handing Rhian a bowl of sweets.

"Take these out to the hall, *milady,* and bring yourself right back here."

Oh, heaven help her. Had the woman guessed so soon? "Hawise—" Rhian pleaded.

"Go. Do as I say."

As Rhian turned to leave, Hawise added, "Right back here. No mincing in front of the men. Leave them for the others."

Mincing in front of the men, indeed. Rhian looked over those gathered in the hall and curled her lip. There wasn't a single man here who warranted any sort of attention from her. *Mincing.*

It would take more than a drunken sot to reduce her to that type of behavior. She approached the head table on the raised dais at the far end of the hall. Not even those seated in this place of honor captured her attention. Least of all the man in charge of the hall, who leaned so heavily on the table that his face was nearly in his food.

Certainly not the man situated to the right of the seat of honor. She wondered if he could see through eyes so red. Rhian gingerly stepped over the man she'd hit earlier and placed the bowl of sweets on the table.

Before she could beat a hasty retreat back to the kitchens, a hand grasped her wrist. "Ah, there you are, my lovely."

She glared at the man holding her arm. "Let me go. I have work to attend to."

He towered over her, easily pulling her closer. Close enough to feel the hardness between them. "Yes, my lovely, you do." The man tightened his hold, grinding his growing manhood against her stomach.

"Sir, do nothing you might regret later." Her legs shook, but she refused to let him see any fear.

"Regret?" He leaned down. His blue eyes were glazed by drink and a look she recognized as lust. Surely the drink he'd consumed blinded him.

"Oh, aye, regret and more." Rhian blinked twice to make sure her sight did not deceive her.

Hawise nudged the young blond serving girl closer to the man. "Why would you want a scrawny girl like this?" The older woman nodded toward Rhian, before directing the drunken guest's attention to the now flirting buxom blonde. "Not when this one here would be more than willing to serve your needs."

Thankfully, the man's gap-toothed smile was diverted to the other girl, giving Rhian a chance to pull free. She waited for no orders from Hawise before escaping back to the kitchens.

With Hawise fast on her trail. "I told you to return immediately. Can you not listen?" She dipped a ladle into the water bucket and handed it to Rhian.

"Thank you." Rhian swallowed deeply, allowing the cool water to wash away the lump that had formed in her throat. "I tried to return. As you could see, I was detained."

"And I saw that you did little to free yourself."

"What was I supposed to do?"

"Kick him. Use your knee. How do you survive on your own?"

Rhian lifted her head. "I have survived quite well until now."

"Aye. Under your father's tender care." Hawise leaned against a support beam before sinking down onto a low stool. "Do not speak lies, I am too old and tired for them. You are no more a servant than I am a lady."

"You cannot be certain of that." Rhian paused to weigh her words. She could not afford to give away too much. "It matters little. I will be gone soon."

Hawise flapped a drying rag in the air and laughed. "Where will you go, child? A woman traveling alone is fair game for all manner of cutthroats and predators."

"I will manage." She'd managed so far these last few days. In a manner of speaking. To be honest, she'd happened on Browan Keep quite by accident. At the time it'd been a blessed sight. Now, Rhian wondered if it was more of a curse than blessing. "Perhaps one of the men out there needs another servant."

Hawise laughed herself breathless. Finally, gasping for air and wiping the tears from her eyes, she asked, "Pray tell, how pleased do you think their womenfolk will be when the lord and master arrives home with a strange female in tow? Not just a female, but an unmarried one such as you?"

"Such as me?"

"Unmarried. Young. Unmarred by pockmarks or worry lines. Just the sight of your smooth face will send the women into fits."

"What are you yammering about?" Rhian frowned. "I am filthy, ragged. I have nothing to call my own." She tugged at the high neck of her faded yellow gown. The coarsely spun cotton had not seen a dye bath in more years than she could imagine. It hung on her like the sack it would soon become. "Even this is…borrowed. There is not a lady in the world who would envy me anything."

Hawise rose and waved her hands in the air. "Girl,

you are a fool, nothing but a young fool. I should wash my hands of you and be done with it."

"Ale!" Shouts for drink echoed down the corridor connecting the kitchens and larder to the hall.

To escape Hawise's senseless babbling, Rhian grabbed two ewers of ale in each hand, then again headed toward the great hall.

"We will finish this!" The older woman's warning followed her down the corridor.

Finish it indeed. Rhian knew that Browan Keep would be far behind her by the full light of day. Hawise could finish her lecture alone.

Since many of the men had already fallen asleep in various spots along the floor, Rhian worried only a little about being pawed upon as she deposited the pitchers of ale on the tables. Quickly finishing her task, she turned back to the kitchens, then looked toward the entry chamber at the other end of the hall.

Here was a choice she could make. Return to Hawise's infernal lecture. Or leave Browan now. The gates were unguarded, she'd not be stopped.

She wiped her suddenly damp palms on the skirt of her gown. She had little else but the clothes on her back. Rhian absently touched the ribbon about her neck. The only item of worth still in her possession hung from the makeshift chain.

The amethyst pendant had been sent to her upon her mother's death a few short months past. An oddly shaped circle, with a crudely etched dragon in the center. Her breath hitched at the pain of a memory still too new, an ache still too raw and horror that still haunted her dreams.

It would be an easy task to leave the hall. None would notice her absence. Surely she could find the stables once outside. Perhaps if none of the stable lads were about, she could coax a horse to follow her out the gates.

Rhian tugged at her bottom lip. If the horse just followed her out of the stables and gates, would that be considered stealing? She knew the answer the instant the question formed. Yes. If caught, she could very well forfeit her life.

She took a deep breath and decided. A horse would require food she did not have. Instead of burdening herself with the added worry, she would walk. As long as she avoided the road and kept to the forest as she had before, it would be safer and quicker.

The decision made, she straightened her back and walked boldly between the tables toward the hall's entrance—in her case, an exit.

As she drew closer, the sound of a commotion from beyond the great doors filtered through to the entryway. Rhian slowed her steps. If more men were coming in, she wished not to be caught up in the middle of their arrival. If she hurried, perhaps she could escape their notice.

Both doors swung open with such force that they slammed against the wall with a crash that reverberated throughout the entire keep. Herb-scented rushes that had been strewn on the floor whooshed past her feet.

Rhian silently cursed. She was too close now to avoid the arriving party. She stooped her shoulders and bowed her head—hopefully in a perfect servantlike manner. Perhaps if she just continued on as if she were about her lord's orders, they would simply let her pass.

Certain the ruse would work, Rhian glanced over her

shoulder one last time before ducking into the entryway, to see if anyone would notice. Undetected, she continued through the archway to the entrance and ran smack into a solid, motionless wall of flesh and muscle covered by hard chain mail.

Chapter Two

"My pardon, milord." The man Rhian had run into did not move. Nor did he say a word. In fact, she suddenly realized that those gathered around him held their collective breath.

Dread curled up from her toes. She closed her eyes for a moment before reopening them and lifting her head until her neck stretched. Only one man could be that tall.

Her single-word curse was far from silent and far from servantlike.

"My, my, such a charming greeting. It matches your lovely attire." His leaf-green eyes staring down at her narrowed. "Ah, now I realize my mistake. I have spent this last week searching for a *lady.*"

Rhian knew that his sarcasm was directed at her curse, the ragged dress she wore, her tousled and snarled hair, the streaks of dirt on her now flaming face. Nay, she neither sounded, nor looked anything like a lady.

She'd not fall prey to his snide remark. Instead, she

lifted her chin, squared her shoulders and met his glare with one of her own.

He motioned to one of his men before he continued, "Milady Gervaise, David will see to your safety until I am able to relieve him." As an afterthought, he added, "Keep her under close guard. Find a cell, or use your sword if you must, but do not let her escape."

The young man she had spoken with earlier in the bailey unsheathed his sword with one hand, then held out his free arm. "Milady, if you please."

She didn't please, so Rhian ignored him. Instead, she held Gareth of Faucon's stare. Torchlight danced a merry jig off the silver streaks of hair that framed his face. Those few strands stood out boldly from the rest of the inky blackness.

"Still you seek to order me about?" A smile flitted about her lips. "Your commands met with little success before." A glance at her broken and unkempt fingernails told her that she'd be unable to claw into his flesh this time. A daunting discovery to be sure, but not one that spelled defeat. Not yet.

"We can draw blood later." Faster than quicksilver, Faucon grasped her wrist. "It might prove an interesting sport. But for now, just do as you are told."

Before she could tell him what to do with his orders, he added, "Lady Rhian, I will gladly spar with you soon. I may even provide you the means to slit my throat. But at the moment—" he paused and nodded toward the arched opening into the hall "—I have business to attend. Spare us both discovery and unwanted complications."

It galled her to realize the truth in his words. She

could not afford those in this keep discovering that they'd unwittingly aided a runaway from the king. Her inability to explain would indeed bring about many complications. Nor did she wish for those here to learn she was not what she pretended to be.

Rhian showered Faucon with what she hoped was a withering glare, before hastening back to the kitchens with David fast on her trail.

Any warrior worth his salt knew the advantage of surprise. Gareth of Faucon was no different. He'd learned many lessons from his older brother Rhys—among them the usefulness of surprise in making an entrance.

His advantage would have been lost at another keep where he and his men would have met armed resistance had they ridden through the gates without announcing their presence. However, Browan's gates were unguarded. A mistake bordering on treason.

Gareth stepped through the archway and looked out across the great hall. He doubted if those men facedown in the rushes on the floor would notice his arrival for days to come. Apparently not all fell to the floor in a drunken stupor.

One man had found his unnatural sleep with the aid of an earthen jug. It didn't require much thought to guess who had put him in that position. Obviously, Lady Rhian had been displeased with the man.

Most of those still coherent sought a willing body to share their pallet with this night. From the seductive laughter of the servants, Gareth wagered that not many pallets would contain a single occupant.

Since he and his men had not rushed the hall brandishing their weapons, they'd not drawn any attention to themselves. His exchange with the Lady of Gervaise had been brief and unnoticed. Nay, the usefulness of surprise had not been lost in Browan Keep.

An occurrence that would never happen again.

Gareth nodded, silently beckoning his men to follow him, then strode toward the center of the room. "Where is Sir Hector?" His shout captured the attention of all gathered.

Which surprised him, since he'd thought they appeared to be exceedingly drunk. To a man, they turned toward the head table where a poorly dressed figure staggered slowly to his feet. "I am here. Who asks?"

It was all Gareth could do not to supply the answer immediately. But he'd no wish to give any information away until he was close enough to see it clearly register on Hector's face. He continued across the floor, pausing only when he reached the foot of the dais.

"Gareth of Faucon." He handed the man a missive from King Stephen. "Your new overlord." The man did not need to know that the boon granting him control of Browan Keep would not be legitimate until after he delivered Rhian to her kin. A minor annoyance that would be accomplished soon.

His foresight did not go without reward. After glancing at the wax seal, Hector's mouth dropped open, then closed, then opened again reminding Gareth of a beached fish.

Sir Hector scurried around the high table as fast as his unsteady legs could carry him and held out a hand, motioning toward the chair at the center of the long table. "Milord, please, join us." He waved toward a servant. "Bring some food and drink."

"Nay. Belay that order." Gareth flicked a pointed glance toward his captain, then he slowly walked to the other side of the table. Before he reached Browan's seat of honor, his men had positioned themselves strategically throughout the hall. Not one door, corridor or stairwell was left unguarded. He knew without turning around, that his own back was also well protected.

Gareth sat down in the high-backed chair and turned his attention back to Sir Hector. "Do you find your service here unacceptable?"

The man appeared genuinely confused. "Nay, milord. Not at all."

"Then perhaps you could explain a few things to me."

Hector moved closer to the table. "Would you care for a private conversation?"

"Nay." Gareth nodded toward the others. "Since my questions also involve the other men, this will suit."

Those who were not overcome with drink moved closer to the dais. Gareth studied each man, wondering if any would ever be worthy of serving him at Browan Keep. The men who were able to stand steady on their feet peered at their more drunken comrades. They mistakenly thought the sodden members of this crowd would be the ones in greater disfavor.

They couldn't be more wrong.

Gareth leaned forward on the table. "Pray tell, Sir Hector, how many men guard these walls?"

A frown marred Hector's forehead. It was hard to determine whether the expression held from confusion or thought. "There are two on each gate, main and postern and six scattered along the walkways, milord."

Quickly schooling his own confusion to remain hidden, Gareth asked, "And these men are loyal?"

"Aye, sir. Without a doubt." The man's chins jiggled with each nod of his head. "Every one of them would give their life for this keep."

A loud expletive escaped Gareth's mouth as he rose in such haste that he knocked the high-backed chair to the floor. He pointed at his captain of the guard, Edgar. "Secure this keep. Now. Permit no one else in or out."

After his captain and half of the men promptly left to do his bidding, he turned back toward Sir Hector. "It seems there is a problem."

The man's eyes grew large as he wrung his hands together. "M-milord?"

Sword clanging at his side, Gareth headed toward the exit. "Since the walls and gates are unguarded, there are ten missing men." Hector gasped, then followed as fast as his obviously now sobering frame would allow. He was nearly trampled by Faucon's remaining men rushing to catch up with their lord.

Gareth paused at the entryway and yelled, "David!" Regardless of what he found outside, he wanted the lad and that black-haired she-devil secured in a chamber above.

It took several breaths before David arrived in the hall holding a rag to his bleeding head with one hand and pulling a woman along with the other. Unfortunately, the woman was not the Lady Rhian.

The pain started in Gareth's temples and quickly rushed to settle directly above his nose. He squeezed his eyes closed and wondered if this was what the moment before death would feel like. A sudden pain and visions of his life running through his mind.

He opened his eyes and waited for David to explain, praying silently that the explanation would not be what he feared.

"Milord Faucon." The squire stopped just out of arm's reach. "She hit me." His high-pitched voice gave hint to his lingering surprise. "With a kettle pot. She hit me." He pulled the woman before him. "And this…this one here tripped me so I couldn't catch the lady."

"Lady?" The older woman shook her wrist out of David's grasp. "Why, she be no lady. Just another kitchen wench." Her laughter sounded more like a cackling hen. The sound grated on Gareth's already throbbing head.

She finally ceased the irritating noise and looked at him. "Your boy here will make a fine soldier." The woman's sarcastic tone was lost on no one. "He was so busy eyeing the other girls that he failed to see the pot coming."

David sought to hide his flaming face by staring at his toes. However, tipping his head down did nothing to hide his reddening ears.

Gareth spared David a well-deserved tongue-lashing. In truth, the fault was his own. He should not have sent a lad to do a man's job. What made him think that David would actually use his sword on Lady Rhian? While the lad was tried in battle, he had not the experience to handle a headstrong woman. A lesson his squire was learning the hard way.

For now, he glared first at David, then at the older woman. "That *kitchen maid* is Lady Rhian of Gervaise."

When the woman's expression didn't register surprise, Gareth narrowed his eyes further. "As well you were aware…ah, forgive me, but your name seems to have escaped me."

"Hawise." Sir Hector provided the answer. "She is in charge of the kitchen help."

"I didn't know for certain she were a lady." Hawise's whine intensified as she twisted the skirt of her gown between her fingers. "I only guessed."

Gareth pointed at Hawise. "If you would like to retain your position in this keep, you will take David here and the two of you will find Lady Rhian and escort her to my chamber."

"Chamber, milord?" Hector croaked.

Gareth spared only a brief glance for the man. "Aye. You heard me correctly. A chamber. One with a door that can be barred."

David shuffled his feet. "Milord Faucon, how…"

Gareth raised his hand, cutting off the squire's question. "Two of the other men will assist you." He couldn't believe he'd said that. The idea that it would take four people to retrieve one woman was unthinkable—unless of course that woman was the Lady Rhian.

A maid cleaning up broken earthenware from the floor caught his attention. Against all common sense he revised his order. "Four of the other men will assist you."

He turned and left his men to argue over the honor of helping David and Hawise. He was certain the losers would demand their weight in drink or gold by the morrow.

A matter he'd concern himself with later. At this moment there were other matters to attend—like discovering how ten men disappeared.

The crisp night wind buffeted him as he crossed the foot planks and stepped onto the wallwalk. Colder than normal, it sent a foreboding shiver down his spine.

Gareth shook off the unfamiliar feeling and surveyed the yard below. Torchlight glinted off the forms of those already searching for the missing guards. Not a single nook or corner would be left undisturbed.

A figure too small to pass for one of the men darted across the yard. When the semiconcealed form disappeared into the shadow of the stable, Gareth took chase. She'd not escape that easily.

Rhian pulled the hood of her mantle more tightly around her face and ducked into a narrow crevice between the stable and the wall. She knew from the shouts of the men that they were on a mission to find something. She just hadn't determined what that something was as yet. Nor did she truly care. She had her own mission—to escape Faucon.

Not only Faucon, but the King and any who would seek to deliver her into the hands of her kinsmen. For ten and nine years her mother's *beloved family* had not so much as acknowledged her existence.

Rhian knew little about them. Only what had been whispered behind her back. It was rumored that they were spawned from the devil. Now, after her father's death, they sought her return to their fold. They sought to marry her to one of their kind.

She'd sooner die.

Her father had raised her alone and they'd managed

quite well without her mother's family all these years. Somehow, Rhian knew she'd find a way to manage without them now.

After taking a deep breath she hazarded a quick glance around the corner of the stable. Rhian swallowed her curse. Of all the bad luck.

She ducked back into the crevice. Pressing her back against the wall she prayed that Faucon had not seen her. With the direction her luck had taken of late, she'd sooner count on cunning.

If she could not cross in front of the stable to reach the gate, she'd slip behind the building. She inched along the stable, away from the bailey, farther into the darkness. Her foot hit something solid, stopping her escape.

Rhian pushed against the object to no avail. Unwilling to give up the building's protection, she reached down to shove the blockage out of the way. Her fingertips met stiffening flesh.

She squatted. Gingerly patting the object, she identified the form as a body—a lifeless body. Her father's love of battle had made her well familiar with dead bodies. Continued exploration revealed chain mail covered in a sticky substance she guessed would prove to be blood.

She scraped her hand across the dirt, seeking to remove the blood before wiping her palm and fingers with the edge of her mantle.

Short of saying a quick prayer, there was nothing she could do for the man. So she rose and stepped over him. Only to trod on what she knew would prove to be another body.

Fear slithered through her limbs. Not of the dead, for they could bring her no harm, but of the killer. What if he, or they, was still about? Rhian's stomach twisted. Suddenly, the idea of slipping into the total darkness behind the stable held little appeal.

"Nay," she whispered to calm her racing imagination. The corpses were cold and nearly stiff, surely they were murdered some time ago. Perhaps while everyone else drank and made merry in the hall.

She shook her head in disgust. Had Sir Hector placed guards about, maybe this would not have happened.

Guards.

She frowned. These men were in armor, could they be the absent guards?

She paused, listening to the shouts of Faucon's men in the bailey. Their brusque cries of "Nothing here," and "Nay, nothing," made it obvious that they searched for something. She took another step and nudged yet a third body. Could this be what they searched for so carefully?

Rhian fisted her hands at her side and inched back toward the bailey—away from the dead men. "Holy Mother of God, what do I do now?" If she left without telling anyone of her discovery, she'd not be able to sleep nights. Yet, she'd have to give herself up along with the bodies. Nay. She stopped her retreat. There had to be a way around this dilemma.

While she was seeking to formulate a plan, a hand clamped down on her shoulder. Before she could force a scream past her suddenly constricted throat, a man asked, "Out for another breath of fresh air?"

She didn't need to turn around to know whose fingers bit into her flesh. "I was seeking a way to avoid you, when I tripped over a few dead bodies." She saw no reason to lie.

Faucon released his hold on her shoulder, bringing her a brief measure of relief before he grasped her wrist. After shouting for his men, he ordered, "Show me."

"They are no more than two steps straight ahead, milord."

Gareth took the torch from the first man who arrived and went to inspect Rhian's claim, tugging her along.

Rhian was unable to stifle her gasp at the sight of the men. She'd been right—the stickiness she'd felt had been blood. The bodies were covered in it, just like the two men who'd been killed at Gervaise Keep after bringing her the amethyst pendant.

Her head spun. There couldn't be a connection. Her stomach rolled. The only thing linking Gervaise and Browan was her. She fought to hold her fear at bay.

Faucon turned to his captain. "Edgar, see Lady Gervaise safely to her chamber."

When his captain offered his arm as an escort, Gareth laughed before securing Edgar's hand around her wrist. "Under any other circumstance I would not need to say this, but since she has already escaped twice now, let me make myself clear. On no condition are you to release your hold on her until she's ensconced behind a locked chamber door that you will then guard until I relieve you."

Edgar bobbed his head. "Aye, sir. You can count on me."

Rhian wanted to rail against this ill treatment, but as the torchlight danced off the bodies, her throat constricted, effectively choking off her words. Perhaps there'd be a sense of security behind a guarded and locked door.

Gareth waited until Edgar led an oddly silent Rhian

away before kneeling over the bodies. At first glance he'd assumed their throats had been slit. But their chain-mail coif protected them from head to shoulder.

While he tried to ascertain how they died, Hector arrived. "Milord, I heard that you—" The man's sentence ended abruptly on a strangled gasp.

"Aye," Gareth agreed with the man's response. "Are these Browan's men?"

"Yes." While Sir Hector had regained control over his initial shock, the remnants of a tremor still shook his voice. "Who could have done this?"

"Have any strangers been permitted into the keep of late?"

"No." The man seemed to reconsider his answer. "The only stranger recently has been the woman you called Lady Gervaise."

Gareth didn't doubt for one heartbeat that Lady Rhian would cherish slitting his throat, but neither did he believe she would do so to another.

"There is so much blood." Hector studied the bodies, then asked, "How did this happen?"

"I'm not certain." Gareth stood. "Perhaps a thorough examination will shed some light."

Sir Hector turned toward Browan's guards and ordered, "Take the bodies to the hall." He then turned back to Gareth. "Have any more been discovered?"

"Nay. The others—"

Their discussion was interrupted by a hue and cry from the bailey. Both Gareth and Hector rushed toward the commotion.

Gareth drew his sword before pushing through the gathered crowd. "Hold! What goes here?"

The din subsided and one of Browan's men limped forward. His torn and dirty garments hung from his frame. He glanced from Gareth to Hector and back, then explained, "We were attacked from behind before we could give warning."

"By how many?" Gareth asked.

The man looked to his companions before shrugging. "I would guess eight or so." The others nodded in agreement.

Sir Hector asked, "How many of you survived?"

The man's eyes widened. "We are six here." The others stepped forward. Each looked as beaten as the next, but at least they were alive.

Gareth answered their unspoken question. "Three were killed. One is still missing."

Then he scowled in thought. Eight men had slipped into Browan undetected. The same eight men had done this much harm to Browan's guard. Either the eight were highly skilled, or someone had helped to arrange this ambush. If so, for what purpose?

He turned his attention back to the guards, asking, "Did your attackers say anything?"

One offered a hesitant reply, "Aye, sir. They asked where the princess slept."

"Princess?" Gareth and Sir Hector asked in unison.

The guard shrugged. "I told them there weren't no princess here, but they just laughed and hit my head."

Hector surveyed the bailey and turned to look at the tower. "What would a princess be doing here?"

Gareth followed the other man's gaze. A multitude of torches lit the bailey and more blazed from the walls.

Far from a rich keep to begin with, the sparse light

accented the poorly constructed outbuildings, weak sections in the curtain wall and the downtrodden appearance of the keep in general.

The daunting prospect of reconstruction was overwhelmed by one question. *What princess?*

A flicker of light from an upper arrow slit in the tower caught Gareth's attention. Without turning, he issued an order to Sir Hector, "See that the bodies are taken to the hall and see that these men are cared for, too."

"Milord?"

He heard the question in Hector's tone. Instead of answering, Gareth only waved one hand in dismissal before leaving to seek answers to his own growing questions.

"You what?" The leader of this small band of men slammed an underling against a tree. He held his forearm across the trembling man's throat.

"Milord, by the time we made certain the guards were well cared for, Faucon had arrived and we were unable to capture the woman."

With nothing but a quick flick of the wrist, a razor-sharp weapon slit the underling's throat.

The leader faced the others. "This will not happen again."

Chapter Three

Rhian paced the floor of what could only be considered a makeshift cell. With a guard at the door, and the inability to come and go at will, what else could she call this chamber?

She surveyed the small room. Chamber? In truth it was little more than an alcove with a door. She'd seen larger storage huts.

But the size of her makeshift prison was the least of her concerns.

In the last sennight she'd gone from the Lady of Gervaise, to Faucon's charge, to runaway, to servant and now to prisoner. Those would have been a great many changes over the course of a lifetime, let alone seven days.

What would she become next? An unwilling bride to some heathen devil worshiper?

Not if she could help it.

The question was how to prevent it from happening?

She paced back across the room. Each footstep she

took across the cold, bare wood floor increased her sense of defeat.

Nay. She could not give up so easily, not yet. Not while she breathed. She would do whatever became necessary to regain her freedom and her peace-filled life. She would make any sacrifice, any compromise that would provide her a way out of the life King Stephen had arranged for her.

There'd been so much blood.

The unwelcome memory of the two messengers from her mother's family stabbed at her mind and knotted her stomach. They'd given her the package containing the pendant and spoken privately to her father at length before taking their leave.

The next day, their blood-covered bodies had been found just outside the walls.

Rhian shivered.

Perhaps being in a guarded cell might be a good thing. Even though she chafed at the forced confinement, she knew a measure of safety. Although, that was not Faucon's intent.

Then again, she could also understand Faucon wanting to make certain she did not escape him again. After all, he was only following King Stephen's orders.

She paused by the lit brazier seeking warmth. Nothing stopped the spring's night breeze from turning the chamber to ice. The small brazier would have to be kept burning many hours before its heat would fill the room.

Hours that Rhian did not intend to spend in this cell, or this keep. She clenched her teeth to hold back a scream of frustration.

The thought of being confined was nigh on unbearable. Yet, the thought of escaping into the forest held much less appeal than it had just a short time ago.

Even without these strange murders, she felt buffeted from all sides—King Stephen, her mother's family and Faucon. Why could they all not just leave her alone? Or at the very least why could they not treat her in a manner befitting her father's daughter?

Rhian stomped over to the pallet in the corner, plunked down on the lumpy mattress and sighed heavily.

Why? Because now she was nobody. Nothing.

With her father's death she had ceased to exist. King Stephen had already given her home to another. Her possessions had been carted away with a promise to have them returned to her upon her arrival at her new home.

She'd been left with only what King Stephen had decided she required for her journey and little else.

Rhian absently touched her pendant. What would her future hold? She knew not her mother's family. Were they truly disciples of the devil, as she'd heard whispered?

She closed her thoughts against the possibility. It mattered little. She'd find a way to escape the future.

The door to her cell banging open with a thud against the wall startled her out of her contemplation. Now that Faucon had arrived, she wondered what his mood would be.

Would he seek to make her pay for running away and thwarting his mission? Would he be angry that she'd hit his squire with the kettle?

He was a huge man compared to her father, or to any other man she'd ever known. She knew full well the distance her father's wrath could travel. What about Faucon's?

In all truth, he'd held his anger well so far. A shiver of dread snaked down her spine. With the unknown danger already stalking her, she wished not to deal with any more.

Faucon stared at the door, now half hanging from a broken leather hinge. With a curse he ordered his captain to find someone to fix it.

All of her emotions raced to the fore: dread, fear, guilt, and at his curse, they tripped out of her mouth as a nervous laugh. Rhian slapped a hand over her mouth hoping to stifle the sound.

Faucon spun around and glared at her. "I am happy I could amuse you."

She arched one eyebrow, then returned his glare.

He inspected the small chamber, then walked across the room and held his hands over the brazier. "You will need more coals. And a bed instead of that pallet."

Relieved that he was not roaring at her, Rhian patted the straw- and herb-filled mattress on the floor beneath her. "This will do fine for the short time I will remain at Browan."

"Oh?" Faucon did not move from his position by the heat. Instead, he only shot her a look she couldn't decipher. "And when do you plan on departing?"

"As soon as possible."

"And where will you go?"

Rhian shrugged. "It matters little as long it is away from where you think to deliver me."

Faucon crossed his arms against his chest. "Where I

think to deliver you?" He shook his head. "Nay, milady. 'Tis where I *will* deliver you. What makes you think you have a choice in this matter?"

"It is my life you play with, Faucon. Not yours. Not King Stephen's. *My* life."

"Spoken like a spoiled child who knows not their place in the world."

"Ah, that is where you are mistaken. I know full well my place in the world. It is nowhere."

Faucon rubbed the bridge of his nose while he walked over to the narrow window opening. "If a king goes to such lengths to ensure your future is secured, I would say you have a place in the scheme of things." He turned back to look at her. "Why do you not agree?"

Rhian scooted back on the pallet and leaned against the wall. "He sends me to a family who has not noted my existence since the day I was born. A family I know nothing about except what I've heard whispered in corners when they thought I couldn't hear."

"I do not believe you would permit rumors and innuendo to overrule common sense."

"What if those rumors hinted at devil worship and Satan's trickery? Would that not make a sane person take pause?"

Faucon's shoulders rose and fell. "Perhaps it might be better to see for yourself. To determine firsthand if the stories be rumors or truth."

Rhian laughed softly. "Oh, aye. A fine thing for a man to say. If the rumors turned out to be truth you could draw your sword and fight your way out if need be. What will I do to protect myself?"

"You?" He looked at her in surprise. "You set out through a dark forest alone to escape me. A feat that could very well have earned you death, or worse."

Rhian felt the heat of embarrassment on her cheeks. "I fail to think when I am angry."

"Truly?" He rubbed his forearm, bringing more heat to her face. "I find that hard to believe."

"If your sarcasm were any thicker, you'd drown in it."

"And if your nails were any longer, I'd have bled to death."

"A strong warrior like you? I doubt that."

He stepped away from the wall and tapped a hand against his chest. "Ah, she thinks I am a strong warrior. My heart will burst at your kind words. I could take that as a compliment."

"Take it as you wish."

After shaking his head, Faucon sighed, then asked, "Where will you go, Lady Rhian? What will you do? How will you live?"

Rhian sat up. "You will release me?"

"Not while I draw breath."

"Why not, Faucon? I am nothing to you."

This time, he laughed softly before answering. "Nothing? Milady, you are the task that will secure my own future."

"How so? What can I possibly have to do with your future?"

A dark look crossed his face. For a moment Rhian thought she caught a glimpse of pain, or regret. It flashed through his eyes so quickly she wasn't certain if she had imagined the display of emotion or not.

"Let us just say that completing this task for the King

will go a long way toward bringing me back in his good graces."

She frowned. What could Faucon have done to lose the good graces of his king in the first place? "What—"

"I am certain we both have past experiences we would prefer to forget." He spoke before she could finish asking her question. "Even you."

"Me?" Rhian shook her head. "No. Nothing I can think of at the moment."

"No? Tell me something, *Princess,* why are there men looking for you?"

Her heart jumped. Her father had always called her his princess as an endearment. It sounded strange coming from another. "*Princess?* I am not certain who you are speaking to, but since only the two of us are in this chamber, I can only assume you are confused."

"Some of Browan's guards were only beaten, not killed. The men who murdered the others asked the whereabouts of the Princess."

Rhian's mouth went dry. "Have you discovered how the others died?"

"At first glance it appeared their throats were slit. But the chain mail would have made that difficult." Faucon's eyebrows met as if he was considering the method of death even now. "I am certain once the bodies are cleaned up that we'll be better able to discover how they died."

She rubbed her throbbing temples. "What does that have to do with me?" She needed to think this through before telling him what she knew. Would it help or hinder her cause? She couldn't decide right at this moment and the men were already dead, so speaking out would do nothing for them.

"Little things. The fact that the murderers are seeking someone. Or that Browan Keep is so poor that nobody of any consequence would come here knowingly, unless of course they were hiding. And the fact that you are the only stranger to have happened upon Browan mere days before this attack on the men."

"From that you have determined that I am the woman they seek?" It was all she could do not to roll her eyes. She would have come to same conclusion if she'd been in Faucon's place, but she'd not tell him that.

He said nothing. Just stared at her.

"Faucon, it is nothing more than a coincidence. I only happened upon Browan while walking through the forest. If anyone had been following me, I would think they'd have captured me before I entered these gates." When his expression didn't change, she asked, "Have your men found the murderers? Are they still within the gates?"

"Nay. They have searched every corner here and found nothing."

"Then whoever it was, obviously isn't looking for me, else they'd still be within the walls."

"Perhaps."

A small little voice inside her heart urged her to tell Faucon all. Her mind bade her wait a little while longer. Confused, Rhian sighed. To tell or not? She stared up at him. "Faucon…" *No. Wait.*

"What?"

"Nothing, Faucon. Never mind."

He crossed the floor and stood over her. "Nothing? It sounded like more than nothing."

Leaning back on the pallet, Rhian craned her neck

back to look up at him. A position that simply would not do. "Either go stand across the room—" she extended her arm "—or help me up."

"Nay." He made a big show of crossing his arms against his chest and shaking his head. "I rather like our positions."

But when she waved her hand at him, he relented and pulled her to her feet. His palm was warm against hers, chasing away the chill. Rhian stared at their entwined fingers.

Faucon brushed his thumb across the back of her hand. The small movement chased the breath from her. *Good heavens, what was this? And why did his hand engulfing hers feel so right?*

Rhian backed a step away and looked up at him. Even though she now stood, she still had to tip her head back to look at his face. *Far too tall.* She really did not like men who were so much taller than she. It put her at a disadvantage.

Firelight danced off the silver strands of his otherwise black hair. *Far too wolflike.* She'd never been fond of wild animals. They were too unpredictable.

His jewel-toned eyes glimmered like emeralds against his sun-darkened skin. *Far too searching, too knowing.* How would anyone keep secrets from eyes that seeking? He'd eventually be able to discern her thoughts without any words being spoken. Did he already know that she hid secrets from him?

His square-shaped jaw clenched and unclenched. *Far too strong.* Stubborn men irritated her beyond belief. They were no fun to argue with because they either lost their temper too quickly, or they sulked in silence.

Without releasing her hand, he tugged her against his chest. *Far too muscular.* She rested her forehead against his chest, fighting to clear her suddenly foggy mind.

Faucon lifted her chin with one finger, then stroked her neck. To retain a semblance of balance she closed her eyes and placed her other hand on his shoulder. *Far too broad.* Men with broad shoulders assumed the world and all its troubles could rest upon them. For an instant she wished he could carry her troubles.

"Rhian."

His deep voice whispered across her ear like a warm caress. *Far too inviting.* A voice like that could convince her to… Why he could…and she would… and they—

He lightly brushed his lips against hers.

She leaned closer. Her heart jumped to her throat. Her pulse raced in expectation.

He slid his arm across her back, holding her to him. This time his kiss was far more than a feathery brush. Insistent. Searching. Exploring.

When he ran the tip of his tongue across her lower lip, Rhian gasped at the bolt of fire and ice that rushed clear to her toes. He was everything she disliked in a man, yet she would willingly—

Dear Lord, what was she thinking?

Rhian shook her head and pushed against his shoulder. "Release me."

Faucon instantly unlaced his hand from hers and stepped back, shooting her a rueful look. "I can't imagine what I was thinking."

To her amazement, a flush of red crept up his neck. Since he didn't spin any excuses, oddly enough she believed him. And that belief made not telling him what she knew even more of a crime.

Still, Rhian kept her distance. "There is no need to apologize." When he didn't protest the apology he hadn't given, she walked toward the window and stared out at the twinkling stars. "I was obviously thinking the same thing."

She heard him approach. Just his nearness put her senses on alert. He caused her heart to race, her breath to catch, her throat to close and her skin to tingle. Rhian knew with a certainty that this sudden unnaturalness, this inability to think clearly, was not a good thing. Thankfully, when she lifted a hand as if to ward him off, he stopped.

Faucon cleared his throat. "Honesty. What a unique attitude."

"It would be rather hard to lie would it not?" *Then why was her conscience snickering?*

"Perhaps. But would it not be expected?"

She turned and looked at him. "How so?"

"A man alone with you in an empty chamber. Would it not make more sense for you to feign the injured virgin?"

And far too arrogant for his own good. "And why would I do that?"

He shrugged. "Had someone walked in, would it not have been the best way to avoid unwanted gossip?"

"Even had someone seen us, I need feign nothing. For one thing I care not what others may or may not think. For another, I *am* a virgin and the only person that will concern is my husband the day we marry."

Rhian paused and bit her lower lip with indecision. When her conscience threatened to choke her, she finally said, "Faucon, we have another concern at the moment. Something of more importance than unwarranted gossip."

The tone of her voice, the squaring of her shoulders and the serious, unemotional look on her face, drew Gareth forward. He leaned against the wall on the other side of the window, hoping it was far enough away to make her feel at ease and to calm his still-racing heart.

This woman with her midnight-black hair and shimmering blue eyes could yet prove to be his downfall if he did not watch himself.

Something about her, from her lips that silently begged to be kissed, to the way she fit so perfectly in his arms, screamed a warning. Rhian of Gervaise would prove to be heaven or hell, and nothing between.

A risk Gareth did not want to take, yet could not seem to avoid. If he were a praying man, he would be on his knees now.

Instead, he softly prompted, "And what concern might that be, Lady Rhian?"

He watched her take a deep shuddering breath and for a moment wondered if he truly wanted to know.

"The bodies in the bailey." She rushed into her explanation. "The blood—so much of it. I've seen that before at Gervaise. Two messengers from my mother's family were killed the same way outside of our gates. The killers were never found."

She wrapped her arms across her stomach, but never paused. "At first it was thought their throats had been slit, but after a closer inspection it was discovered that someone had pierced the vein in their neck with something sharp, like a nail. Which would explain the vast amount of blood, since it would have spurted out and—"

Gareth raised his hand. "Enough." He quickly digested all she'd just told him, then asked, "There were no clues, no witnesses? Nothing to give any hint who they were or where they were from?"

"No." She shook her head. "My father's men searched for weeks to no avail. Everyone was questioned, but nobody had seen or heard anything."

Gareth rubbed the space between his eyes. "And now the only additional thing we know is that they seek a woman." He lowered his hand, glanced at her, and then turned his attention out the window. "A princess, to be precise."

"I can assure you I am no princess."

Many a comment rushed to his mind at her declaration, but he kept them to himself. Instead, he asked, "You mentioned two messengers. What did they want? What message did they bring?"

Rhian slipped her hand down the edge of her high-neck gown and pulled out a pendant. "They brought this to me, along with the notice of my mother's death."

He reached out to touch the amethyst, pausing to ask, "May I?" When she nodded, he held the stone, looked at the dragon etching, then he turned it over in his hand. He was certain it was only his imagination that made it feel alive, pulsing under his touch. He wondered aloud, "Why is it so warm? As if it's been held over a fire?"

She snatched it from him and tucked the pendant back inside her gown. "It is only warm from being against my skin."

Gareth watched the pendant slide into place between

her breasts and wondered if her flesh could be that warm without causing her pain. He stepped back, grasping for a different subject. "You said they brought word of your mother's death?"

"Aye." Rhian's voice was a near whisper. "I did not even know she'd been alive all those years."

"She did not live with you and your father?" Yet another mystery.

"No. I never knew her."

"You did not find that odd?"

Rhian shrugged. "Odd? I had been told as a small child that she had died. Why would it appear odd?"

"So your father lied to you."

Her eyes filled with unshed tears. "Obviously." The choked word seemed torn from her lips. She walked away from the window to stand before the brazier.

"Did the messengers tell you anything about her?"

"No. I did not speak with them."

"Did you ask your father for an explanation after the messengers left?"

Rhian looked at him, her eyebrows raised. "Would you not do so? Of course I did."

He ignored the tartness of her tone. "And?"

She turned back to the brazier, seemingly intent on chasing the night's chill from her hands. "I was told that it no longer mattered. That they'd made the best decision for me and for them. I had little choice but to assume the subject was closed."

This was becoming more of a quest than he'd first thought. Why could it not have simply been as King Stephen said? He was just to deliver an heiress to her mother's family for her marriage. That was all. No words about mysteries, secrets or murders. Hardly a simple task.

"Your father died shortly after that, did he not?"

Rhian only nodded.

"Would I be too bold if I asked how?"

"Nothing as dramatic as a murder. He was thrown from his horse and died instantly."

Maybe not dramatic, but he could hear the pain and grief in her voice. "I am sorry for your loss, Lady Rhian."

She met his gaze and held it for a brief heartbeat. "Thank you."

"And now I am to take you to your mother's family and your new life in Caernarvon."

"No."

"No? What do you mean by that? I cannot let you escape again."

Her bitter laugh grated on his ears. "With these latest murders, I have no intention of escaping. I meant that my mother's family is not in Caernarvon. That is only where you will leave me."

"Leave you?" Her statement confused him. "I will not leave you until I see you safely ensconced with your family."

"Then, Milord Faucon, if the whispering servants are to be believed, you will be traveling to Ynys Môn, Anglesey and not Caernarvon."

Gareth's breath caught in his chest. "Druid's Isle?" He silently chided himself. Rumors and only rumors. There would be nothing satanic on the isle. Even if there were a few outcast druids residing there, they would have nothing to do with Rhian.

"Now do you understand why I have no wish to join my beloved family? Why I fought you so hard?" Her voice shook. "Why I would rather risk my safety running away than let you lead me to their tender embrace?"

He caught a flash of fear in her eyes and fought the urge to offer comfort. A fight he quickly lost as he crossed to stand behind her.

Gareth rested his hands on her shoulders. "Do not fear rumors, milady."

Rhian leaned back against his chest as if seeking the comfort he offered. "I cannot help myself." She turned and rested her cheek against his chest. "I would rather stay here and fight the devil I know, than the one I have never met."

"Devil? Rest assured, I am no devil."

She snaked her arms about him. He closed his around her. "I did not mean you. I meant this desire I feel when you are within my reach."

Gareth stared down at the top of her head. Amazing. A woman who did not faint at the sight of dead bodies. One who would run away and perform manual labor as a servant rather than permit him to escort her to her family. A woman who physically fought him—a seasoned warrior with more than twice her strength. A woman who met and returned his desire with enough honesty to admit it.

A woman who would be worth calling wife.

He swallowed. *Where had that ungodly thought come from?*

Chapter Four

Gareth stretched his suddenly tight neck. King Stephen had given him a task to complete in a short period of time. He needed to keep his mind on his responsibility and not senseless thoughts that would only get him into more trouble.

And dallying with ladies brought nothing but trouble. His brother, Darius, was proof of that. It was best to dally with whores—at least their fathers would not bring the wrath of God upon you, or your family.

Rhian looked up at him. "Now I have shocked you with plain speaking. Should I care what others think?" She waited for a response. Her piercing blue gaze steadily, silently demanding an answer and sending his thoughts into a worse muddle.

Finally, he answered, "It would take much more than words to shock me." Gareth diverted his attention to the brazier. But the small fire pot only reminded him of how heated his blood raced while he held her.

He looked out the arrow slit at the stars. The twinkling lights made him wistful, longing for the days when his actions were not watched and analyzed, when his words were not scrutinized by those seeking to besmirch him or his family.

"Nay, Rhian, your words do not shock me. However, this lack of concern for your reputation does."

Her brittle laughter was muffled against his chest. "I find your concern…touching. And unwarranted."

"As long as you are under my charge, my concern *is* warranted."

"Then release me from your charge." When he didn't respond immediately, she stared up at him again.

Gareth sighed before leaving his stargazing behind and returned her stare. "Nay, milady, that I cannot do."

She stepped away from him and faced out the window. He came behind her and rested his hands on either side of the narrow opening, effectively trapping her with his body.

They were so close, the heat of her anger threatened to burn through his armor to his chest. When she straightened her spine and squared her shoulders, he fought the urge to back away from what would surely be an argument she would not win.

"Faucon, if you possess a drop of mercy, let me go. Do not do this."

"Nay. I fear we are fated to spend a few more days in each other's company."

She tipped her head to one side. Her half-braided hair gently swung in the same direction. The pale, smooth skin of her neck provided a stark contrast to the blackness of her hair.

It also provided a welcome distraction from this conversation. Gareth lightly stroked the curve of her neck with his thumb before resting his hand on her shoulder. The tightening of her muscles did not make the flesh beneath his thumb any less smooth, any less inviting to his touch.

A shiver visibly rippled down her neck before she jerked away from his touch. "Stop that."

Fascinated by her skin's response, Gareth ignored her order and stroked her neck again. His effort was rewarded when again a tiny tremor vibrated beneath his touch.

"Are you certain I should stop?"

Rhian shook her head before clearing her throat and answering, "No."

He dipped his head and brushed her neck with his mouth. She trembled against his lips.

Rhian closed her eyes. This was insane. They were arguing about his mission, about releasing her. Yet when he stroked her neck with his tongue the arguing fell to the wayside. She tilted her head to the side, offering him more of what he sought.

The notion that a simple touch of his lips to her neck could cause this flare of desire to rush through her body was unthinkable. It was unimaginable. It was… She leaned against his chest… It was as real as the stars in the sky.

He held her close, his fingers splayed across her stomach, the tip of his thumb resting beneath her breast. When the floor seemed to shift beneath her feet, she reached up and threaded her fingers through his hair.

The bulge against the small of her back let her know that desire coursed through his blood, too. He trailed his lips up her neck, pausing only to whisper in her ear, "Kiss me, Rhian."

His last kiss had left her confused and breathless. Would it be as heady this time? She turned in his arms and stared into his shimmering, half-closed eyes for a few heartbeats, before pulling his head down.

He held her tightly, her breasts nearly crushed against the hardness of the armor protecting his chest. The uncomfortable embrace was soon forgotten as his coaxing mouth captured her full attention.

His lips sought a response from hers and she answered willingly. A flash of realization captured her mind and her heart as his tongue slid against her own.

His arms around her, the feel of his lips on hers, was right. Almost as if it was meant to be this way. Soon she would be delivered to a family who'd ignored her existence for a lifetime, then to a man she did not know. A stranger the family who'd abandoned her had chosen.

Her heart ached for a return to the life she'd shared with her father. Years filled with someone who loved and accepted her as she was. Years when she did not have to make decisions that went against everything she'd been taught, everything she believed.

As if sensing her mind's distance, Gareth growled softly, bringing her thoughts back to him, to them. To what she might be able to have for the few days remaining to her.

His gentle touch let her know that he would not harm her. He would do nothing that she did not want. Rhian clung tighter to him. What did she want him to do?

She wanted him to cherish her, to hold her, to take her to heights she'd only heard about from gossiping servants. She wanted him to ruin her for any other. She wanted him to release her. She moved against the bulge in his groin and swallowed his moan.

Gareth broke their kiss, pulling her head against his chest with a shaking hand. "Rhian, we must stop this."

She took hope in the fact that he did not release her. She could feel the rapid, strong beating of his heart beneath the armor digging into her cheek.

Rhian knew that her success or failure would be determined by her next few sentences. After summoning all of her courage, she leaned her head back and captured his overbright gaze. "Faucon, let me escape. None need know."

He closed his eyes tightly as if in pain and shook his head. "I cannot. I must fulfill my orders." When he opened his eyes, he looked down at her with a small smile curving his lips. "My future depends on this mission."

It was now or never. She had to decide her course of action in a heartbeat.

Rhian slid a hand up his chest, reached up and traced his half smile with a fingertip. "I will make you a deal, Faucon."

He grasped her finger gently between his teeth and teased it with his tongue before stating, "I am near afraid to ask what this deal might be."

She swallowed, seeking the courage to continue with her lie, before finally finding the words. "I will not try to run away again if you will…" She sucked in a quick breath. "If you will take me."

A frown marred his forehead. "Take you?" Realization widened his eyes. "You cannot mean—"

"Yes, I do. Take me with your body, Faucon." She

glanced away, then back before continuing, "Teach me the ways of lovers."

His heavy groan gave her hope. "Do you know what you ask?"

"I would not ask if I did not know."

"But you are to be—"

She cut off his words by placing her finger over his lips. "Married. Yes, I know that. I will be married to a man I do not know. A man whose kiss I may not like. A man my unknown family has chosen." She traced his suddenly tight lips with her fingertip. "Do I not deserve to enjoy being kissed? Do I not deserve a few nights of shared passion?"

Rhian knew she was rambling, but she hoped her lengthy plea would keep him from detecting her true motivation—escape from her fate. "Do I not deserve to hold a memory to my heart? Something to remember when the nights get cold and the days are too long?"

She was unable to read his stare. He did not appear shocked. But neither did he appear to be thrilled with her offer.

Rhian stepped away from him and looked at the floor. "I am—"

The sound of men coming down the hall leading to her chamber cut off her apology.

Gareth gritted his teeth at their approach. With an effort he didn't realize he possessed, he brought his wildly thudding heart under control before his captain entered the room with two other men.

"Milord, we will have this door fixed in but a few moments." At Gareth's silence, Edgar prompted, "Milord? You do want us to fix the door, yes?"

Gareth waved for the men to continue. "Yes."

He wondered if his voice sounded as hoarse to his captain as it did to him.

While the men worked on the door, Edgar offered, "I will relieve you, so you can go below and eat."

Gareth cleared his throat. "Perhaps later."

He wanted to kick himself. He knew his clipped responses would make his man aware something was not quite right.

Rhian turned back to the window, leaning her forehead against the wall.

Finally in control of his racing desire, Gareth faced his captain and motioned the man to join him outside of the chamber.

"Have all of Browan's men been accounted for?"

"Aye, milord. Three dead, six with minor injuries and one who was worse off. They found him crawling out of one of the storage sheds. He is hurt, but will recover."

"Good. Were they able to provide any further information?"

Edgar shook his head. "No. But nobody has truly questioned them in detail. Would you like me to bring them to you for interrogating?"

"No." That was the last thing Gareth wanted at the moment. "Let them rest and I will talk to them on the morrow."

"Aye, sir." Edgar peered around Gareth. "They are almost done with the door. Are you certain you do not wish me to relieve you?"

It was all Gareth could do to hold back his laugh. "I am fine, Edgar. See that the others get some food and a place to sleep for the night."

Edgar frowned before saying, "You need sleep more than the rest of us. I can—"

"No."

The captain stepped back from Gareth's near shout. "No need to tear my head off, milord." He peered at his lord from beneath bushy eyebrows for a moment before a smile crossed his face. "Oh, I see. You have plans for the evening."

"In a manner of speaking, yes. I plan to spend the night guarding my charge."

Edgar's eyes widened. His mouth dropped open. After blinking a few times, he frowned, then asked, "Alone? In her chamber? Milord, do you think—"

Gareth cut his man off with a raised hand. "I try not to think of anything other than the successful completion of my mission for the King." To reassure Edgar, he added, "I will sleep on the floor, by the door, not in her bed."

Edgar waggled his eyebrows. "Excellent idea, milord. I will see to the men. Then I will return to guard the door from any who would seek to disturb you...or the lady."

Gareth bit the inside of his cheek to keep from responding to his captain's obvious opinion. The less said, the better. "That is fine, Edgar. I will see you on the morn."

After Edgar went below stairs, Gareth waited until the men were done with the door before reentering the chamber. He closed the door behind him and dropped the locking bar into place.

Rhian hadn't moved. Her slumped shoulders spoke volumes to him. He imagined that she was embarrassed, perhaps now even regretted her boldness.

What fanciful ideas had she been concocting with her

brazen offer? There was little doubt that the lady was up to something. Most likely she was seeking yet another way to escape her fate.

She'd admitted to being a virgin, but she seemed more seductress than virgin. So her outrageous offer seemed even more absurd. Was she truly that desperate to ruin her future? Or had she lied?

Did it matter to him? Shamefully, he had to admit that no, at this moment it did not matter in the least. Her offer appealed to him more than he could explain.

On one hand the mere idea felt right. As if it was meant to be. On the other hand, he was intrigued by her attempted manipulation and wanted to see how far she'd go. Would she complete the act? Would he? This was not a way to regain honor. It was more like another test to see if he truly had any honor left.

He leaned against the door. "Rhian."

She turned around, but kept her face averted.

"Rhian, I would like nothing more than to give you a night of passion. But not if you have changed your mind."

She took a step toward him, stopped and looked at him. "This will remain between us? You will tell no one?"

He started across the floor toward her. His steps slow and steady, unlike his racing heart. "I do not run to all with tales."

"You will not think less of me?"

"I thought that others' opinions did not matter."

She frowned. "In this, yours does matter."

He stopped an arm's length in front of her, praying his tongue would find the right words. "You offer me what no other woman has ever even hinted at. How could I think less of you?"

"Will you think less of me in the day's light?"

Gareth shrugged. "I do not think so, but I do not know for certain."

Rhian rolled her eyes. "Well, do you think any less of any woman you have…that you've…" She stopped, obviously unable to find a word for the act.

While it would be amusing to see what word she eventually conjured, Gareth saved her the search. He reached out and ran a finger down her arm before lacing his fingers through hers. "I would not know, Rhian. Whores are not generally still around by the day's light."

With a gentle tug, he pulled her closer until she rested against his chest. "If you have changed your mind, I will go now."

She shook her head. "Nay. You touch me and I want more. I do not wish for you to leave."

"And when you speak so, I have no wish to leave." He tipped her chin up with the side of his thumb. He searched her eyes, looking for any sign of wavering, any uncertainty and found none in her seemingly guileless stare.

She was willing to risk much in this bid for a night of passion. He still did not believe for one heartbeat that she would carry this through to the end.

Gareth briefly touched his lips to hers, before releasing her. "Since neither of us wish for any others to know what we are about," he said while pulling his tunic off over his head, then unbuckling his sword belt. "You will have to help me out of this armor."

Rhian laughed softly before stepping back to tug at the laces holding the mail sleeves and his hauberk together. "I have played squire before."

Her fingers shook as she worked the bindings. It was all she could do to not tear at them, to quickly divest him of his clothing and fall together to the mattress.

Anything to get this over with before she lost all nerve. *What had she been thinking?*

A few hours ago, the mere suggestion of lying with a man seemed insulting and degrading. Only a cheap whore would permit herself to be used so.

What was she? By offering herself, hopefully in exchange for her freedom, was she any better than those who offered their bodies in exchange for coin?

Since she was the one who would do the using, Rhian felt lower than a whore. What was the penance for such wanton, deceitful behavior? At the moment, she didn't know. But she doubted if it'd be anything pleasant. In the recesses of her mind, she wondered how long she'd burn in hell.

Finally, the bindings came loose and she slid the long sleeves off his arms. "Bend over." When he followed her bidding, she tugged at the armor until it finally slid over his shoulders and head. Too heavy and cumbersome for her to handle, she let it fall to the floor with a thud.

He quickly released the bindings of the mailed chausses protecting his legs and tossed them atop the growing pile of armor.

While he stood upright, Faucon peeled his quilted hacketon and sweaty woolen shirt off with one fluid swipe and tossed both on the growing pile. Relieved of the added weight of armor, he stretched and rolled his shoulders.

Clad only in braies and boots, he worked his muscles. Rhian sucked in a sharp breath. Muscles rippled across his chest, bulged and relaxed in his arms and corded in his neck. She had assumed the armor and the clothing added bulk to his size. She'd assumed wrong.

By the heavens he was larger than she thought. How in the name of God had he gotten that big? Surely he'd not been born twice the size of a normal babe. His mother would have died in childbirth.

Rhian's mouth went dry as she knelt to unlace his boots. He ran his fingers through her hair. She jumped at his touch and came eye level with... By all the saints she could not do this.

But she had no choice. Her numb mind could think of no other way to defy the fate planned for her. She bit her lower lip before returning to the task at hand, but her hands fumbled with the laces. The sudden ineptitude brought tears of frustration to her eyes. *Fine whore she would make.*

Faucon bent over and stayed her useless fingers. "Rhian, let me." He released her, sat down on a bench and removed his boots.

She stood, frozen in place, unable to think, or to move. Rhian felt his attention sweep over her before she hesitantly met his gaze.

He briefly closed his eyes and shook his head before beckoning her with his forefinger. "Come here."

Somehow, as if in a strange dream, she found her feet taking her toward him. Slowly, like a condemned person walking toward her own death.

Faucon pulled her down on his lap, held her against his chest and stroked her back.

Several moments of silence passed before Rhian released a huge breath and relaxed against him.

He rubbed his cheek against the top of her head. "We

do not have to continue. If you want to cry hold, we can stop now."

Cry hold? Rhian frowned. Did she want to stop? Would that not be admitting fear? Admitting defeat? Since when did she let fear of a thing stop her? But would it not be a wiser move?

This indecision would drive her mad.

She turned to look up at him. "Just tell me if I need be afraid."

"I thought I was a devil you did not fear."

Rhian groaned. She had declared that, hadn't she? "Perhaps I was a little hasty. Should I fear the devil I know?"

"I cannot force myself to believe you would have ever considered so bold a move if you truly feared me."

Heat filled her cheeks. Rhian admitted, "'Tis not exactly *you* that I fear."

Faucon's soft chuckle raced warm across her heart. "Your imagination is far-reaching. It is not as if I will impale and kill you."

At the absurd vision his words created in her mind Rhian had no choice but to laugh.

Faucon tipped his head to one side, shot her a boyish-looking half smile before asking, "Would it upset you to know that I have not the vast experience you seem to believe I possess?"

Rhian sighed. Then pulled up the skirts of her gown and turned around on his lap. With her legs astride his, she placed her hands against his chest.

"Disappointed?" His deep voice rumbled up from his chest.

Rhian smiled up at him. "Disappointed?" She shook her head. "Nay, Milord Faucon. I am relieved."

Chapter Five

"Relieved?" Gareth wondered how any feeling of relief fit into their current situation. His heart pounded like a hare caught in a hunter's snare. If relief truly coursed through her veins then he was obviously doing something dreadfully wrong.

Rhian answered, "Aye. Relief. You will not be disappointed by comparing my fumbling against countless other women."

Gareth nearly choked on her skewed logic. But with her fingertips tracing a path across his chest and her legs straddling his, any logic was fast slipping away.

She rubbed her cheek against the hair on his chest before scooting closer. "What do we do now?"

He knew what he should do. Leave. Stop. Do nothing to dishonor her, or himself any further. But a driving need to know how far she'd take this game urged him on.

He could take her like a whore now. No niceties. No kissing or stroking. But regardless of how she was acting at this moment, Rhian was not a whore and did not deserve so little regard.

Gareth slid his hands around her back and worked the laces holding her gown in place.

Hands that could deftly wield a sword with deadly accuracy, shook. Would he manage to undress her before she cried hold? Gareth gritted his teeth in an attempt to refrain from simply tearing the thin fabric of the gown from her body.

Rhian sat patiently, but he saw the corners of her mouth twitch in what he knew would have been laughter at his fumbling had she not bit her lip.

"Laughing at me?"

She shook her head. "No. Never." He heard the amusement in her unsteady voice.

Finally, the knot came free and he slid the laces from her gown. Rhian slipped her arms easily out of the overlarge dress, letting the fabric pool at her waist.

Gareth traced a fingertip down her neck and across one shoulder. Her flushed skin was soft beneath his touch. As he stroked along the edge of her chemise, his fingers itched to caress her breast. He yearned for more. But when he caught her gaze, she closed her eyes and turned her head away.

What he yearned for mattered little. She was not doing this out of desire, he'd known that. It would be an easy thing to goad her into completing the act she'd been foolish enough to begin, but he'd not have her without the desire. Nor would he have her at the instigation of a lie.

His heart steadied to a sure and even thudding, heavy in his chest. Gareth dipped his head and kissed her shoulder, her neck before brushing his lips against hers.

He whispered into her ear. "We would disappoint each other if one of us were no longer willing."

"Nay, I am still—"

He caught her chin and turned her face to his. "You are what, Rhian? Willing to barter yourself for a memory? To ruin yourself so completely? For what, Rhian? Your freedom?"

When she didn't respond, he asked, "Do you think me a complete imbecile? That I am so eager for a woman that I fail to know when I am being manipulated?"

She could not hold his gaze and closed her eyes. "I thought that…" Her words trailed off.

"You thought what? That I would let you escape if you gave yourself to me?"

Rhian shook her head. "No." A shuddering sigh escaped her parted lips. "Perhaps."

He released her chin. "There is no need to whore yourself for something that will not happen."

When she leaned away from him, he warned, "You will not escape again."

The look she turned on him was as stormy as a windswept sea. "I may not escape, but I will not stay where you take me."

"That is your choice to make when the time comes."

Rhian wanted to scream in frustration. He had caught her in a moment of indecision and she could not deny his accusation of seeking to manipulate him.

However, she would expect him to be angry at the discovery. His kindness confused her. But that was beginning to prove a common happening of late. She could do nothing but concede defeat—this time.

"So what do we do now?"

Gareth nodded toward the door. "Edgar stands guard out there. My leaving would only create difficulties we do not need at this moment."

"How will you leave in the morning?"

"I know my man." He pulled her gown back up over her shoulders. "He will leave long enough to attend Mass." His fingers lingered on her skin momentarily before he rose, shifting her off his lap as he stood.

Gareth grabbed his shirt off the floor, pulled it over his head and walked toward the corner of the small chamber. "You, milady, can sleep on the pallet."

"You can't sleep on the floor."

"Fear not, you will be quite safe."

Lingering desire laced his voice, making it deeper than normal. The raspy tone sent a shiver of regret down her spine. "I fear not for my safety."

He settled his frame down onto the floor, with his back propped up against the corner. "Perhaps you should."

Candlelight played across his face, accentuating dark circles beneath his eyes. A pang of guilt pricked at her. "You will not find comfort there. Take the pallet."

"I have spent the last sennight on the back of a horse." He patted the floor. "This will be more comfortable than a moving beast. Go to bed, Rhian, worry not for me."

She stretched out on top of the pallet. "Do you want the blanket?"

"No."

She snuggled under the cover. How would he stay warm? "Should I build up the fire?"

"No."

"Is there anything—"

"Yes. Be still and go to sleep."

* * *

Gareth awoke to Edgar's voice calling him from the other side of the door. "Milord Faucon, are you awake?"

But it wasn't his captain's question that he found odd. However, the snoring woman draped across his chest was highly out of the ordinary.

While he may have thought it strange now, he obviously hadn't while asleep. His arm was wrapped around her, holding her to him and his one leg rested over the top of one of hers.

Gareth didn't want to disturb her by shouting an answer to Edgar, so he ignored his man's call. After settling more comfortably against the wall, he pulled the cover up over Rhian's shoulders.

This was pleasant. Absently stroking her hair, he realized how easy it would be to get used to waking up in this manner every day.

When her light snoring ceased, Gareth tightened his embrace. "Was the pallet *too* comfortable?"

Rhian stretched, her legs brushed down the length of his, chasing pleasant thoughts from his mind with ones more carnal. She sat up with a yawn. "No. This was the only way I could get you to stop talking in your sleep."

His stomach lurched. "I do not talk in my sleep."

"We were the only two in this chamber and I wasn't talking."

Gareth glowered at her and demanded, "What did I say?"

Rhian shook her head. "Nothing really. Just some mumbled words about not leaving and capture." She touched his arm. "Truly, Faucon, it was not as if you held a logical conversation."

He didn't believe her, but had no choice but to take her at her word. From now on he'd make certain he slept alone.

She stretched again, reaching up, she ran her fingers through her hair. "I must look a fright."

In truth, she didn't look a fright. Sleep still softened her face. Her movements as she stretched lengthened her torso. When she pulled her arms above her head Gareth had to wrench his stare from her breasts. Suddenly, cotton seemed to fill his mouth and mind. He swallowed past the dryness and finally said, "I could have a bath sent up if you would like."

Her eyes lit up. "That would be wonderful. I have nothing clean to put on, but the bath would still be welcome."

"Milord Faucon." Edgar tapped on the door again.

Gareth and Rhian looked at the door, then at each other.

"How does he know you're in here?" Furrows lined her forehead.

Gareth shrugged. "Perhaps I find it needful to let my man know my whereabouts when visiting a strange keep."

"Perhaps?" she asked in a clipped tone before rising. "And perhaps you'll find a way to disabuse him of what he surely thinks happened last night."

"He'll think whatever I tell him to think." Stiff from the cold floor, hungry and needful of the garderobe, Gareth's patience started to wear thin. "He's the captain of my guard, not of my life. Edgar knows his place."

Rhian spared him a darting glare before opening the door and looking at the captain. "Yes?"

Edgar's surprise lasted but half a heartbeat before craning his neck to look around her. "Milord?"

Rhian stepped out of the way and pointed toward the corner. "Over there."

Edgar did her the courtesy of tipping his head in acknowledgment before entering the chamber and approaching Gareth.

"And a fine good morning to you, too, Sir Edgar." Rhian spoke to the empty doorway before closing it. She leaned against the door.

When Gareth jerked a thumb toward her, Edgar stopped and turned around to face her. "I apologize, Lady Gervaise. How are you this fine morning?"

"A little food, a bath and an empty chamber will make this morning nearly perfect."

Gareth knew when to take a hint, especially when it was spoken with a silken voice so fake that it hurt his ears. He stood up with a groan. "I don't suppose Sir Hector had a chamber prepared for me?"

"Aye, sir. It's the chamber next door. Your clothing is there and I took the liberty of requesting a bath be prepared since there was a tub in there already. Hopefully, the servants will arrive shortly because Sir Hector is below awaiting your instructions."

Gareth scooped up what he could of his pile of clothes and armor in one hand, then headed for the door. He stopped in front of Rhian. "I'll have them bring the bath in here. When you are finished, do not leave this chamber until I come back for you."

Rhian just looked at him.

He frowned down at her. "Do not test me. I will do whatever is needful to ensure your safe delivery to your family."

Edgar gathered the rest of Gareth's belongings and left the two alone.

Rhian walked over to the window. "And *I* will do whatever is needful to see that I don't arrive." She turned back to face him, stiffened her spine and jutted her chin a tad higher. "Nothing has changed, Faucon." Ice tinged her words.

Ice and a challenge.

"By all that's holy." Gareth cursed then cleared the distance between them in three long strides. Before she could escape, he wrapped his hand around the back of her head and drew her close.

He dropped his clothes, leaned down and whispered, "Much has changed, Rhian."

Just before their lips met, Rhian sighed, wound her arms around his neck and whispered back, "Show me what has changed, Faucon. Show me."

Gareth paused. Frozen less than a breath away from her lips. Her breathless voice was far too seductive for the anger she'd just displayed. He shook his head, released her and picked his clothes back up. "No. It will not work."

As he headed for the door, he ordered over his shoulder. "Do not leave this chamber."

Her curses followed him out the door.

Rhian couldn't remember a bath that ever felt as welcome or as wonderful as this one. She leaned back against the wooden side of the tub.

At the moment she didn't care that Faucon had ordered it for her. One way or another she'd eventually figure out how to deal with him and his quest for honor at her expense.

Right now, though, the only thing she wanted to do was to soak in this heavenly hot water that the servants had slaved over. The looks on their faces when they'd filled it for her were beyond compare. Yesterday, they'd known her only as Rhian the kitchen wench. Today, she was again Lady Gervaise.

She leaned her head back to rest against the rim and stared up at the curtain surrounding the tub. Private. Warm. What more could she ask for?

The rim cut into her head. A pillow would be nice.

Rhian pushed the curtain aside and grabbed one of the drying cloths that had been left. She folded it up and laid it over the edge of the tub before resuming her soak.

With her arms draped along the sides of the tub and the makeshift pillow for her head, Rhian let the tension leave her body. She'd worry about Faucon later.

Gareth stared at the bodies. Even though most of the blood had been cleaned from them, they presented a grim vision.

Browan's local midwife had been the only one available to call upon and she bent over each naked body, clucking her tongue and shaking her head. Finally, she called, "Milords, come look at this."

Gareth and Hector approached her side. Gareth knew what she wanted to point out to them, but for Rhian's safety, he remained silent.

The people of Browan were unknown to him. Rhian

had already lied to them once. He knew not how they'd react if they learned the murderers had most likely followed her to their home.

The woman poked a bony finger at the throats on each man as she walked around the table that held all three. "What do you make of these?"

Gareth leaned closer. "It appears as if they were pierced with something sharp."

"And round," the woman added.

"A nail?" Sir Hector asked.

She snorted at his question. "A mighty large one." She stuck her index finger into a gaping hole, then pulled it out and held it up. "More like some type of spear."

If someone had thrown a spear it would not have pierced the armor so neatly. Gareth frowned. Even if it had been such an excellent throw, the spear would have gone through the men's necks.

Which meant that someone used a short, handheld spear, or spike of some type and jammed it into the intended target.

"While I can see the advantage of using such an odd weapon to get through the chain mail, why would someone choose that method instead of simply ramming a sword through the chest?"

Hector's useless shrug provided little.

The midwife frowned, then shook her graying head before making the sign of the cross. "There have been tales…"

While waiting for her to continue, Gareth fought back the dread snaking up his spine.

She finally muttered under her breath, "No, it cannot be." Then leaned on the table as if seeking support.

"Go on, old woman," Gareth prodded.

"There are old, old tales of a renegade group of ancient druids who did not kill with metal. They used only weapons made of the wood of hawthorn to murder their enemy." She looked down at the bodies. "This form of death would have prevented the men from shouting for help before they died and would produce much blood."

Gareth reached over and moved her out of the way. He pried the mouth open on one of the men and peered inside. The man's mouth was caked with blood.

Of all the woods that could be used, why hawthorn? He stepped back and looked at her. "See if you can find any slivers in or around the wounds."

He then turned to Sir Hector. "Make sure your gates are double guarded. Put everyone on alert. No man is to be alone at any time."

When both turned to follow his orders, Gareth pulled Edgar aside. "We must leave here as quickly as possible. It is the only way to draw the murderers away from Browan. Send word to Count Faucon that I need more men and I need them now."

"What should I tell him, milord?"

Gareth thought for a moment. The last thing he wanted was for his brother to show up. He didn't need Rhys's help, he just needed some of his men to strengthen his pitiful force.

"Tell him as little as possible. Lie. Tell him that some of our men have become too ill to ride and that I cannot postpone my mission for King Stephen."

"Do you think he will believe that?"

Gareth laughed. "No." Rhys was not that trusting—of anyone. "But he is newly married. His mind will be so occupied with other thoughts that perhaps he will not spend much time questioning my odd request."

Edgar nodded. "Consider it done." He turned to leave, then paused to ask, "Should I use one of Browan's messengers?"

"No." While he didn't relish risking his own men, Browan had already lost three. Since Gareth would be the new overlord here, he'd no wish to earn their malice. "Use our men."

"How many men?"

Normally, one would do. But not now. "Send three. Two archers and one swordsman." Better safe than sorry.

When Edgar left to do his bidding, Gareth glanced at the stairs. Rhian should be dressed and pacing the chamber by now. In truth, he was surprised that she hadn't come down for something to eat.

What was he to do with her? She'd been correct about how the guards died. Could her fears about her family be correct, too? His chest tightened with the sudden need to protect her.

Gareth shook his head. One thing at a time. He had no choice but to deliver her as promised. When that was completed, he could decide what to do next.

For now, perhaps something in her belly would lighten her mood. He grabbed a pitcher of water, a chunk of bread and cheese and headed up with the food to break her fast.

Chapter Six

~~~

Rhian awoke with a start. She'd fallen asleep and now the water was nearly like ice. She sat up, brushed the curtain aside and reached for another drying cloth.

Her hand met empty air.

"What the— Where'd the cloth go?"

Someone shoved it into her hand.

She'd not expected any of the servants to return, but was grateful for the assistance. "Thank you."

She rose and stepped out of the tub. The cold air hit her body, making her shiver.

Rhian wrapped the soft, oversize cloth around her and stood by the brazier.

She brought the last cloth up over her head and started to dry her hair. The familiar scraping sound of wood across the floor let her know that the servant had dragged a stool near where she stood. When the edge of the seat touched the back of her legs, she gratefully sat down. Without turning to see which girl had offered to help her, she again said, "Thank you."

After she finished drying her hair as best she could, Rhian wrapped the cloth back around her shoulders and asked, "Would you be kind enough to find me a comb?"

A comb gently tugged at the ends of her hair. Rhian tipped her head forward. "I'm sorry, I know it's a tangled mess."

The servant patiently worked the snarls out of her hair, lock by lock. The steady rhythm of the comb stroking through her hair and the heat of the brazier did as much to relax her as the bath had.

She closed her eyes and sighed. She'd not realized how much she'd missed having the assistance of a maid. When a gentle tug on her hair urged her to tip her head back, she readily complied. Her hair was combed back away from her face. Once all the tangles were gone and the comb slid easily through her tresses, she heard the servant lay the comb aside before beginning to fluff out the now-curling strands.

"That's not necessary, I will just braid it, thank you." Rhian reached up to stay the girl's hand and froze.

That was not a girl's hand. Her heart slammed against her ribs. Large fingers laced through her own. She sucked in a deep breath and held it a few long heartbeats before turning around to look up at her personal *maid*.

Gareth smiled down at her. Before she could think, or work her mind around another plan to manipulate him into releasing her, he pulled her up from the stool and into his arms.

Her lips opened to protest and he took full advantage of her unplanned response by covering her lips with his own.

With a gentle tug, the drying cloth slid down her

body and hit the floor with little more than a soft rustling of fabric.

Her skin was soft beneath his callused fingertips and he longed to stroke every inch of flesh. The scent of roses from her bath clung to her, filling his mind with unattainable passion.

Gareth broke their stolen kiss and reluctantly released her.

Rhian retrieved the cloth from the floor. Her flaming face and shaking fingers warned him of her ire.

After securing the drying cloth about her body, she swung a hand toward his face.

He easily caught her wrist before her palm made contact with his cheek. "Having felt the flat of your hand once before, I have no desire to do so again."

"You swine." She nearly hissed through clenched teeth.

"I gather you can be a blood-thirsty wench when you want." Gareth smiled down at her, refusing to lose his temper.

"Faucon, I swear—"

"Gareth."

Rhian frowned in obvious confusion.

"My name. It is Gareth." He pulled her closer, moving her arm behind her back. "Say it. Gareth."

She tried to twist away from his hold. "Let me go."

"No." Easily keeping her in place, he repeated, "Gareth. Say it."

Her glare, had it been a solid object, would have lacerated him. "What difference would it make?"

He brushed his lips across her forehead, just grazing her flesh before she could jerk out of his reach. "As one who has tasted your sweet kiss, held you in my arms and felt your answering desire, I think it only appropriate that you use my name."

"Have you lost your wits? I thought you resented my attempts at manipulation."

"I do." Gareth shrugged. "But I find myself unwilling to forget what might have been."

He knew the instant she resumed plotting. Rhian narrowed her eyes and pursed her lips.

It was all he could do not to sputter with amusement when she smoothed the lines from her forehead and plastered on a smile filled with more artifice than he'd ever seen, before winding her free arm up and around his neck.

"Then let us not dwell on what might have been."

He leaned down and whispered into her ear, "Gareth."

Rhian lifted her face and whispered back, "Gareth."

"Again."

"Gareth."

His name, whispered in a soft rush of air, felt like a caress against his cheek.

With her lips against his, Rhian whispered again, "Gareth."

He knew, somewhere in the back of his mind, that her compliance was nothing but a ploy, but for just a heartbeat he wanted to believe otherwise. Gareth released her wrist and gathered her into his embrace, cutting off another whisper of his name with his lips on hers.

Against all logical thought and common sense, his heart pounded inside his chest. What he knew to be true and what he wished melded until the truth became lost in a murky haze of longing and need.

God help him. It would be all too easy to forget she sought only freedom.

With a breathless sigh of surrender, Rhian clung to him. It was all she could do to remember that this was nothing more than a game. A game she had no choice but to win.

But with his hand cupped around her neck, gently stroking her flesh with the side of his thumb, remembering anything was incredibly hard. And with his other hand tracing a line of fire down her spine before coming to rest on the fullness of her hip, it became nigh on impossible.

And with his lips on hers, demanding and receiving a response filled with a returned passion, she felt guilt and shame crowd into her heart.

God help her. She wanted to play no games with this man.

He didn't deserve such treatment from her. He only sought to do as his king bade him and to regain what he had surely mistaken as lost honor. She could not play the whore to trick him.

Unable to hold back the cry tearing at her throat, Rhian pushed away, breaking their kiss and embrace on a shuddering sob. "Stop. Faucon, stop."

She caught her breath and looked up at him. His darkening stare only filled her with more shame. Rhian gently touched his cheek. "Gareth. I am sorry. I…" Uncertain what to say to take away the anger raging in his gaze, she let her words trail off and dropped her arm.

Before she could turn away, he threaded his fingers through her hair to hold her in place. "No apology is required. I knew what you intended and I willingly joined in your game."

She flinched as if struck before shaking her head.

"No more, Faucon." When his fingers tightened in her hair, she lifted her gaze from the floor. "Gareth. I cannot deny that I desire your touch. But I promise I will attempt no more ploys at your expense."

He coaxed her forward. Easily drawing her to rest against his chest. "No more than I can deny my desire for you, Rhian."

The steady thumping of his heart beneath her cheek lulled her to relax against him.

"I promised only to deliver you to your family."

She tensed at his statement.

He brushed the top of her head with his cheek. "I made no promises on what happens after that."

Rhian backed slightly away and stared up at him. Hope, newly forming, urged caution. "What do you mean?"

His smile helped to relieve her hesitancy. "I mean that while I may deliver you, I have no orders regarding what happens next."

"Then—"

"Rhian," he interrupted her question. "I cannot see past this moment. You may find that you genuinely like your family and the man they have chosen."

At her snort of disbelief, he continued, "On the other hand, you may not. I made a vow to King Stephen guaranteeing your safe delivery. I will see that vow fulfilled. However, if you decide you do not wish to remain, I will see you safely to wherever you wish to go."

She was amazed. "You will split hairs for me?"

Gareth shrugged. "I prefer to look at it as following orders precisely."

"This will not cause trouble for you in the future?"

"Why should it? Only a churl would leave a lady in a place she had no wish to remain."

"Why should I trust you?"

"Because I have not lied to you. Nor will I." He paused, apparently contemplating his next words. "However, you must make me a vow in return."

Warning bells rang loudly in her mind. "A vow?"

"Aye." He lifted one eyebrow, as if daring her to refuse. "You will not seek to escape and you will give your family a chance before deciding one way or another."

"They have not..."

"A chance, Rhian. I only ask that you give them a chance. You know not what their reasoning, or their circumstances have been."

"But I have heard—" She stopped herself and mulled his vow over in her mind. He was giving her every opportunity to accept or decline what fate had demanded. Finally, she agreed. "It is a bargain."

"Good." He pulled her close for a moment, before dropping his arms to his sides.

To fill the suddenly uncomfortable silence, Rhian asked, "I do not suppose I have any clothing available?"

He nodded toward the pallet. "Over there."

As she walked toward the pallet, she asked over her shoulder, "Will you assist me?"

Gareth's heart somersaulted in place. "No." He headed toward the door. "I will find you a maid. Now."

"I never would have taken you for a coward, Faucon."

He heard the laughter in her voice; it raked across him like a knife. But when he turned to glare at her, he saw the teasing smile.

Instead of glaring, he bowed. "Milady, I freely admit

my cowardice in this instance." Rising, he added, "This mere mortal man would rather face a sword unarmed, than be subjected yet again to the enticing sight of your perfect flesh. A sight that would surely chase the breath from my body."

"My, my. We do have a way with words, do we not?" She turned toward him and started to unwind the cloth from around her body.

He managed to choke out, "We try." Before hastily leaving the chamber.

Rhian was still laughing to herself when the door reopened.

Gareth stood in the doorway with Hawise at his side.

Rhian's laughter stopped abruptly. She looked at the two of them and then focused on Gareth. "You cannot be serious. Her? My maid?"

He shrugged. "It is the best option considering the needs of the moment."

Hawise looked from Rhian to Gareth and back to Rhian before hitching a thumb at Gareth. "Have you compromised yourself with this one here?"

Rhian knew that the woman's boldness was warranted, but if she didn't put Hawise in her place from the beginning, there'd be more sarcasm to deal with later. She drew herself up to full height and pinned the former cook with a stare that made full-grown men back away. "That is none of your concern."

Hawise shook her head, not in the least bit perturbed. "Nay. I thought not, but it was amusing to ask."

Rhian blinked.

Faucon laughed.

When Rhian turned the same stare on him, he saluted and backed out of the room. "I feel certain that I leave you in good hands."

Hawise laughed. "See, that look only works with men, milady." She crossed the chamber and began picking up the gowns Rhian had strewn across the pallet. After a quick glance at the pallet, she clucked her tongue. "You need a bed."

Rhian rolled her eyes. "So I have been told. Instead of wasting time telling me what I do or do not need, why don't you just act like a simple maid."

Hawise dropped the gowns and shook a finger under Rhian's nose. "You may find it an easy thing to thunk a smitten lad upside the head with a cooking pot and make good your escape, but I will not be so easy to elude."

"You think you could stop me?" Not that it mattered after the vow she'd given Faucon, but Hawise's attitude was unacceptable.

"You may be taller, but I am bigger than you. And Faucon's gold is more than enough incentive to see that you behave."

"Behave?" The insult fueled her outrage. "Behave?" She'd find a way to repay him for his kind consideration. "I will not stand here and be insulted or scolded like some toddling child."

"Then do not act like one."

"You are to be my maid, not my keeper."

"Perhaps you need speak about that with Lord Faucon."

Rhian narrowed her eyes. "What does that mean?"

"It means, milady, that he has explained all to me and I will see that his wishes are carried out."

That unsatisfactory answer, and a wildly growing curiosity to know what she faced, prompted Rhian to ask, "What exactly did Lord Faucon explain?"

While returning to straightening out the clothing, Hawise answered, "That by King Stephen's orders he is escorting you to your family." She paused to smirk at Rhian. "And that it would be best for all concerned if you were to arrive there...*untainted* is the word I think he used."

The woman's sudden cackling broke into her explanation. The sound grated sharply on Rhian's ears, but clenching her jaw did little to stop the irritation.

Hawise wiped tears of laughter from her eyes before continuing. "I believe his lordship meant *uncompromised* but did not have the wherewithal to say so."

"You can cease tossing that word in my face."

"I only wished to use a term you would understand. A fine young lady like you shouldn't be subjected to crudities."

Rhian clenched her hands at her sides, stared up at the ceiling and cursed. After exhausting herself of every swear word she'd ever learned, she took a deep breath that did little to calm her frazzled nerves. "I doubt if there is a crudity I am not aware of. But on the off chance that I am incorrect, let me assure you that Lord Faucon is in no way concerned about my virginity."

The lie tripped off her tongue so easily that she felt compelled to expound. "He is concerned only with appearances. It will serve him better if I do not arrive at my family's home with any rumors or gossip trailing my heels." She glared at the other woman. "Understood?"

Hawise flapped a chemise and gown at her. "As you

say, milady." She then pulled the drying cloth from around Rhian and dropped the chemise over her head. "You will need much more practice at lying than that pitiful attempt if you seek to have any believe you."

Rhian groaned from inside the garment. This was not an argument worth continuing. She could not win. Hawise would never let her.

Instead, she bit the inside of her mouth and permitted the woman to help her dress in silence.

Once she was clothed, had eaten and was finally, blessedly alone, Rhian stared out the window.

Not one thing was turning out the way she'd planned. Gareth had somehow set everything askew—including her senses.

Her stomach fluttered. Just thinking about him drew unwarranted responses from her body. If she was to honestly consider the man her family had chosen, a fondness of any sort toward someone else would be wrong.

She shook her head. Precisely the reason she should not risk further contact with the man.

So what to do now?

The door to the chamber opened. Since the guards Gareth had placed at her door didn't announce anyone, Rhian assumed it was Hawise returning and didn't turn away from the window until a hand grasped her shoulder with a hurtful, unfamiliar hold.

She jammed her elbow sharply backward until she made hard contact with her visitor, then spun around to see who she'd hit.

Rhian gasped as she realized her visitor was an assailant. A man, she assumed he was a man by his height, wearing a black hood that concealed his face and head stood just inches from her, rubbing his side where she'd planted her elbow.

She could only see his eyes and they flashed with a hatred she'd never before witnessed. A hate so deep and cold that it chilled her through to her soul.

"Who the hell are you and how did you get past the guards?"

He didn't answer. Instead, he made a move to grab her again. Rhian quickly ducked out of his reach.

She ran toward the chamber door, but was forcibly stopped when he caught her by the arm and threw her on the pallet. While she tried to catch her breath, he dropped to kneel over her and asked, "Where is it?"

She stared at him. "Where is what?"

"The amethyst dragon." He grasped her shoulder in a hold that she knew would leave bruises. "Where is it?" His voice was a near growl.

Rhian immediately reached for her pendant. It was gone. She'd been so used to wearing it of late that she'd not noticed its absence. She didn't remember taking it off. Where could it have gone?

The man cursed, then straddled her.

Rhian opened her mouth, but he cut her scream off with his hand.

He loomed above her. "They await the dragon. Tell me where it is and I will make your death quick." He leaned closer. "Do not tell me and I will see you suffer."

"The guard at your chamber door died quickly." He pulled something out from beneath the opening of his tunic and held it before her. "You decide."

Rhian swallowed and forced herself to focus on the object. It appeared to be a tiny wooden sickle, but the end was more flat than hooked. Not taking the handle into consideration, the entire sickle was no more than the size of a hand, but the tip looked more like a spike—Her heart ceased beating.

This is what killed the messengers at Gervaise and Browan's guards.

"I see you understand. Good." He dragged the tip of the weapon lightly across her throat. "Now, where is the dragon?"

She shook her head slightly.

He pulled the weapon across the top of her skin, down her neck, over her collarbone and hooked the end of it in her gown. With nothing more than a quick flick of his wrist, he tore through the fabric.

"Why are you not wearing your mother's gift?"

Rhian blinked several times. How did he know it came from her mother? Who was he?

He toyed with the sickle, running it back and forth over her exposed flesh and up to her neck before caressing her cheek with the side of the weapon.

"They will be disappointed. The dragon would have gained much power from resting between your breasts." He emphasized his words by drawing his weapon down the valley between her breasts.

She fought back a sob of fear. Her body trembled. With his instrument of death away from her throat, she tried to twist free of him. But kicking her legs and bucking to throw him off did little good. Her long gown hampered her attempt and he was too heavy for her to budge.

He just tightened his knees against her sides and stared down at her. "When you are finished, you will answer me."

Dear God, she did not want to die. But she didn't know where to find the pendant. A tear escaped and ran down the side of her face. She squeezed her eyes closed, hoping to prevent any more from escaping. Fear was a useless emotion. It would not help her stay alive.

He slid his hand from her mouth, only to immediately grasp her chin in a hold that threatened to break her jaw.

"Now. One more time. Where is the dragon? I have not all day. They await."

"I do not know."

He dragged the point of the sickle sharply across the top of her shoulder. Rhian gasped at the flare of pain. Blood coursed down her shoulder as it trailed hot to the pallet.

"We can do this the hard way if you insist."

Her arms and legs trembled at his statement. Her stomach knotted.

He slapped his hand over her mouth and nose, cutting off her breath and stared into her eyes, mumbling words she did not understand.

His black pupils seemed to flare with life and Rhian felt as if her soul were being drawn from her body. What trickery of the devil attacked her?

The room began to spin, slowly at first, picking up speed with each rotation. Rhian grasped the covers beneath her in an effort to still the sickening twirling.

Again he mumbled unintelligible words and she felt her heart beat slow.

"Rhian! Go. Escape now!"

She heard the woman's order as if it came from within her head, but she had not the energy to obey.

Something brushed her cheek. A warm breath? A gentle touch? She closed her eyes.

"For the love of God, Princess, move!"

Another voice joined the first one in her mind. This one sounded oddly like her father's.

"Now!"

At the urging of both voices together, Rhian bucked as hard as she could, unseating the man and scrambled away from the pallet. Screams of fear tore from her throat. Fear of the man and fear of the voices.

Of a certainty, Satan had entered her chamber. Unable to gain her feet, she half lunged and half crawled for the door.

The man shouted for her to stop and then fisted his hand at the ceiling, yelling, "You will not win." He turned toward Rhian with his weapon held before him. His wild eyes pinned her with a look that promised a gruesome end to her life.

Rhian raised her hands before her as if to ward him off and screamed again.

The door to her chamber slammed against the wall, barely missing her.

Gareth spared her but a brief glance before he drove his already drawn sword through the man's chest.

Edgar, Hector and two others raced into the small chamber, filling it with men, shouts and drawn weapons.

Rhian curled into a ball, her head on her knees and leaned against the wall.

"Cease." Gareth silenced the men immediately. He took one look at Rhian and as he lifted her into his arms, he ordered, "Get that midwife and Hawise into my chamber now."

Sir Hector looked down at the dead man on the floor, "But, milord—"

With an effort, Gareth held back a curse and a growl. "He is going nowhere. Guard the chamber until I return."

Rhian clung to him, her sobs broken only by the shudders coursing through her. Gareth carried her into his chamber, but when he went to lay her on his bed, she nearly choked him in an effort to hang on.

After gathering her securely into his arms, he sat down on the bed, bent his knees to help hold her against him and rested his back against the wooden headboard.

He brushed the hair from her face, smoothing it back behind her ear and noticed the blood. His heart slammed against his ribs. "Jesu, what did he do?"

She shivered silently against his chest.

Gareth willed his hands not to shake with rage. His anger and the sudden stab of fear slicing through him would do her no good.

He forced logic to come to the fore. She was alive. He needed to keep her that way for King Stephen. He felt his mouth twist with a wry smile at the lie he told himself.

"Rhian." He rested his chin on the top of her head. "Rhian, I must see to your wounds."

She burrowed closer to him.

Gareth sighed as he gently cradled her head against him. "This is my fault. I never should have trusted your safety to anyone but myself."

When she still didn't respond, Gareth looked for apparent head injuries. His pulse leaped when he found none. What *had* this man done to her? "Rhian, speak to me." Worry sharpened his voice more than he intended.

But at his harsher tone, she took a shaky breath, then asked, "Are spirits good or evil?"

Gareth paused. Spirits? What nonsense was this? "Rest assured, that man was not a spirit."

"I know." She leaned back against his arm. "My father ordered me to escape." She furrowed her brow. "And so did a woman."

"Rhian, did he hit you about the head with anything?"

One black eyebrow winged up. "I am not addled. No, he did not hit me." She worried her bottom lip between her teeth a moment before the frown returned. "I know it was my father."

Gareth refused to argue such an intangible topic. Instead, he shrugged. "Perhaps it was. Or perhaps your mind sent the warning in your father's voice so you'd listen."

She shook her head, but thankfully let the subject rest. "Perhaps. Perhaps not."

Since she was still mulling the idea over in her mind, he pulled her gown away from her shoulder. The cut, while not deep, ran the length of her shoulder in a nearly straight line. It stood out angry and red against the purpling fingerprints on her pale skin.

"At least he was good with a knife. This is clean and will mend without much scarring."

"It wasn't a knife."

Gareth looked at the wound again. "Then what was it?"

Rhian visibly shivered. "It was a small sickle." She turned her face into his shoulder a moment before looking back up at him. "It was the weapon he used on the others."

Gareth sucked in a heavy breath. The midwife's worries were justified. "What did he want with you?"

"My pendant. He knew it came from my mother." Her voice sounded small, confused.

He longed to take her fear away, but knew that could only be accomplished by the passing of time.

She continued, "There are others, nearby. They need my pendant, but I know not why."

He glanced at the opening made by her torn gown. "Does he have it?"

Rhian rested her hand on her chest. "No. I cannot find it. I didn't take it off, yet it is gone." She tipped her head. "Do you think *they* removed it?"

"They who?"

"The spirits. Perhaps they took it from me to keep it safe."

Gareth groaned in exasperation at her fanciful thoughts. "You were wearing it this morning when you awoke, yes?"

She nodded. "Yes."

"But now that you've had your bath and have gotten dressed, it is missing."

Again she nodded.

"Then it is more likely that the chain broke and it is lying at the bottom of the tub, or on the chamber floor somewhere."

Rhian shook her head. "It was not on a chain, but a ribbon. The ribbon was new and would not break on its own."

"Maybe the water weakened it. Or maybe it came untied."

"It was knotted."

"Rhian—" A knock at the door interrupted what would have been a lecture on the uselessness of wishful thinking.

He straightened his legs and kissed her on the forehead, before lifting her to sit on the bed. "It is Hawise and the midwife come to attend your wound."

When he rose, she grabbed his hand. "You will not leave?"

Gareth looked down at her. The fear still tingeing her voice shone starkly in her wide eyes. His heart went out to her. He longed to take her back into his arms and protect her from any evil, now and until his heart ceased to beat.

He lifted her hand to his lips. "I will be in the chamber next door." He kissed the back of her hand. "Both doors will remain open. If you need me, just call out my name and I will be back before your next heartbeat." Reluctantly, he released her hand and went to the door.

After giving the two women his instructions, he waited until they went about their business. Hawise fussed over Rhian like a mother hen while the midwife checked for injuries.

"Why has he not returned?" He knew. They all did. The man they'd sent into Browan hours ago must surely be captured—or dead.

They could do little but wait for their informant to supply them with the details.

The man slammed his fist into a tree with a curse. "This will not work. From now on, I will deal with these matters on my own."

He pierced each man with a hard stare. "Pack your gear. They will be hunting us now."

He then looked toward the keep. "Farewell for now, Princess. Faucon will soon lead you and your bauble straight into my waiting arms. That will give me half the key I need."

His maniacal laugh filled the forest.

Chapter Seven

Gareth studied the dead man on the floor of Rhian's chamber. Browan's guards had removed the hood concealing his face during their search of the body.

The sight of the man's features had momentarily surprised Gareth. The man looked like Rhian. The same shockingly black hair fell in shorter waves about his head.

The jewel-tone blue eyes, staring unseeingly from beneath finely winged eyebrows, lacked only Rhian's spark of life.

The straight nose and full lips could have been hers. Only the shape of the chin was different. This man's squared chin was softened to a more feminine shape on Rhian.

When Edgar sidled up, Gareth asked, "Do you see anything odd about this man?"

"Besides the fact that he's dead?" Edgar looked away from Gareth's scowl before turning his attention to the man on the floor. Finally, he asked, "Does the lady have a brother?"

"Not that I am aware of. King Stephen said she was an only child."

"A bastard perhaps?"

"That is a possibility, but why would he try to kill Rhian?" Gareth walked toward the tub as he continued, "He wanted her pendant. But if that was all he wanted, there was no reason to also seek her death."

He reached into the now cold water, felt along the bottom until he found the missing piece of jewelry. Gareth dangled it from the unbroken and still-knotted ribbon. The amethyst dragon shimmered in the sunlight streaming in through the window.

The facets of the hazy gem reflected the light and appeared to glow from within. Making it appear that somehow the dragon's heart had flared to life.

Gareth pushed aside the fanciful thought and caught the pendant in his hand. Imagination or no, he could not deny the heat of the amethyst against his palm.

"What is so special about a piece of woman's jewelry that someone would kill for it?" Edgar asked.

When the captain approached, Gareth tossed the pendant to him. "I see nothing special about the bauble. What about you?"

Edgar held it up to the light for a better examination. After a few moments, he shook his head. "I see nothing special."

To better study the stone dangling from Edgar's fingers, Gareth narrowed his eyes. The gem did not shimmer or glow. It looked like nothing more than what it was—a dragon carved into a piece of amethyst.

He moved back to where the body lay. "This man confirmed what Browan's guard said. There are others about."

His statement prompted Hector from his silent position by the door. "Did he say where?"

"Not that I'm aware." Gareth glanced down at the body. "From the look of it, I'd say they are inside the walls somewhere."

"Nay." Hector visibly paled. "We have searched and found no one. Where could they hide?"

Gareth nudged the body on the floor with the toe of his boot. "I have no answer to that other than the simple fact someone obviously managed. Or they have hidden themselves so well that their presence was missed during the search last night."

"Or someone is hiding them," Edgar suggested.

Sir Hector's face reddened. He nearly bristled with outrage. "No one from Browan would be so bold." He turned a questioning look on Edgar. "Perhaps one of your men carelessly hid the villains."

Edgar tossed the pendant to Gareth before facing the other man. "Faucon's men are not careless. If they were, they wouldn't be a Faucon guard."

"And that little mishap with the boy permitting the wench to escape?" Sir Hector made a sarcastic snorting noise, before asking, "That was not careless?"

Edgar fisted his hands. Gareth shoved the now warm pendant inside his tunic and stepped between the men. He glared down at Edgar, who instinctively backed away. He then turned his attention to Hector. "The *boy* is still a squire. He will learn. The *wench* is Lady Rhian of Gervaise and you will not forget that again."

Hector shrugged. "The lad failed in his job and goes unpunished. The *lady* came here disguised as a servant and lied to all. It will be hard to remember which role she is assuming at any given moment."

Before another word left Hector's mouth, Gareth reached out, grabbed the front of the man's tunic in his hand and lifted him from the floor. In two strides he crossed the room to slam the man against the stone wall and held him there.

Mere inches from Hector's face, Gareth smiled. "Now that you are of a height to look me in the eyes, perhaps you will hear me more clearly." The only muscles in Hector's face that moved were the ones that widened his eyes.

Certain he had the man's full attention, Gareth continued by asking Edgar, "How is David currently occupied?"

Edgar stepped forward to answer, "He is cleaning and sharpening every sword in Browan Keep."

"Does the punishment fit the crime?"

After a brief laugh, Edgar admitted, "Aye. He should now remember what a sword looks like. If nothing else it will be a long while before his attention to duty is diverted by wenches."

Gareth pushed into Hector's chest until the man squinted. "When I arrived here and found the gates unguarded, I could have dismissed you immediately. Without question. You were in charge until my arrival and you failed in your duties, gravely. Had I chose to dangle your severed head from a pole, none would have questioned my decision." He released the man and watched him crumple to the floor before adding, "You will show my men and the Lady Rhian the respect due them, or you may still find yourself dismissed—or worse."

Without waiting for a response, Gareth quit the chamber, with Edgar on his heels. "Milord Faucon?" Gareth waved the man's question off, motioning for him to follow.

When they reached the bailey, Gareth quickly assessed the security of the keep. As usual, the inner yard was a beehive of activity. Many people—guards, servants and freemen scurried about while performing their duty of the moment.

He scanned the walls, before asking, "You sent to Rhys for men?"

"Yes. They should arrive within a day or two."

"When they arrive, post them on the walls. There is not enough manpower there to protect this keep from even a small army."

The casual entry of a wagon caught his attention. Browan's guards had done nothing more than simply wave the driver through the gates.

Gareth headed toward the wagon, shouting, "Driver. Hold."

When the wagon came to a stop, the driver peered down at Gareth through red-rimmed eyes. "Sir? Is there a problem?"

"That depends." Gareth pulled the tarp off the back of the wagon, exposing eight wooden casks. "What do you carry?"

The man sputtered before answering, "Just wine, milord."

Edgar drew his sword. "Wine?" He looked toward Gareth. "There is enough wine in storage to last a lifetime and more."

The driver covered his nervous laugh with a strangled

cough before exclaiming, "Ah, but Sir Hector does like his drink."

Gareth could not argue the truth in that statement. He completed his circle around the wagon and leaped up into the seat next to the driver.

After wrapping his arm around the man's now trembling shoulders, he suggested, "Well then, since there is so much of the grape available, what say the three of us open one or two and sample the wares?"

"I beg pardon, milord, but I am not a drinking man."

Gareth pulled the man tighter against his side. "No?" The overpowering scent of stale wine assaulted his nostrils. "Then you bathe in the wine?"

"Milord, I—"

Gareth heard the swoosh of the arrow's approach an instant before it reached its intended target. One heartbeat he was baiting the driver. The next, he was staring at the still-quivering shaft of an arrow protruding from between the man's eyes.

In the next heartbeat he released the man, letting him tumble to the ground, sprang from the seat, drew his sword and stood next to a near-frantic Edgar.

The captain's sharp shout of "Faucon! To me!" broke the silence that had fallen over the bailey.

Faucon's ten guards came from every direction at a dead run. In varying stages of dress, they circled the wagon with swords drawn.

Activity in the bailey had ceased. While a few peered from behind windows and doorways, or around corners, not a soul was to be seen in the open.

Gareth studied the walls, then turned his attention to the keep itself, before glancing at the deceased driver.

His heart raced. From the angle the arrow protruded, he could make only one deduction. "That arrow came from the keep."

Edgar glanced around him toward the driver, before he nodded in agreement. "Aye, 'tis my thought, also."

"I must see to Lady Rhian."

"Milord." Edgar grabbed his arm. "Wait. Let me go first."

With an easy jerk, Gareth pulled out of the man's hold. "Had they wanted me dead, I would be standing before heaven's gate now."

His concern for Rhian prompted him to hurry, but before starting back to the keep, he ordered, "I want a Faucon guard posted at every entrance to the bailey and the keep itself."

After the men dispersed to do his bidding, he looked back at Edgar and added, "Get rid of this wagon. Stow the wine someplace secure until we can determine what may or may not be wrong with it. Then keep an eye on Hector. I trust him not."

Edgar quickly sprinted around Gareth and stopped in front of him. Drawing himself to full height, which brought him almost to Gareth's chin, he said, "Milord, I cannot leave you unprotected. I cannot, I will not do anything so foolish."

Gareth slowly drew up one eyebrow. "You cannot? You will not?" He shoved Edgar aside and continued toward the keep. "I really must have my brother explain this lord-captain relationship to me again. I seem to have forgotten the order of command."

"Milord." Edgar's tone turned pleading. "Please, 'tis your brother I must answer to if anything should befall you. Comte Rhys would gladly have me drawn and quartered alive, or worse, if anything happened."

Gareth stopped, but he did not turn around. "Do you think the day will come when you no longer fear my brother's wrath over my own?"

"No."

If he'd learned nothing about Edgar in the many years they'd been together, he knew that at the very least the man was honest. Gareth shook his head. "I am no longer in swaddling clothes. Nor do I need a nurse-maid." He resumed striding toward the keep. "However, if you feel the urge to assume that position, you are free to return to Faucon. I am certain my sister could use your services."

"Nay. I ask your pardon, milord."

Gareth glanced up at the sky. "Dear Lord, give me patience." To Edgar he said, "Granted. Now, go do as I bid."

While Edgar looked far from pleased, he answered, "Aye, sir."

Never one to lie abed when nothing was physically wrong, Rhian leaned against the wall in Gareth's chamber for support while she gazed out the narrow window down at the bailey. Gareth and his captain appeared to be discussing something when a wagon entered unchallenged.

The two men approached the driver and when Gareth jumped up onto the seat next to the man, she heard the twang and swoosh of an arrow being released from somewhere close above her.

Her breath caught in her throat. Her heart jumped, stilled and then raced with fear.

No longer able to stand upright on her shaking legs, Rhian slid to the floor. Dear Lord. If that arrow found its mark and Faucon was dead, what would she do?

The faint sound of a door banging shut drifted through the fog of fear. With Faucon out of the way, would they now come for her? She had not the strength left for any more fighting this day.

On her hands and knees, she frantically looked around the chamber, seeking a place to hide. She scurried into the alcove off the side of the room. Surely even a keep as poor as Browan would have a hiding place in the master's chamber.

She patted desperately at the walls. On her near cry of despair, the back wall moved slightly beneath her hand. With a quick prayer that it would close silently, she scrambled behind it and held her breath as she pushed the panel slowly back into place.

She heard footsteps descending the stairwell and slid the wall faster. With a short sigh of relief, she gave thanks that it moved without noise. As soundlessly as possible, she scooted back as far as she dared into the blackness of the hidden room and curled into a tight ball.

The door to the chamber opened and closed. Two sets of feet walked about the room, passing her hiding place more than once.

Sweat covered her body. Could they hear the heavy, rapid pounding of her heart? Could they smell her fear?

When the two spoke to each other, it was in an unfamiliar language. Rhian frowned in concentration. The only words she could make out sounded something like *aimitis dragan*.

Did they seek her amethyst dragon pendant? What

was the importance behind this piece of jewelry her mother had sent her? If it meant the difference between life and death, she'd gladly part with the bauble.

But she had a feeling that simply handing the pendant over would not be enough. Her gut instinct warned that they'd still seek her death.

And Rhian truly didn't wish to die.

Finally, after what seemed an eternity, the men gave up their search and left the chamber. Uncertain whether they would return or not, Rhian stayed in her position and waited. For what she knew not.

A few dozen rapid heartbeats later, the door to the chamber opened again. She sucked in her breath and listened as this time only one set of booted footsteps crossed the room. The clinking of spurs told her that it was not either of the men returning.

She heard the scraping as he drew his sword from its wooden sheath before he walked to the window, then to the bed. He then passed in front of the alcove.

She gasped as the panel slid aside. Rhian knew she'd not be able to defend herself, even if a weapon were at hand. She was still in too much pain from her earlier bout with the hooded man and now stiff from being curled in a ball in a cold, dark and damp closet. She wasn't certain she'd be able to move, let alone fight.

Unwilling to see the end of her life, she covered her face with her hands, closed her eyes as tightly as possible and prayed silently for a quick end.

Nothing happened.

Rhian frowned before warily parting her fingers and opening one eye to peer out at the lurking danger.

A pair of arresting emerald eyes stared back at her.

Gareth waited until his heart resumed a more normal rhythm before drawing in the shakiest breath he'd ever heard. "I thought you were dead."

Rhian sucked in a huge lungful of air before admitting, "I thought the same about you."

"How long have you been in there?"

She stuck her one hand up. "Mere moments, or a lifetime. I cannot decide."

Gareth grasped her hand. "Can you stand?" When she winced in pain, he reached in and lifted her up into his arms. "This suits my needs better."

Rhian wrapped her arms loosely around his neck. "Your needs?"

Her voice shook. He glanced at her and saw the glimmer of unshed tears. Whether from fear or pain, he knew not. Nor at this moment, did he care. "Yes. My needs. This will assure me that you are well and alive."

"That would make a difference to you?"

He wanted to shout that it would make a great difference. But ever-present caution ruled. She was still promised to another. To hide what he really felt, he teased, "It would be highly annoying to explain your death to King Stephen."

"Ah, yes. I imagine it would be."

Her answer gave Gareth pause. He had expected at least a touch of sarcasm. Her ordeals this last day had obviously taken more from her than he'd imagined.

Gareth sat down on a high-backed chair and cradled her on his lap. Rhian put up little more than a token fight when he refused to release her. Instead, she gave in and rested her cheek against his chest with a sigh.

"I thought the arrow was aimed for you." Her voice was little more than a whisper.

"No. It was meant for the wagon driver."

"It came from above this chamber." Before he could interrupt, Rhian rushed on, "I heard the bowstring and the arrow. Then the men rushed down the stairs. That's when I hid."

"Did they enter this chamber?"

She shook her head. "Aye. The only words they spoke that I could understand sounded something like amethyst dragon."

"I do not understand. Even if the guard had to leave for a moment, this door should have been locked." Gareth could not hold back the anger in his voice. "Why was it not?"

"Because I didn't think about it." She shrugged. "I have never lived anywhere that required me to hide behind locked doors."

"Obviously that has changed. How long ago did the men leave?"

Rhian shrugged. "Perhaps a few moments before you arrived."

"I saw no one on the stairwell. Could you tell which way they went when they left here?"

"Nay." She shook her head. "I paid no attention. My heart was beating so loudly that I would not have been able to discern their direction." She paused. "They did not go back up the steps. I would have heard the squeaking from the loose boards."

He frowned. Was it possible that somewhere between this chamber and the stairwell more than one secret passage existed? He'd have to grill Hector.

Gareth reached into his tunic. "Here. I found your pendant."

Rhian held it aloft and twirled the ribbon. The gemstone glimmered in the light. "Is it not beautiful?"

"Not exactly a term I'd use to describe it."

She leaned back and looked up at him. "Why not?"

He winced as the heat of embarrassment rushed up his neck. It would be a fine thing for a warrior to admit—fear of a bauble. "I swear the blasted thing is cursed."

Gareth felt every muscle in Rhian's body stiffen against him. She looked at the pendant and then back to him. "You feel it, too?"

"Feel what?"

She reached over, took his hand and placed the amethyst in his palm. She kept her gaze locked on his as she curled his fingers over the gem. "Tell me you do not feel the heat."

Although he wanted to, he couldn't lie. He did feel the warmth flare hot against his palm. "I do."

Rhian smiled. "Thank the Lord."

"Pardon?"

She laughed before answering, "I thought it was just my imagination. I am glad to know I am not alone in this."

"Well, I would greatly prefer that you were." He opened his fingers, the pendant resting on his palm. "I should keep this until you are safe with your family."

"No," Rhian disagreed. "I cannot let you put yourself in danger for me."

He glared at her. "I am better able to fend for myself than you are. If they truly desire the pendant and by some quirk of fate capture you, they would have to keep you alive to find it."

She finally gave in. "You keep it safe until this journey has ended."

He slipped the ribbon over his head and tucked the pendant inside his tunic. The gem rested warm against his chest. "Any idea why they seem to value it so much?"

"No. But since they seem ready to kill to possess the dragon, it is worth something of value."

Gareth rested his forehead against hers. "I will guard it for you until you are delivered to your family." He paused and stared into her suddenly smoldering gaze. "I have sent for additional men. They should arrive tomorrow or the next day."

She kissed his chin. "We will resume our journey then?"

"Aye." He slid his arms around her and placed a chaste kiss on her forehead. "We will." He rose, sliding her to her feet. "And I will leave you to rest for the coming trip."

As he headed toward the door, she asked, "Could you not use a little rest yourself?"

Gareth paused at the door. "Yes, I could." He glanced over his shoulder and smiled. "But I would find none here in this chamber."

Chapter Eight

"Not again." Rhian stared in disbelief out the narrow window in Gareth's chamber—now her chamber. With a sharp curse and furiously beating heart, she headed for the door.

A mere two days ago an archer had barely missed taking Gareth's life and now another sought to finish the deed?

Not if she could prevent it from happening. With the Lord's blessing and quick feet, perhaps she could stop the man from striking again.

With a guard on her heels, she raced down the steep steps to the Great Hall, through the entryway, out the doors and across the narrow footpath to the wall.

Quickly surveying the area where she'd seen the man dressed all in black with a bow slung over his shoulder, she spied the top of his head. Rhian slowly traversed the wallwalk, toward the man.

Gareth kept the new visitor to Browan in his sights at all times. If Sir Melwyn, Captain of Comte Faucon's guard, thought to catch him unaware, he'd be sadly disappointed.

When Edgar and David walked out of the stables, Gareth motioned for his captain to join him.

After sending the boy on his way, Edgar approached. "Milord, any word from Faucon?"

"Aye, of a sorts." Gareth nodded toward the ladder Sir Melwyn had just ascended. "My brother's captain just slipped in for a visit."

"What is he doing here?"

"That is what I'm waiting to find out."

Edgar hissed in a breath and pointed toward the other end of the wall. "Milord, I think Lady Rhian is out to discover that for herself."

Gareth darted a quick glance toward Rhian and back to Melwyn. Faucon's captain was now ducked down behind some barrels. The tip of his bow bobbed in and out of sight before he reached up and pulled an arrow from his quiver.

With a curse, Gareth headed toward Rhian. She would have no idea that if Melwyn was readying an arrow that it was not meant to cause harm. And Melwyn had no way of knowing what happened the other day.

Rhian saw him approach and shouted, "Faucon!" She pointed toward Melwyn. "There is one of the murderers."

Then everything happened at once. Melwyn dropped his bow and stood. Browan's guards raced along the wallwalk and grabbed Melwyn. Edgar choked in his effort to hold back his laugher. Gareth's men gathered in the center of the bailey with varying degrees of amusement on their faces.

Browan's servants and villagers raced to the bailey

with clubs, pikes, pitchforks or whatever implement of death they could find, with varying degrees of revenge on their tongues.

Sir Hector blustered out of one of the storage huts, paused at the ladder leading up to where Melwyn was being held and ordered, "Throw him in chains."

For a moment, Gareth wondered whether to laugh or curse. Since neither would help, he pushed through the assembly, grabbing Edgar as he passed.

Just before reaching the ladder, he shouted, "Cease!" The noise dulled to a smattering of grumbles. Gareth ordered Edgar, "Good Lord, man, get him down here."

He then stood on the bottom rung of the ladder and looked out over the crowd. "This man is not a murderer."

Rhian cried out, "He had—"

"Stop!" Gareth's near roar stopped her words instantly. "This is the Captain of Comte Faucon's guard."

The crowd physically backed away. Whispers of "devil's guard" reached his ears.

Amused that the reputation Rhys had intentionally created seemed to suit his brother, Gareth left it alone. After all, who was he to question his brother's decision? Especially since it had the desired effect—women left him alone and men thought twice before doing battle with the Comte of Faucon.

It was not as easy to ignore Rhian's curse before she turned and marched back toward the keep. But Edgar and Melwyn were descending the ladder and he had to ensure Melwyn's safety before he could do anything about Rhian's anger. He stepped off the ladder and waited for the men to join him.

The crowd dispersed. Sir Hector ordered his guards

to return to their duties and headed back toward the storage hut. Gareth turned his head toward his own men and they went about their duties without any further orders.

Melwyn reached the ground and handed Gareth a missive. "From your brother."

"And how is Rhys?"

Melwyn looked from Gareth to where Rhian had disappeared into the keep and back before replying, "I would say he's only slightly more occupied than you."

Edgar nodded his agreement.

Gareth ignored them both and unrolled the message from his brother. A quick scan of the note confirmed he had been correct. Comte Faucon was far too involved becoming acquainted with his new wife to need his entire force. He'd sent a score of men with Sir Melwyn and enough supplies and arms to last a month.

He slipped the note into his tunic and studied Melwyn. The captain would never change. No matter how many years went by, Melwyn would always be dark, short and mean looking. Perfectly suited for his role as the devil's right hand.

"Good to see you again, Sir Melwyn. What are you doing here?"

"I grew tired of watching the lovebirds." He perused Browan Keep, obviously seeing everything that was wrong. "Tell me this is not yours."

Gareth clapped the man on the shoulder and laughed. "Not until I deliver the lady to her family."

"Perhaps you should fail. This will cost you a fortune."

"And then some. I know. Edgar and I would appreciate any advice you can provide on fortification. I want to get the building under way as soon as possible."

"A raging fire would be a good place to start." He looked pointedly at Gareth. "And some guards who knew their duty would help."

Edgar stepped in. "Those were Faucon's guards at the gate. They knew we were expecting reinforcements from the comte."

"I am not dressed like one of Comte Faucon's men."

Edgar visibly bristled. Two Faucon captains together would not work well to anyone's benefit. Gareth intervened. "Sir Melwyn, you could dress as a midwife and my men would know you on sight."

Melwyn conceded that point with a nod. He then asked, "Do you realize that you are being tracked?"

"Yes. The events of the last fortnight have been…interesting." Gareth waved toward the keep. "After you signal your men, Sir Edgar will fill you in on the details while I inform Lady Rhian of our resumed journey."

"When do you wish to start out?"

"If the three of us can devise a plan suitable for all, I would like to leave under the cover of darkness—tonight."

Edgar offered, "Combined we are a force of thirty-six men. Browan has fifteen that are healthy. Ten of those are good men. I've made no determination on the other five, although I have decided they are worth watching."

"Do they huddle together?" When Edgar nodded, Melwyn's eyes lit with an unholy fire. "Split the five up. Two stay in Browan, three travel with the others. It will be easier to see which way their allegiance lies if they are separated."

Gareth could only imagine the tricks Melwyn would employ to get the men to show their hands. Rhys's captain was a crafty dog and no trick was too low for the man to use. A handy trait at times like now.

Gareth glanced toward the keep. "The two of you decide which men stay and which ones travel. I want Edgar here." When his captain jerked back in surprise, Gareth added, "The men and others at Browan need to get used to following your orders and the sooner the better. It will be easier for you to gain control if I am not here."

"What about Hector?"

"I have no use of him."

Edgar shook his head. "Nor do I."

"That is possible. Still, it will give you a chance to see if any here have the least amount of respect for the man. Perhaps you can find a place for him. If not, so be it."

"If Sir Edgar is to remain here, then he needs more of Faucon's men to stay. Is this Sir Hector controllable?"

"As long as he is not left to his own devices." Gareth shrugged. "The man only needs to be told what to do and he does it."

Edgar glared at Melwyn. "I can deal with Sir Hector. However, if anything befalls Lord Gareth, I will have your head."

Melwyn snickered. "If anything befalls your lord, mine will have my head before you get a chance."

"He will have to run me down first."

"I am sure that will not pose a problem for the comte."

"Good Lord, I am surrounded by bearded nursemaids carrying swords." Gareth rolled his eyes. "You two women work out the details, prepare the men and I'll go over the plans later."

When Gareth turned to leave, both men replied, "Aye, sir." Before resuming their boastful bantering.

* * *

Gareth paused at the open door of Rhian's chamber. She and Hawise were discussing the rather dubious topic of men. A conversation he had no wish to hear, as it would only lead to arguing.

His sister, Marianne, had more than once engaged him in conversations about what she called pigheaded men that only led to verbal wars.

He knew Rhian was angry. The way she'd marched off the wallwalk and into the keep had made that plain. He'd no wish to start this journey tonight under a cloud of silence or willfulness.

Gareth raised his hand and knocked on the doorframe.

Both women turned to look at him. Rhian rose, then dropped into a curtsy. "Milord Faucon." Venom dripped from her voice. "To what do we owe the honor of your visit?"

Hawise lifted her nose in the air and turned away.

Gareth glanced inside the door to make certain there were no armed men ready to slit his throat. He crossed to Rhian, took her hand and tugged her against his chest.

Hawise stood. "Milord!"

He ignored the woman. Instead, he placed a finger beneath Rhian's chin and lifted her face to his. Thankfully, she was unable to arm her eyes. Otherwise the ire shooting from them would have killed him as surely as an arrow to his heart.

Gareth lowered his head and whispered in her ear, "I apologize for shouting at you."

When he looked back at her, he saw the emotions dance across her face. Anger rapidly faded to shock.

Shock relaxed to a smile. But when she returned his look, she narrowed her eyes.

"You think to catch me off guard with an apology you do not mean."

Gareth felt his lips twitch. She was quick. "It was worth a try, was it not?" He stole a kiss from her parted lips before releasing her.

Yes, she was still angry. He could see it in the tightness of her jaw. But her eyes danced with suppressed amusement. Surely that was a good sign?

She spun away from him and stood behind Hawise. From over the top of the older woman's head, Rhian asked, "Did you truly find it necessary to humiliate me in front of everyone?"

He shook his head. "I did not realize that's what I had done."

"Then what exactly did you think you were doing?"

"Stopping you from either getting killed or making a complete fool of yourself and me."

Rhian crossed her arms against her chest and tilted her head. "And how were either of those things going to occur?"

"It appeared to me as if you were about to attack Comte Faucon's captain. I have no ability to foretell the future, but I am fairly certain that Melwyn would not have taken an attack lightly."

"Your brother's captain would attack a woman?"

"Melwyn would defend himself against an attack and then discover he'd harmed a woman."

"As if that would matter to him."

"For heaven's sake, Rhian, the man is not a monster. But he is trained to fight, to kill and then to ask questions."

She tossed her head. "What an odd order of things you men seem to follow."

Gareth pointed at Hawise. "Get out."

Rhian stayed the older woman with a hand on her shoulder. "Stay."

Gareth took one step toward them. Hawise scurried from the chamber, closing the door behind her.

With another toss of her head, Rhian turned her back on Gareth and crossed to the window. "Since this conversation will go nowhere, you can leave, too."

She felt the heat of his hand as he grasped her shoulder and spun her around. Rhian had not even heard him cross the distance between them.

"I am going nowhere."

His deep voice rumbled against her ear. His warm breath against her neck sent shivers down her spine. Someday she'd learn how he did that—but not today.

Rhian warred with herself. Push him away and force an argument? Or give in and choose another day, another time and another argument?

She threaded her fingers through his hair and sighed before resting her cheek against his chest. "I wish not to argue with you."

"Then do not. Accept my apology. I truly did not want to see you get hurt. Nor did I wish to explain to my brother how his captain was injured."

Rhian gazed up at him. This time she saw no sarcasm, or hint of teasing in his gaze.

She saw only the heat of desire flare to life. It warmed her, chasing away any lingering resentment.

"I do. I accept your apology and I am sorry to have acted so rashly. But I saw only a man seeking to kill you."

His soft chuckle reverberated against her chest. "I assumed that's what had happened. Edgar is explaining all to Melwyn now."

"What was the man thinking?"

"He only thought to catch me off guard and bid me his brand of good day."

"I would think a simple *hail* or *good day* would suffice."

"You do not know Melwyn." Gareth tightened his embrace. "At this moment, I can think of a thousand other things I would rather discuss than my brother's captain."

"Such as?" She turned her face up to his, expecting and receiving his kiss.

A kiss that turned her limbs liquid and her blood hot. Rhian briefly wondered if she would simply melt, and then as her toes curled, wondered if she would even care.

He stroked her back. Ran a hand up her side, brushing against her breast.

She leaned tighter against him, wishing for more than just the feel of his lips on hers and his caress.

The door to the chamber opened. "Enough!" Hawise strode across the room. "I said, enough." The woman touched Gareth's arm.

He broke their embrace, slowly. Obviously as reluctant to stop their interlude as much as she. He brushed a quick kiss against her forehead and stepped back.

Rhian glared at Hawise through eyes still foggy with desire. "Thank you."

Gareth turned around and cleared his throat before taking a seat on the bench. "The reason I came up here…one of the reasons I came up here was to let you know that we are leaving here tonight."

"Tonight?" Rhian and Hawise stared at him.

"Yes." He nodded. "I thought it would gain us time and perhaps a measure of safety to leave under the cover of darkness."

Rhian wondered about the wisdom of that choice, but kept her thoughts to herself. It was entirely possible that he might be correct.

Gareth looked at Hawise. "Can you ride a horse?"

The woman shook her head. "I have never had the opportunity to try."

"I should have considered that before." He frowned. "We have not the time for you to learn now."

Rhian offered, "There are hours before night falls. I can teach her how to stay on the saddle. She can learn anything else as we go."

"I have no desire to leave Browan." Hawise looked from one to the other. "This is my home. I have never been farther than the village and at my age have no wish to venture farther now."

"We have little choice," Gareth tried to explain. "I cannot deliver Lady Rhian to her family in the company of only men."

"King Stephen did not take that into consideration before, so why is it important now?" Rhian asked.

A dull flush raced up his neck answering her question without words. But he answered anyway. "I would say things were a trifle different then."

Hawise snorted and flapped her apron at him. "Ah, I see. You worry that if she arrives without a lady's maid that they will wonder about her chastity."

Now the heat of embarrassment warmed Rhian's neck and face. "Exactly."

The older woman paused. She appeared to be thinking. Finally, she asked, "How long will you be gone?"

"I hope to return to Browan within a fortnight," Gareth answered.

"And you will be sleeping where?"

He hesitated before saying, "In the saddle or on the ground."

Hawise blanched. "Ack. I am far too old for either."

"There might be another way." Rhian frowned, then paced the distance between Gareth and the window. "The supplies will follow in wagons, correct?" When he nodded, she continued. "Let Hawise travel with the wagons. We can await their arrival near my family's abode before entering. None will be the wiser."

"A supply cart is not exactly the most comfortable way to travel."

Rhian agreed, but Hawise countered, "It seems to me that it is the only option that will suffice."

Gareth gave in to the idea, but warned, "Once we are on the road, we cannot turn back if you change your mind."

"Understood."

He rose. "I will finalize the plans with the others. I am sorry for the rush, but you need to be ready to leave after sunset."

Hawise headed for the door. "Then I best be packing." She paused and turned back to look at the two of them. "Try to behave while I am gone." She made a show of leaving the door wide open before she finally left.

Gareth took Rhian's hand in his. "I hope this plan of yours does not prove a bad idea."

"That makes two of us."

He pulled her close. "Since this may be the last time

we are alone, I want you to know that I will protect you from any harm whether it occurs during the journey, or after."

Her heart turned over itself. She placed a hand against his chest. His heart beat strong against her palm. "I am holding you to that, Faucon."

Chapter Nine

"Milord Faucon!"

At Melwyn's shout, Gareth brought his horse to an instant halt on the forest path and turned around in his saddle. If Melwyn found it necessary to raise his voice, something was wrong.

This was the first time Melwyn had made personal contact in the two days they'd been on the march to Rhian's family.

Gareth and six of the other men had ridden alongside Rhian, with the horsedrawn carts close behind. Melwyn and ten others had formed a circular perimeter around them.

In between the two parties was a tighter perimeter of four men who carried reports back and forth. They'd been guarded on all sides and had been in constant verbal communication.

Gareth broke away from his party and rode out to meet Melwyn. The captain brought his horse to a nervous prancing stop alongside. "Milord, two are missing."

The hairs on the back of Gareth's neck rose. "What do you mean by *missing?*"

"Vanished. Men and horses. The reports started coming in slower. I called for a roll and when two did not respond correctly, I made the round myself and discovered they were gone."

"When?"

"Not long. By my best estimation, I would gather sometime late this morning."

Gareth looked up at the sun. The denseness of the forest filtered out most of the light, but from the angle of the rays that broke through the foliage, he guessed it to be around noon now.

How could this have happened? "You used a rotating roll call?" He knew that his brother used that method on occasions when he was with those he did not trust. Melwyn would have done the same. Each time a roll was called, they would send back their different responses with the messenger.

"Aye."

A sick churning started in the pit of Gareth's stomach. He sought to shake the notion forming in his mind, but could not. Finally, he asked, "Do you know which man is the spy?"

Melwyn nodded. "Aye."

Gareth cursed, but it did little to lighten the heaviness in his chest. All four of the messengers were his men. Not a man from Browan as he'd believed, but one of his own.

"Bring him in. I want an explanation before he draws his last breath."

Melwyn reached out and briefly touched Gareth's

shoulder. "If it is any consolation, I suspected Browan's men, too. If you would prefer, I can deal with this myself."

"No." Gareth sat straighter in his saddle. "I do not need any to save me from my duty." It seemed that for most of his life someone had stepped in to deal with matters when things began to go awry. First his father, then his brother. It was time he dealt with matters himself.

A smile crossed Melwyn's face as he leaned back and nodded. "Aye, milord."

Gareth glanced over at Rhian. Concern furrowed her forehead. He knew without a doubt that the men did not leave their posts willingly. "Close ranks."

"I have seen to that."

They were in an area that Gareth did not know. The nearest keep could be miles away and even then, he had no way of knowing if those inside would provide protection.

While the denseness of the forest was useful for cover, it did not enable the men to fight at the best of their ability. And he needed them at their best. "We will stop at the first clearing and await whatever they have planned."

"I will pass the word."

When Melwyn rode away, Gareth passed the word to the men in his group that they would stop at the next clearing.

He rode next to Rhian with guilt eating away at his gut. He'd sworn to protect her and now she was in danger because one of his men turned traitor.

"Gareth." She leaned toward him and he dreaded the question he knew was coming. "All is not well, is it?"

It would be easier if Rhian was stupid. He could then

lie. But Gervaise had not raised a dolt. She would see through any fabricated tale he created.

"No. All is not well."

She tipped her head back and quirked an eyebrow at him expectantly. "And?"

"And what? I cannot tell you much more than that."

"*Can*not, or *will* not?"

Gareth looked over his shoulder at the others. While each face displayed varying degrees of alertness or weariness, they all showed signs of concern. Melwyn's uncharacteristic shout had alerted all to danger of some sort. His own order to stop at the next clearing had only increased their awareness.

He turned back to Rhian and spoke loud enough for all to hear. "Two men from the outer perimeter are missing."

"Which two?"

"I did not ask. We will know that soon enough."

Rhian asked, "Is there any clue as to how this happened?"

"Aye. We have a traitor in our midst."

The men behind them gasped. Gareth trained his stare on the trees dead in front of him.

From the corner of his eye, he saw Rhian flinch at the various murmurs from those behind him.

However, it was the wagers that set his nerves on edge. The men were betting on whether the traitor would be from Browan, or Faucon.

Gareth said nothing. In truth what could he say when he'd wondered the very same thing.

The wagering became louder, angrier as the two groups began to size each other up. This had to stop. Now.

Rhian must have seen his fingers reach toward his

sword, because she quickly laid a hand on his forearm before reminding those behind, "It truly cannot be wise to bait your overlord."

A couple of the men made choking sounds as they swallowed their laughter. One or two apologized.

Gareth doubted if they meant it, but the matter wasn't worth arguing over. Right now, the important thing was to see to Rhian's safety.

And with the clearing straight ahead, he'd be better able to carry out that mission.

After dismounting, Gareth ordered one tent to be erected for Rhian and Hawise. While not as safe as a solid structure, it would provide a better measure of safety than the open air.

He saw Rhian grimace when he assisted her from her horse. "Stiff?"

She leaned against him and shrugged. "A little. After not riding every day for a time, it will take a day or two before my muscles no longer revolt."

He waited until she found her legs, then led her over to a log just beyond the edge of the clearing to sit down.

"Do you think they will attack?"

The shakiness evident in her voice belied the calmness of her features. Her only other outward show of worry was the way she folded her hands together as if in a clenched position of prayer.

Gareth glanced up at the sky, then into the surrounding woods. "Had they wanted the advantage of surprise they would have already done so."

He raised a hand toward Melwyn as Faucon's captain and the men with him entered the hastily made camp.

Gareth stroked a finger down Rhian's cheek before tilting up her chin.

"I am only certain that they will not give up their hunt for your pendant. Whether they attack here, now or later remains to be seen." When he caressed her cheek, she leaned into his palm and closed her eyes.

His heartbeat kicked up a notch and the coolness of the forest turned warm.

Gareth cleared the tightness in his throat before adding, "Whatever happens, I will see to your safety before my own."

Rhian grasped his hand and placed a kiss on his palm. "I thank-you for that, but would wish that you'd see to your own, too."

As if through a fog, Gareth heard footsteps approach and a snort of disgust before Melwyn muttered, "Good Lord above, not you, too."

Rhian frowned in confusion. Gareth gently squeezed her fingers before releasing her hand, then turned to Melwyn with an air of presumed innocence. "I fear I am at a loss as to what you infer."

Melwyn looked from Rhian to Gareth and shook his head. "Is this a disease you Faucons all contracted at the same time?"

"Perhaps we caught it from you." Even though Melwyn was only a few years older than Rhys, Gareth added, "After all, you have been married since the dawn of time."

"Hardly." Melwyn made a show of rolling his eyes heavenward. "You can ask my wife, but I am certain we never sat around cooing like lovebirds."

Rhian shifted on the log, drawing Gareth's attention.

Her gaze darted everywhere but to him or Melwyn and her face glowed with a pale shade of pink. They'd managed to embarrass her. To lessen her discomfort, he waved Melwyn off. "You are imagining things that do not exist, old man. See to the wagon and I will join you in a moment."

Surprisingly, Melwyn didn't continue the bantering; instead he left with another snort of disgust as his only comment.

Gareth reached down and pulled Rhian to her feet. She belonged inside the safety of the tent, not out here in the open. "I'm sure that after spending half the day with no one about except my men, Hawise would like your company."

Rhian shrugged. "I doubt that. She has probably enjoyed their companionship."

As if to lend weight to her words, Hawise's boisterous laugh drifted across the clearing as she playfully slapped at the man seeking to assist her from the wagon.

Rhian nodded toward the scene. "And I guessed correctly."

"Yes, well, then maybe you should go rescue my men by taking your maid inside."

He led her across the clearing to the tent the men had erected for the women's use. "This tent will be surrounded by guards at all times. You can be assured that you and Hawise are safe with the men here. However, do not leave the tent unless you have an escort or two."

Rhian's eyes widened. "Do you think they are close? Will they attack?" She placed her hand against his chest. "Do you think if we just gave them the pendant, that they would go away?"

He longed to gather her into his arms and offer assurances against her worries, but he could not do either. There were too many others about who knew they were escorting Rhian to her family and future betrothed. He'd not have tongues wagging because of his longings.

And he could not assure her that danger was not at hand. It was. He'd not lie.

"We will know how close they are when the rest of the men arrive at camp. I would imagine they will wait until sunset to take any action. However, I do not think it will be an outright attack."

Rhian stepped back and looked up at him. "What makes you think that?"

"The guards at Browan said that eight men had attacked them. I killed one in your chamber. Even if there were more outside the walls, they could not have hidden a force of many. We would have seen them, or evidence of them."

She looked around the camp. "So there are enough men here to defeat them?"

"Yes. Of that I am certain."

"But if they don't attack, what will they do?"

Gareth didn't want to frighten her, but she'd be better off warned and on guard than unaware. "They only want you and the pendant. It would be easier for a man or two to slip into camp and take you than it would be to attack so many men."

Rhian gasped and lifted a hand to her throat as if to ward off the fate that had befallen the others killed by this enemy. "Give them the pendant."

"No." Gareth shook his head. "Too many have already died for it—"

She reached toward his neck. "Then give it to them."

He grasped her shoulders and held her away. "Think, Rhian. They must believe that this pendant holds some type of power. If you place the bauble into their hands, what happens then? Do you truly think they will stop their terrible deeds once they hold any type of power?"

She stepped out of his hold, toward the tent. "No." As she turned to enter the tent, she looked over her shoulder and warned, "I expect to hold you to your word. No harm will befall me. And, Faucon, you best take care of yourself, too."

"Rest assured, I intend to do both."

A commotion at the edge of camp caught his attention. The men were bringing the traitor in.

When Rhian backed out of the tent, Gareth pushed her back through the flap. Ignoring her look of mutiny, he called for Hawise and ordered both women to remain inside the tent. He then ordered six men to surround the tent and threatened them with a fate worse than death should they fail in their duty.

He met the arriving party at the center of the clearing. The men literally threw the traitor to the ground at Gareth's feet.

While the thought that one of his own men could do something so dishonorable still twisted at his gut, his shock grew at the discovery that it was a man he'd considered a friend.

He stared down at Richard, remembering the times they'd fought side by side. And the nights they'd spent drinking and carousing. Friendly wagers. Shared jokes. Easy laughter. Gareth ached with what duty now required.

Sword drawn, he stood over the man, his throat

tight with fury, his chest heavy with betrayal. "Explain yourself."

On his knees in the dirt, Richard stared up at him. It was obvious the men had not been gentle when they brought him in.

Blood ran from his crooked nose and split lip. His torn tunic lay in disarray over his dirt-caked armor. The bindings securing his hands in front of him had cut into the flesh on his wrists.

"You have always had everything, Faucon. Everything. The finest horses, the sharpest sword. Women fawn over you, men jump at your command."

Gareth unlocked his jaw enough to say, "You have lacked for nothing."

Richard spat in the dirt at Gareth's feet. "I have taken your leavings and they no longer satisfy me."

Envy and greed. Two useless emotions that could spell a man's doom. "How much did it take to betray a man you called friend, Richard?"

"More gold and riches than a man could carry. A position of honor in their court. A life to rival your own."

Gareth wanted to rage aloud. When had this happened? Why had he failed to see it coming? Instead, he swallowed the bile in his throat and asked, "How many and what did they look like?"

Richard's unsteady laughter caused a couple of the men to step back. "I will tell you nothing."

Gareth lifted his sword. "Then you will die like a dog."

"Wait." A moment of sanity crossed Richard's face. "If I tell you?"

"Then you earn the chance to defend yourself."

"I can take you, Faucon."

Gareth's laugh drew a few gasps from those standing in the circle around them. "I would give all to see you try."

Richard heaved an unsteady breath of air before beginning. "One man. He was always hooded. I know not his name." After another gulp of air, he added, "After the lady escaped. The man approached me as I kept guard one night."

"And you sent him to Browan?"

"I told him we were headed that way, yes."

The men surrounding them uttered curses. Gareth quelled their voices with a look before he asked, "So you sacrificed our friendship, your honor, your name and your life for promises from a man you know not?"

When Richard didn't respond, Gareth continued. "Men died because of your envy and greed. Others, men you have trained and fought beside are now missing. Have you no shame? No guilt? Any words of comfort for their families that might help them make sense of their loss? A tidbit I might carry to them in an attempt to help them come to terms while facing their future without their loved one?"

Richard shouted, "Nay! I owe them nothing."

Gareth quickly sliced through the ropes binding Richard's arms. "Get on your feet."

The man slowly rose, keeping his hate-filled glare trained on Gareth. "I cannot fight you bare-handed, Faucon."

Gareth reached out and took the sword Melwyn held. He tossed it to Richard, who caught it midair. "Come, traitor. Come taste death."

Richard grasped the sword with both hands and slashed at Gareth. "It will be your death we feast on this night."

Gareth deflected the man's blow. "I have not lost a

sword fight since I left the nursery." He sliced his own weapon through the air, opening a gash on Richard's arm. "I will not start with you."

Richard steadied his sword. "It will be my pleasure to turn your luck." He lifted the length of steel and fended off Gareth's thrusts.

The circle around them widened. From the corner of his eye, Gareth saw the two women standing amongst the men. Melwyn stood behind Rhian, one hand on her shoulder, the other clutching a dagger.

If anything happened, Gareth knew Rhian would be protected.

The muscles in Gareth's arms and shoulders burned. The heavy weapons were not meant for prolonged sword fights.

Sweat dripped down Richard's forehead. The man stumbled slightly. Gareth took immediate advantage and slammed his forearm into Richard's face.

Quick to regain his footing, the man came back at Gareth. A small sidestep and Gareth avoided Richard's blade.

Gareth whipped around and slapped the side of Richard's head with the flat of his blade as the man's momentum kept him moving right past Gareth.

Richard hit the ground howling, but he again stood up, stiffened his spine, straightened his shoulders and lunged forward.

Gareth smiled bitterly. The man would not win, but at least he would die fighting. He parried Richard's blow and pushed the man back.

The circle of men around them widened farther, giving the two combatants more room to move.

Richard held his sword low and came at Gareth for an undercut.

Gareth heard the swoosh of an arrow as it whizzed by his head and lodged between Richard's surprise-widened eyes.

"Take cover!"

Chapter Ten

Rhian watched in stunned silence while everything happened as if in a waking dream. One heartbeat ago she'd held her breath, while Gareth and his man fought to the death.

The next, an arrow appeared out of nowhere to end the man's life. Melwyn had bodily tossed her into the tent. Now, Gareth's men scattered for cover behind trees, supply barrels or the wagon while seeking an enemy who'd vanished.

"Are you daft?" Hawise grabbed Rhian's arm, pulling her away from the flap and back into the relative safety of the tent. "Get back in here."

Rhian shook off the woman's hold. "Let me go. I need to see—"

"No!" Hawise hung on with both hands, digging her fingers into Rhian's arm. "You need do nothing but keep your head in here."

Rhian gave up trying to pull away. The older woman released her and stood before the now-closed tent flap.

"Those men do not require your help. You would only distract them from their duty."

She realized the truth in Hawise's logic. With a sigh of exasperation, Rhian plunked down on a stool. "That may be true, but not knowing what is happening will only make me worry more."

The men's shouts and curses filtered through the tent wall. But there were no telling sounds of metal striking metal accentuating their loud cries. Nothing to hint at a battle being waged.

Rhian could only assume the enemy had slipped away as easily as they'd arrived—undetected by any. Who were these men who attacked and then slipped away without anyone seeing? Were they demons who tormented her? How did one fight a demon? No. It was not a demon who had shot arrows or punctured men's throats.

The thought turned her blood to ice and sent prickles of fear down her spine. As long as they—whoever they were—roamed free, all would be in danger—especially Gareth. Dear Lord, she could not permit anything to happen to him.

She jumped to her feet. "I cannot bear not knowing."

Hawise quickly pushed her back onto the stool and then rummaged through her small pile of belongings. She pulled out a wineskin and a small mug, which she then filled and handed to Rhian. "Here, drink this. It will help ease the wait."

Rhian sniffed the brew. The unfamiliar scent of a sweetened, fruity wine wafted across her nose. The scent was light in comparison to the rich and spicy brews her sire favored.

The maid waved her to drink. "Go on. 'Tis only wine mixed with water, honey, fruit pulp and soothing herbs. The midwife makes this remedy special for me. Helps to calm my moods."

Rhian asked, "And you partake of this remedy often?"

Hawise sniffed. "Aye. Since my dear Henry passed on it makes the nights more bearable."

Rhian held the mug toward Hawise. "I think I will be fine without this, but I thank you."

More shouts erupted from right outside the tent. Someone stumbled against the side of their temporary dwelling, sending Rhian's heart to her throat. She took a second whiff of the liquid before downing the contents.

It ran across her tongue and down her throat like cool, liquid silk.

Hawise laughed and poured another cupful. "Drink up, milady, before you know it tomorrow will be here and we will be on our way again."

As Rhian downed the second cup, Gareth stuck his head inside the tent. "Is all well in here?"

Hawise lifted her wineskin and winked at him.

Gareth frowned, but another outburst from the men required his attention. He looked at Rhian and urged, "Be careful." Before rejoining his men.

Rhian laughed. The sound seemed to come from far away. "Be careful of what?" She looked at Hawise. The older woman swayed on her feet before spinning around.

Rhian shook her head. No, Hawise was not spinning, she was…or was it the tent?

The maid took the mug from her hand. "There, there,

milady, all will be well now." She then helped Rhian up from the stool and led her to the back of the tent to lie on a pallet she'd prepared on the floor.

After she helped Rhian ease down onto the makeshift nest of covers, Hawise pulled the edges of the fur blankets over her. Rhian snuggled under the soft warmth.

It was hard to breathe in the overly warm cocoon. But Rhian could not find the strength to push the covers from her face. Her arms refused to move and when she tried to tell Hawise to uncover her, the words came out sounding like a whispered mumble of nonsense.

Between the heat, the lack of air and the spinning floor, Rhian knew only one thing for certain—something was not right.

She thought Hawise laughed before the woman shouted for Faucon's men. Then the sound of footsteps pounding on the ground around the tent reached her inside her dark soft cave. The men surrounding the tent answered Hawise's call.

Rhian tried to make sense of the conversation taking place at the flap of the tent, but her concentration faltered when she felt herself being pulled across the ground.

The covers wrapped around her protected her from scraping on the hard dirt and rocks. Suddenly the ground was no longer beneath her. Someone had pulled her upright and then tossed her, still in the blankets across the back of an animal. By the smell, she was certain her conveyance was a horse.

The clopping of hooves, the strange voices speaking words she didn't understand and the sick jolting from the animal beneath her were her last coherent thoughts before the swirling darkness engulfed her.

* * *

Gareth cursed as the last small group of men came back into the camp. They'd been unable to find the enemy. The curs had released one single arrow and then vanished.

He and his men would catch a glimpse of one of them and would take chase only to find empty air. Unwilling to send all of the men out searching, he'd sent a few at a time and so far, each group had returned empty-handed.

Enough was enough. The sun had begun to set and he would not play this game of hide-and-seek into the night. Instead, he ordered the men to eat and rest in shifts, making certain the entire perimeter of the camp stayed guarded at all times. They would leave at first light.

He and Melwyn would take turns watching the guards. The lesson he'd learned this day rankled. How many times had he raged at his brother for trusting no one—not even family?

And how many times had Rhys laughed, pitying him for what would someday be a hard lesson?

That day had arrived. It galled him to know his brother was right.

Gareth swore it would not happen again. His trust would not be lightly given to any.

After reviewing the plans for resuming their journey with Melwyn, Gareth mentally prepared himself for a barrage of questions from Rhian and entered the tent.

Everything he saw and didn't see, besieged him at once, sending thought and logic into a confusing mass of rage.

Rhian was not in the tent.

Hawise was gagged and bound.

The pendant burned against his chest.

Without backing out of the tent, he shouted, "Melwyn!"

Faucon's captain barged into the tent with his sword drawn.

Gareth forced his racing blood to calm enough to regain the ability to think. He took the gag from Hawise's mouth and cut her free of the bindings, all the while firing questions at her. "Where is Rhian? What happened here? Who did this? Why did you not call for the guards?"

At his last question, Melwyn opened the tent flap with the side of his sword and yelled, "Faucon! To me!"

Faucon's guards appeared instantly. Melwyn set two of the older men to work searching for any trail, or hint of what may have happened.

Hawise twisted the hem of her skirt in her hands before using the fabric to dab at her eyes. "I know not what happened." She waved toward the remaining guards. "One moment I was talking to them and when I turned around, I was gagged before I could find the wits to scream."

"And Rhian?" A part of Gareth feared the worst, yet the pendant resting hot against his chest gave him a thread of hope. They wanted the amethyst dragon and would keep her alive until they possessed the bauble.

"I am sorry, milord…." Hawise choked on the words. "I know not. She was already gone."

Gareth's stomach fell, then quickly rose to his throat at the maid's statement.

Melwyn made a guttural sound in his throat before stepping into the conversation. "Gone? How?"

Hawise shook her head. "I do not know."

"Surely, you heard something," the captain prompted. "She did not leave without some type of fight or argument."

Again, the maid shook her head. "I heard nothing."

Gareth frowned. He did not believe her for a heartbeat. When he stared at Hawise, the maid looked everywhere but at him.

She lied. Why? What was she hiding?

As much as he wished to discover the reason for her falsehoods, they were wasting precious time. He could not very well beat the answer from an old woman.

He fastened his coif up over his head, pulled on his mailed gloves, spun around and brushed past Melwyn as he ducked out of the tent.

"I want that woman out of my sight. Escort her back to Browan." The enemy was after the pendant, they'd not chase a maid and a few men back to the keep. "Tell Sir Edgar that I want her confined. I will deal with her later."

His brusque order to the guards caused Hawise to exclaim, "Milord, I did nothing."

Gareth paused. He then turned around and looked at her through the open tent flap. "Aye. You did nothing to protect your charge."

"Milord Faucon." The guards Melwyn had sent to find clues beckoned him and the captain. "We found their trail."

The torch Melwyn held aloft permitted them to see the telltale signs of a large bundle having been dragged from beneath the back wall of the tent.

Gareth remembered that Hawise had lifted a wineskin and winked at him when he'd stuck his head inside to check on the two of them earlier. Had Rhian become intoxicated and fallen asleep on a pallet?

He glanced at the tent. Or, he wondered, had Hawise drugged her? Were his suspicions unfounded? Prompted only by Richard's treachery?

Gareth didn't know and had not the time to dwell on speculation—not now. Later, after he had Rhian safe. Only then would he sort through fact and fallacy. Now, however, he followed the trail until it disappeared into the forest.

It took all of one heartbeat to decide his course of action. He dismissed the two men before reaching up to tear the knotted ribbon from his neck. Gareth handed the pendant to Melwyn. "This is what they seek. Keep it safe. Let none know it is in your possession."

Melwyn dangled the ribbon in the torchlight. "'Tis nothing but a bauble."

Gareth took the torch from the captain. "I thought the same. Obviously, the thing is worth something to someone."

Melwyn tucked the pendant inside the small leather pouch he wore strapped to his belt. He studied Gareth intently. "What are you planning?"

"To find Rhian."

"Alone?"

Gareth nodded toward the camp. "There is little choice. I trust none here but you. However, I need you to stay with the men and make certain that maid is escorted back to Browan. Send a missive along for Edgar. Tell him to chain her somewhere until I am free to deal with her."

Melwyn opened his mouth, then quickly closed it at Gareth's hard glare. The tightening of his lips gave evidence to his disapproval.

Finally, he nodded. "Lord Faucon, go find your lady."

"She isn't—"

Melwyn's snort of laughter stopped Gareth's denial. The captain continued, "I will see to things here and be at your back within hours."

Gareth didn't doubt that for a moment. He turned to leave and was stayed by Melwyn's hand on his arm.

When he looked over his shoulder at his brother's captain, the man smirked before suggesting, "Do yourself a favor. Either claim her as yours, or let her go."

Gareth paused. Would honor be served by doing as Melwyn suggested?

"The King cares naught about this woman." In his typical and familiar fashion, Melwyn saw straight through to Gareth's thoughts. "Stephen cares only that the next time a battle wages you do not join those who retreat. This little task is nothing more than your punishment for what happened at Lincoln. See it as nothing greater."

His words stung. Gareth's guilt over his actions at Lincoln burned anew. He'd followed his overlord's lead instead of the king's orders. A mistake many made that day, allowing Stephen to be captured.

What others had done mattered little to Gareth. He had only to answer for his own shame.

"Take her if you must, Gareth. Stephen will not care. If you cannot bring yourself to take her, then marry her. Bring her riches, great or humble, to Stephen and all will be forgotten."

Gareth tucked Melwyn's advice into the back of his mind. Something else to think on…later. He flashed the captain a wide grin before raising one eyebrow and saying, "For one who claims to have no use for women, you certainly seem intent on seeing me shackled."

Melwyn cuffed him none too gently alongside the head. "Be on your way, pup."

With a quick laugh, Gareth headed into the forest, following the trail left in the dense underbrush.

The hairs on Gareth's neck quivered. This was too easy. Something was not right.

Not one night sound broke the unnatural silence of the forest. No rodents rooted for food. No owls hunted in the trees.

Only the sound of crunching twigs and dried leaves beneath his footsteps sliced through the blackness of the night.

He backed off the trail, blending into the darkness of the forest.

The cool night wind brushed over Rhian's face and limbs. She squinted against the fire's light flickering in her eyes.

When had they released her from her furry cocoon? How long had she been unconscious? She glanced up at the night sky. The moon was overhead. It was the dead of night.

The sound of feet pounding wildly in rhythm to a beating drum cut through the fog in her mind.

Memory rushed in. She sprang up with a gasp at the stiffness of her limbs.

And then she gasped again at the strange and frightening sight before her. Creatures of the forest danced upright around the blazing fire. Deer, bear, wildcat, fox and wolf stood on their hind legs and circled the growing flames.

The wolf swiveled his head and stared at her. Rhian realized these were no animals. They were men wearing the pelts of the beasts over their heads and shoulders.

She looked across the fire and saw others watching the dancers. Others who wore the black hoods she'd come to fear.

What had happened came rushing back with a force that took her breath away.

Hawise had drugged her.

Why? Why would the woman who'd done nothing but help her since her arrival at Browan suddenly seek to bring her to danger's door?

Rhian remembered naught of being taken from Gareth's camp. Only hazy memories of waking long enough to have yet more of the sleeping draft being forced between her lips. How many hours or days of dreamless sleep had passed?

She rolled her shoulders, working the kinks from her neck and back. Rhian knew the time could not be measured in hours. Mere hours could not account for the pain shooting through her body.

However, the sharp burn in her muscles meant that for the moment, she was still alive. For that she was grateful.

Rhian lifted a trembling hand to her throat. These men wanted a pendant she no longer possessed. Would they spare her life in hopes she'd lead them to the amethyst dragon they so desired?

A hand touched her hair. Rhian jumped. She'd been so lost in thought that she'd failed to hear any approaching footsteps.

"Ah, Princess, the game is up." He lifted her hair, slowly stroking the long braid.

Rhian's heart slammed against the inside of her chest. The gathering fear threatened to burst through bone and flesh.

His deceptively gentle touch stilled. "You had the chance to decide your fate." He tightened his grasp on her hair and tugged Rhian's head back until the pain flared like fire on her scalp.

Between his hood and the darkness of the night, she could discern little more than his outline in the flickering firelight. Twin flames reflecting in the pupils of his eyes caused her heart to beat even faster, harder. The soulessness of Satan shimmered from his stare.

He leaned closer, whispering, "Now *I* will decide your fate."

He slid his fingers along her exposed throat, up and back down the side of her neck, then beneath the edge of her gown and across her collarbone.

She cringed beneath his touch.

He reached lower, between her breasts, his fingers stroking her skin, searching. Her flesh crawled.

With a harder tug on her hair, he stretched her head back farther until she was certain he'd snap it off of her shoulders. "You know what I seek. Where did you hide it?"

His tone held no note of mercy. And his lifeless stare promised terrors she could hardly imagine.

Rhian shook her head as much as his tight hold would allow. "I do not have it."

He leaned even closer. He brushed his cloth-covered cheek against her hair, before asking, "Where is it?" His hot breath seared each word into her ear.

"Safe from you." That was not a lie. It was safe—for now.

To her surprise, the man released her and came to stand before her. He was dressed in black, from head to toe. Every article of clothing from the hood concealing his face, to the boots covering his feet, blended into the darkness of the night.

Rhian shivered. The roaring fire behind him made him appear more satanic than before.

He bent over and traced her jawline. She jerked away from his touch. He threaded his gloved fingers through her hair and roughly pulled her up from the blankets.

"The woman said you wore the pendant at all times."

A gasp of surprise escaped her lips before she could swallow the sound. What had Hawise been thinking? She knew what these monsters did to the guards at Browan. What did the woman think they'd do to her?

Rhian barely managed to swallow a groan of dismay. Did Hawise detest her so thoroughly that she cared not?

"Ah, I see you know who I mean. Aye, Princess, it was easy to pluck your maid. A few coins in her palm and the information that you alone had brought the evil to Browan made attaining her help an easy task."

"I brought nothing to Browan. You did that."

When he twisted her hair in his hand, Rhian thought he would yank it from her scalp. Her eyes watered from the burning pain on the back of her head.

"But you…you were the stranger living a lie in their midst. It was a simple chore to sow seeds of doubt in her mind. A few whispered words of witchcraft and the devil were all it took to make the good woman turn against you."

His evil laugh chilled her blood. He slid his free arm around to her back and dragged her tight against him.

"No God-fearing woman wants a devil-worshipping whore living nearby."

When he ground the hardening bulge in his groin against her, Rhian leaned her chest against his. He sneered down at her. "Do not think to ply a whore's trick on me. It will not work. You will not sway me from my goal with promises of the flesh."

Rhian held his gaze while silently praying that her stiff limbs would heed her bidding. She judged his height and rammed her knee into his groin as hard as she could.

His bellow of pain and rage rang in her ears as she jerked out of his hold. She flinched at the pain as she tore her hair from his now open fingers.

She spun around and raced toward the forest, stumbling on unsteady legs as she ran. The remains of the drink that had been forced on her settled in her head as a dull thudding. She blinked her eyes to keep her vision from blurring.

"Stop her!" The pounding of the dance stopped as all now rushed after her.

In the wavering light from the fire, she thought she saw Gareth standing at the line of trees surrounding this clearing.

"Gareth!" she called out his name, her voice breaking on a sob. But when she blinked again, he was gone.

She heard cursing directly behind her, before a body hit her back as if it had flown through the air.

"Got her!"

Rhian screamed and twisted beneath the weight holding her down. "Let me go. I don't have it. It is not here."

The weight lifted and she was yanked unceremoniously to her feet. She did not need to open her eyes to know who held her in a grip that promised death.

He dug his fingers into her upper arms and shook her until Rhian was certain her head would fly off her neck.

Curses winged from his mouth. Some in a language she could not understand. However, the snarl in his voice gave evidence to his anger at her action. She could not mistake the rage directed toward her.

"If you ever try a trick like that again, you will die."

She didn't doubt that his threat was in earnest. Nor did she doubt that given the chance, she would repeat the act.

He shook her again. "Did you hear me?"

Instead of answering, she stiffened her spine, raised her head and stared at him.

When the man lifted one hand, as if to strike her, Rhian held her ground. She would not give him the satisfaction of her fear.

"Before I am finished, you will choke on your stubborn pride."

She saw the glove-covered hand coming toward her and gritted her teeth, silently hoping she wouldn't scream.

Chapter Eleven

Suddenly, before the man could strike her, Rhian was yanked from his hold. His fingers gouged into her arm, but his failed attempt to keep her prisoner did nothing more than bruise her as she was torn from his grasp.

The instant she was free, the fingers on her shoulder relaxed and slid down to curl around her wrist.

She hadn't been seeing things in the woods. She knew by his touch, by the sureness of his movements, by his harsh whisper as he ordered her to move that it was Gareth.

His presence sent life flowing into her limbs and a spark of hope to flare in her heart. Quickly, before those assembled could react to her escape, they ran into the cover of the woods.

Rhian held up the skirt of her gown with her free hand and silently followed Gareth, trusting him to guide them around trees and over logs that were invisible to her in the darkness of the night.

The enemy took no pains to hide their pursuit. Instead of creeping to mask their approach, they crashed through the forest, breaking twigs, stumbling over fallen trees, cursing and shouting at each other and at her and Gareth.

Rhian hazarded one look over her shoulder and sucked in a deep breath. Torches flickered close behind.

She knew that if caught, they would die.

Sensing her slight hesitation, Gareth pulled her alongside of him. "Do not look back." Without stopping, he draped his arm across her shoulders. "Trust me."

His whispered plea against her temple chased away some of her fear. "I do."

He nodded toward his right side. "It is just a short way farther."

She wondered what lay ahead, but her question dissolved at the sound of another crash coming from a little closer behind them.

Gareth grabbed her hand and picked up their already breathless pace.

The unseen path beneath her feet seemed to angle upward. Unable to keep up with his long stride, Rhian tugged on his hand, willing him to slow down.

His unspoken answer was to pull her around, in front of him. With a firm hand against the middle of her back, he urged her to hurry. She had little choice but to obey his prompting—it was that, or to permit those on their trail to catch them.

Rhian refused to give in so easily to what would be certain death. Her breath hitched at the thought, giving her an added measure of renewed strength and resolve.

She stumbled over rocks and around trees. Sweat

dampened her scalp, plastered her gown to her back and trickled between her breasts.

Gareth knew his success at taking Rhian out of the enemy's grasp had been due to the advantage of surprise. While they'd left an obvious trail, they'd expected more than one man to follow them.

He'd skirted around the guards watching for a group of men to come to her rescue. They'd not noticed a lone man slinking toward their camp.

However, he'd not taken her physical condition into consideration. Her labored breath and unsure footing spoke loudly of her exhaustion after being drugged and kidnapped.

As much as he wanted to stop and let her rest, he could not. They had no choice but to gain the safety of a hiding spot he'd discovered on his way to her rescue.

A cave on the other side of the summit was concealed by boulders. There would be no trees or bushes to hide them as they slipped into the narrow entrance. Only the remaining darkness of the night could provide the secrecy they required.

Gareth glanced up through the now thinning canopy of trees above them. The moon was beginning its morning descent. They had to move quickly. A task easier said than done in the near blackness of the forest.

He held his breath to stop the sound of his heart beating in his ears and listened to the sounds of the night. Nothing broke the eerie quiet.

The men still followed, as he'd expected, but they'd long ago ceased their shouts to each other. They were reserving their strength for the ascent up the side of this mountain.

After making certain he and Rhian were still on the winding path around the growing field of boulders, he glanced briefly over his shoulder. Aye, the men followed. The flickering light from their torches as they searched for their prey bobbed in and out of sight.

Each time he'd checked their progress they appeared to be a little closer. He'd not let them recapture Rhian. Soon the dirt, tree roots and rocky path would give way to nothing but rocks and boulders. Rhian needed to regain some of her strength for that part of the climb.

Gareth reached out and found a smooth-faced boulder. He touched Rhian's shoulder. "Stop."

As he sat on the edge of the large rock, he assisted her up on top. "Climb on my back."

"You can't carry me."

He grasped her wrist. "Either climb on my back, or I will carry you over my shoulder."

"Well, I—"

Gareth stood and leaned his shoulder into her stomach, prepared to sling her across. Rhian pushed him away. "Fine, turn around."

When he presented his back to her, she wrapped her arms around his neck, commenting, "This is insane."

Her words ceased when he hooked his arms beneath her knees and rose. "Just hang on."

He choked at her hold around his neck. She instantly loosened her grasp and he headed up, toward the cave.

At first the added burden made his gait uneven. But he quickly adjusted and soon his strides were long and steady.

Rhian rested her head on his shoulder. "Will they stop chasing us?" Her breath warmed the side of his neck.

"Nay." He answered, seeking to curtail her shiver of fear as it rippled against his back. He briefly tightened his arms around her legs. "Take heart. They will not catch us."

"I will hold you to that, Faucon." Her lips brushed against his ear. A soft flutter that arrowed directly to his heart.

Gareth swallowed hard against the unfamiliar emotions churning in his gut and chest. Surely it was nothing more than concern for her well-being that caused his innards to clench in a manner that felt suspiciously like an illness.

He paused to catch his breath and clear his befuddled mind.

Rhian shifted. "Gareth, I am too heavy for this. Put me down. I will not delay our escape." In an attempt to pull her legs free from his hold, she leaned harder against him, pushing her breasts against his back.

A flitting vision of holding her this way before him—with her arms wrapped around his neck, her legs around his waist and her breasts against his chest—propelled him into action. Anything to drown out the memory of Melwyn's suggestion to take her.

Gareth managed to choke out a strangled, "Nay," before resuming their ascent.

By all the saints above, had he lost the ability to reason? He was on a mission for the king. One that would prove his honor, or bring about his and Rhian's deaths if he did not keep his mind on the task at hand.

Yet he found himself bewitched by nothing more than a whisper, the caress of a warm breath against his ear. Aye, he'd lost his mind.

And stood in immediate danger of losing his heart, too.

A loss he would face when the time arrived. For now, Gareth drew his focus back to the rocky path beneath his feet.

The climb grew steeper, steadily angling sharply upward. Soon, it would no longer be possible to carry Rhian.

He nearly laughed at the absurd twinge of regret the mere thought of releasing her summoned.

Rhian rested her cheek against Gareth's shoulder. The stiffness she'd encountered upon waking up in the enemy's camp had left her limbs. The crisp night air had done much to help clear the drink-induced fog from her mind.

There was no logical reason for her not to walk on her own two feet. She snuggled closer against his back, burying her nose against the warmth of his neck. No logical reason at all.

But she could think of many illogical ones.

She rubbed her cheek across his shoulder. He provided warmth against the chill of the night.

She inhaled deeply and breathed in the lingering traces of sandalwood. Of all the unpleasant scents she could detect—smoke, sweat, horseflesh—it was the sandalwood that drifted beyond her nose to calm her unsettled mind.

She pressed closer against his back and felt the rise and fall as he breathed. The sure and steady movement went far to ease her fear.

She tightened her legs around his waist. The long skirt of her gown had bunched up past her knees. The flexing and stroking of his callused fingers against her exposed flesh curled her toes and made breathing difficult.

She laced her fingers tighter together to keep from slipping her hands beneath the fabric covering his chest.

She longed to feel his muscles expand and contract as he sought his way through the darkness.

Rhian swallowed. Aye, her thoughts were illogical. Out of character. Completely inappropriate.

And impossible to ignore.

A rock slipped out from beneath his foot. He stumbled. Quickly regaining his footing, Gareth paused.

With a twinge of regret, Rhian slid her legs down his body, rested her cheek against his back for a moment before reluctantly unlacing her hold from around his neck.

Cold air replaced the warmth of his back against her breasts, sending a shiver down her spine.

Gareth lightly stroked her cheek before sliding his hand down her arm and grasping her hand in his own.

"It is truly just a little farther. Up over the top of this mountain is a cave. We are nearly there."

Rhian shook her head. "Oh, aye. You said that earlier. Just a little farther."

"You needed the lie then."

Even though she was unable to see his face, she could hear the smile in his words.

She felt him turn against her shoulder, back toward the way they had just traversed. She joined him and noted with relief, "I no longer see their torches."

"Aye. With luck, we have increased the distance between us."

As they resumed their climb, she prayed he was right.

Tree roots no longer littered the unseen path. Now, only rocks and boulders barred their way. She followed him closely as he picked his way carefully between the overlarge stones.

Rhian tripped over a dislodged rock and slammed her

knee down on the hard uneven surface. Momentarily stunned, she bit back a frustrated cry of pain.

Gareth scrambled to her side. "Are you all right?"

She clenched her jaw at his nearly whispered question. No, she wasn't all right. She was tired of climbing in the dark and now, if she wasn't mistaken, the wet warmth on her knee was blood.

She rose and gingerly tested her leg before saying, "I am fine."

Gareth knew she lied. He could hear it through the pain evident in her voice.

He'd been wrong in his assumption that she could make this journey. It'd been a mistake to think any woman could accomplish what he expected her to do. But he could devise no other plan than to literally rip her from her enemy's hands and seek shelter in one of the many caves nestled in this mountain.

Gareth rubbed the tightness building between his eyes. They had no other choice. They could not descend without being caught. Nor could they just sit here and wait for the enemy to take them.

He wrapped one arm about her waist, supporting her as she took a few steps. Certain she'd not caused an injury that would prevent her from continuing, he released her and urged, "Let us go."

He led her slowly up to the summit, walking until they could climb upright no longer. Then, on his hands and knees, he tried to find the easiest path. One that would permit them to proceed with the least amount of danger. He tested each step with his hand, making certain the rocks beneath him would not slide and tumble behind him and onto Rhian.

Finally, after what seemed an eternity, the reach before him was naught but air. They'd gained the peak. He turned and pulled Rhian up next to him to sit for a moment on the top.

Her breathing was labored. The raspy, uneven gasps took a few moments to steady. When they did, he heard her inhale sharply at the sight before them.

The moon, already on its descent, was framed by a myriad of twinkling stars against the blanket of a near-black sky.

"A truly heavenly vista, is it not?"

The wistful tone of her voice made him long for things beyond a mere mortal's reach.

Peace and quiet. A warm, safe home with a wife to love and be loved by, and children to carry on his name.

"Yes," he finally agreed. "It is and it will be tomorrow, too." Gareth reached for her hand and rose. "But for now, we need to go."

After one look back at the moon and the stars, she stood and followed him down to a slate rock that projected out from the side of the mountain.

Gareth peered over the edge of the slate. His form silhouetted by the moonlight. He pointed to his left. "Down there is the cave."

The crash of falling rocks and a man's scream sailed over the peak behind them. Rhian's heart raced. If they did not hurry, the moonlight would give them away.

Gareth's whispered curse lent credence to her fears. He grabbed her hand and headed toward the cave. "Stay close. We have little time."

They made it into the safety of the cave with little more than a dozen heartbeats to spare. Gareth pushed

Rhian inside before scrambling through the opening behind her.

"Move back." His near-hissed order sent her scurrying quickly across the slick floor of the cave. Over the loud, rapid pounding of her heart she heard the scraping of rock against rock before a hand brushed her arm.

Rhian jumped. Then, as Gareth pulled her against him, she laughed softly at her overactive fears.

They sat side by side, his arm across her shoulders holding her close. Only the heavy thudding of her own heartbeat echoing in her ears broke the silence.

She held her breath as the sounds of men scrambling over rocks and around boulders drifted into the cave. If the men discovered this hiding place, she would not live to see the sun rise. Nor would Gareth. Surely after the hazards of this climb, God would see them safely through the rest of the night.

Rhian swallowed an unbidden cry. She was not yet ready to die. Especially not over a worthless bauble. The amethyst had already caused her enough grief. They were welcome to it. Her mistake had been in not giving it to them before. A mistake that had cost men their lives and left more in danger.

She reached up and touched Gareth's neck. Unable to feel the ribbon that held the dragon pendant she pulled her hand back. What had he done with it?

He leaned closer and whispered into her ear, "It is safe, fear not."

She whispered back, "End this senseless killing and just give it to them."

Gareth placed a finger over her lips and moved away.

She sucked in a breath of air and held it tightly until he returned to her side.

"I think we are safe." He kept his voice low.

Rhian shivered. "Safe to do what? Stay in here until we die?"

"Oh, now that would truly be a waste." She heard him drag something across the floor of the cave and stop in front of her. "Hungry?"

"Aye." To lend truth to her answer, her stomach growled. "But where will we find—"

Her question was cut off by what felt and tasted suspiciously like a chunk of bread as it was pushed between her lips.

Rhian retrieved the chunk and tore it into smaller pieces. Between bites, she asked, "Where did this come from?"

"The same place this did." Gareth took her hand and placed a hunk of cheese in her palm. "I only brought water to drink and I think there are apples, too."

While she was grateful for the food, she wondered aloud, "How?"

"I found this cave earlier, while following your captor's trail. Since it seemed a good place to hide until Melwyn and the other men arrive, I stashed a sack of rations and weapons in here."

"The men, they left a trail?"

"A rather prominent one. I've no doubt Melwyn will find it easy enough to follow it, too."

For some reason she could not name, her heart tripped over itself. "You came for me."

She heard Gareth snort. "Since we are sitting here together, I would say that was obvious."

"Why?"

The silence grew heavy, making her regret asking. He finally replied, "I made a vow to deliver you to your family. I will honor that vow."

"Oh." Rhian knew not what else she'd expected. But it hadn't been this sudden falling of her stomach. Nor had it been this odd tightening of her throat.

His fingers grazed her cheek before he gently grasped her chin. "Rhian. I would have come for you without a vow to the king."

Her stomach lifted. Her throat cleared. "Oh."

He released her and she heard the rustle of his clothing brush against the rocks. The scraping of his ration bag being dragged to the side followed.

She could not see him, but she felt the heat of his body as he moved nearer. Rhian tipped her head to one side to listen closer to his movements.

His warm breath drifted across her cheek, his fingertips followed. Her heartbeat and breathing paused, waiting to see what would come next—hoping it would be his kiss.

She sighed softly as his lips brushed gently against hers.

Her heart resumed beating with a pace that reminded her of a bird's wings. Rapid and light, it fluttered inside her ribs.

She leaned against him, resting her hands against his chest and returned his kiss. She followed his prompting and parted her lips.

Gareth groaned, breaking their kiss long enough to sit alongside her. Rhian clung to him, willing him not to stop.

He pulled her across his lap and held her cheek against his chest. "This will lead to only madness, Rhian."

She felt the hard pounding of his heart and knew he spoke the truth. But she cared not. She reached up and stroked his stubble-covered chin. "Then lead us there."

Chapter Twelve

Between the growing tightness in his groin and the building thickness in his throat, Gareth knew the path to madness would be a very short one.

With a groan of regret, he leaned back. Cold, damp air rushed to fill the space between them. With the chill came the ability to think.

He brushed the pad of his thumb across her soft cheek before threading his fingers through her hair.

"Nay, Rhian. It would not be right." When she tried to pull away, he held her fast. "It is only the thrill of victory, the rush of heated blood after a hard-won battle that makes us act this way now."

His lie was half-true. The rush of hot blood was familiar, but he'd learned long ago to contain the fleeting thrill of victory.

Rhian rubbed her cheek against his palm. "'Tis more than that, Faucon, and well you know it."

Her lips moved against the flesh of his hand. A slight movement that seared through the calluses on his palm.

He purposely misinterpreted her words. To do otherwise would make the path even shorter. "Aye, 'tis more than that. You are still promised to another." Gareth cringed at the unladylike curses that left her lips.

"What must I do to convince you that I will not honor that promise?"

Marry me.

Those two unspoken words drifted up from deep inside him. Unbidden. Unexpected. And filled with the urgent need to be said aloud.

Gareth bit the inside of his mouth. Hard.

"I will not marry this heathen that others have chosen for me. I would sooner die."

Marry me.

His brothers would laugh until they cried if they could read his thoughts at this moment. He, the one who'd never entertained serious thoughts of tying himself to any woman before, could think of nothing else.

Gareth swallowed. And then there was Melwyn. While his brothers would only laugh, Melwyn would make sport of the idea for years to come.

Rhian placed her hand against his chest. "Faucon, if you will not help find a way to free me from this future fate has planned, I will find someone who will."

Sweat beaded on his forehead. He tasted his own blood on his tongue. "Marry me."

Silence momentarily filled the cave. Not even the sound of breathing broke the tomblike quiet.

"I…I beg your pardon?"

"Marry me." Now that he'd already said it aloud once, the second time wasn't quite as bad. In fact, Gareth suddenly felt like laughing with relief. A response he was certain would not be welcome.

"Marry you?"

He wished he could see her face. Would her features register as much surprise as her voice?

"Aye. You seek a future different from the one fate has decreed for you. Would not becoming my wife fulfill that search?"

She jerked her head out of his grasp and nearly sprang from his lap as if he were suddenly on fire.

"Oh, aye, that would most certainly be different."

The sound of her voice moved away from him. "Rhian, do not—"

Her curse as she slammed her head against the low ceiling of the cave made the rest of his warning unnecessary.

Rhian rubbed her head. Obviously, he was going to warn her not to stand up. But she needed to move. It mattered little if she did so on her knees, she needed to get away from him and his strange way of helping her.

Strange because it sounded, and even worse, felt right. For the first time since her father's death, something finally felt right again. But why did it have to be the most insane idea she'd ever heard?

"I can't marry you."

"Why not?"

Did she detect laughter behind his words? She narrowed her eyes. "Why should I?"

"It would be an excellent excuse not to marry another."

While she never expected a man to declare undying love, she did hope to wed for something more than an excuse not to marry another.

His feet scuffed across the stone floor. Rhian backed

away from the sound until a wet, cold wall stopped her retreat. "Stay where you are, Faucon."

Her words hissed across the space between them, stopping his approach.

In an attempt to sort out this conversation, she said, "Let me see if I have the right of this. You are willing to disobey your liege, destroy your honor and possibly risk the loss of any future entendre to save me from my fate?"

"Simply put? Yes."

She shook her head. "Are you mad?"

"Mad? As in angry, or lack-witted?"

Yes, he was without a doubt laughing at her. "Lack-witted."

"No. I am simply offering you the escape I thought you desired."

What did he expect in exchange? "I have little coin."

"I have no need of your coin."

"A second son with gold. How does that happen?"

He laughed before answering. "My sire acquired enough for all of us and I have a winning sword arm."

"And enough overblown pride to match." Rhian slapped her hand over her mouth. She hadn't meant to say that aloud.

"Yes, true enough."

"The king already granted my father's land and keep to another."

"I have my own."

Rhian pursed her lips. Perhaps the simplest way to do this was just to ask, "What do you want from me?"

"Shared conversation. A warm bed. Children."

Those words, coming from his deep voice, sent a shiver down her spine. She swallowed the lump forming in her throat. "I have brought you nothing but trouble from the moment I was delivered into your hands. Why would you help me now?"

A sudden thought turned her warmth to ice. "If this is your way of punishing me, you need find another way."

Gareth pulled her into his arms. Rhian gasped. She had not heard any sound warning of his approach.

"Punish you?" His breath brushed hot against her ear. "I could have done so at any moment and none would have stayed my hand."

Her stomach flipped at the truth of his statement. She summoned every ounce of bravado she possessed to ask, "So why, Faucon, would you wish to saddle yourself with a wife such as I?"

He threaded his fingers through her hair, up the back of her head, holding her in place for one brief heartbeat before pulling her head back. "Such as you?" His mouth was hot against her neck. "Perhaps because I find you interesting."

She swallowed against his lips. "Interesting." The cave tilted wildly beneath her knees. When she swayed against him, Gareth slid one arm around her and held her close.

"Enticing."

Rhian shuddered when he found the soft spot on the side of her neck. "Enticing?"

He traced the shell of her ear, before breathing, "Challenging."

With a fluid shift, he slid his leg between hers. Every sensation she'd ever known raced to settle low in her belly.

Rhian licked her lips. "Challenging?"

Gareth trailed circles down her back, his fingers coming to rest against the fullness of her hip. He nipped gently at her earlobe and pulled her tight against his thigh. "Exciting."

This was happening far too fast. What felt right only heartbeats ago, suddenly seemed the worst idea in the world.

Rhian resisted the urge to clutch him close. Instead, she pushed against his chest. "Stop, Faucon. Cease."

While he instantly halted his mind-stealing attack on her senses, he did not release her. "You would rather take your chances with this unknown man than with me?"

"I would rather not take any chances at all."

She rested her cheek against his chest and took comfort from the fact that his heart hammered as quickly as her own. "When I asked you to let me escape, you would not. When I asked you to ruin me for another, you refused. Now, you offer me marriage as a solution to all of my problems."

Rhian wished she could see his face. Would he hold her searching stare or would he look away in an effort to hide his true emotions and thoughts?

"Do you think your offer some form of heroism?" She frowned, still trying to make sense of it all. "Are you seeking a way to avoid a previous engagement of your own?"

Gareth rested his forehead against hers and nudged her head back. His lips brushed her cheek. "I cannot see your face. How can I answer your questions in a manner that will enable you to believe me?"

Rhian swallowed the nervous laugh building in her throat. He read her mind—an unthinkable possibility. As disconcerting as it was impossible. She touched his shoulder, feathering her fingertips across the breadth of muscles and bone beneath his damp tunic. "Just answer me, Faucon. I will hear the lie in your voice."

His gentle laugh wisped across her flesh. "And what about the truth? Will you also hear that?"

She shrugged. "I suppose we will see, will we not?"

"I have never been a hero, Lady Gervaise, and I sincerely doubt if offering you marriage would qualify as such."

He pressed his lips briefly to hers. So briefly she wasn't quite certain if it'd been real or if she imagined his touch.

Faucon continued, "And I have no previous betrothal, not even a smoldering liaison to hinder marrying you."

Rhian shook her head. "This makes little sense, Faucon. There is nothing here that would be advantageous for you or your family."

His laughter echoed off the cold stone walls of the cave, bouncing behind them before returning to seemingly mock her worries.

"Have you never seen anyone do something simply because they wanted to? Simply perhaps because it seemed the right thing to do at the moment?"

"That is fine for now, but what about tomorrow or next year? What if this foolish notion of yours no longer feels right then?"

His shoulders rose and fell beneath her touch. "Faucon…Gareth, less than a week ago I sought nothing more from life than a chance to escape my fate and you."

"Do you still wish to escape your future?"

"Aye." She would be content to never visit her mother's people. To never lay eyes upon their chosen mate for her.

"And me?" He traced her chin with the side of his hand. "Do you still wish to escape me?"

Rhian shivered as he explored her face with his fingertips. "Yes. No."

His gentle, seeking touch brushed across her lips before trailing down her neck. "Which is it? Yes or no?"

"I…I am not certain." She gasped when he paused his hand on the swell of her breast.

"Come, come. Surely you have your own mind. Yes or no?"

Gareth nudged her head back up, giving him access to her lips.

He knew she was confused. There was not the slightest doubt in his mind that Rhian was as befuddled as he by his outrageous offer of marriage.

Perhaps he should withdraw the offer until both of them were of sound mind.

Rhian shivered beneath his touch. The slight tremors coursing down her body reverberated against his own. He closed his eyes against the fiery chill. Perhaps he would wait a bit before voicing that idea.

He stroked the side of her neck with his thumb and felt her warm breath against his face. Even without being able to see her, he knew that her lips were so close that the wind would not have room between them.

He tilted his head and closed the minute distance between them.

Her mouth was warm beneath his. Warm and yielding. She parted her lips with little more than a gentle caress from his tongue.

Rhian followed his lead tentatively at first. Then quickly gave herself up to the same fog of desire that beckoned to him.

They teased and explored, taking turns retreating and advancing until the mist swirled around them, catching them both fast in a whispered promise of coming fulfillment.

Gareth wanted more than her kiss, more than an unspoken promise. He wound both arms around her, holding her tight against his chest. She was soft in his arms, lost in the haze and did not protest when he leaned to the side and dropped them from their knees to stretch out on the hard slate beneath them.

He rolled to his back, dragging her along with him until she rested on top.

Rhian scooted farther up his chest, sliding her body up the length of his. When her legs straddled his waist, Gareth was unable to contain his groan of near frustration.

He felt her lips curve into a smile as she swallowed the sound. Determination to bring her to the same level of need urged him on.

He threaded his fingers through her hair and ran his other hand down the length of her side and back up. She trembled against him as he caressed her breast.

The layers of clothing did not hide the desires of her body. Heat nearly scorched his thumb as he teased her hardened nipple.

Rhian's breathing paused a heartbeat before her back rose and fell quickly. Her heart raced against his chest.

But still, not a sound escaped her.

Gareth trailed his fingertips back down her side, over the roundness of her hips and down her thigh.

The fabric of her dress rose on his wrist as he drew lazy circles back up her thigh.

Her soft flesh tensed and quivered beneath his touch. She leaned harder into their kiss.

Gareth untangled his fingers from her hair and trailed his hand down the other side of her body, again drawing her gown up as he repeated his movements until the fabric rested above her hips.

With an effort, he reminded himself that she was no whore. As much as he wanted to simply roll her over and take her now, it would not endear him to her.

And that was the goal.

He dug his heels into the hard slate, amazed that it did not crack beneath them.

While the flesh on her legs had been soft, it was nothing compared to the velvet skin covering her inner thighs.

And while the heat raging through his own blood was hot, it held nothing compared to the flames singeing his fingertips as he stroked along the divide separating her derriere.

She was hotter than anything he'd ever felt. Hot and nearly ready for her lover's touch.

Gareth dipped his hips and quickly slid his other hand between them. Gently stroking and coaxing damp curls out of his way, he found the touch that forced a sound from Rhian's lips.

Rhian couldn't have held back her moan of frustrated surprise mixed with pleasure had her life depended on it. Her legs went stiff of their own accord, at the same time the rest of her body went limp.

Thankfully, Gareth's strong body cradled her own as he worked a strange magic with his hands and mouth.

He would drive her mad. Her stomach clenched low as he slowly stroked with one hand and teased with the other. When she tried to lift her head, he nipped at her lower lip, bringing her back into their endless kiss.

But not even chains could have held her against him when her body seemed to reach for the stars. It was as if every sensation she'd ever experienced settled between her legs and begged for release.

She pulled herself up and gripped his shoulders. "Please—" her words echoed as breathless pants "—make it stop."

His soft, deep chuckle chased away her plea. He stopped the madness for half a heartbeat and she thought she'd go mad with wanting it to return.

Holding her in place on her knees, Gareth slid his body beneath her. Rhian swallowed a cry of dismay when his lips and tongue covered the pulsing between her legs.

But the dismay evaporated as quickly as it came. With his hands firmly holding her thighs and his too-intimate kiss, she was unable to do anything but close her eyes and surrender to the fire silently calling her name.

She spiraled up on a low moan. The stars burst around her and a cry sprang from her lips. Then ever so slowly, she floated back toward the ground.

And Gareth was there to break her fall before she landed on the hard slate floor of the cave.

Rhian drew her legs together and stretched like a cat who'd just been granted a bowl of thick, rich cream.

She arched her body atop of his and felt the hard length of his erection as she slid across it and froze.

Rhian reached up and traced his lip with her finger-tip. "What about you?"

He cleared his throat and wrapped his arms around her before replying, "It is not as if I will die. I am content."

She laughed softly. "You are such a liar."

She felt him shrug beneath her. "Nay. I am nearly certain that no man has ever died from wanting."

Rhian frowned. What could she do? She slid down his body, out of his embrace until she was encased by the muscles of his legs.

Crossing her arms on his thighs, she rested her chin atop them. "Surely there is something that can be done?"

He half rose, grabbed her arms and dragged her back up to his chest. "Oh, yes, there are many things. But I am still waiting for an answer. Yes or no?"

Rhian sighed. "And I no longer remember the question."

Gareth rolled them onto their sides and brushed his lips against her forehead. "Neither do I."

She shook her head before resting her cheek against his chest and threading her fingers through his silken hair. "The answer is no, Gareth. No, I no longer wish to escape you."

She felt his chest rumble before he finally said, "That is good, because I do not think I could let you." He pressed his lips to the top of her head and tightened his arms, pulling her closer. "We have unfinished matters that I long to complete."

Rhian rubbed her leg against his groin. "Are you waiting for a specific time and place?"

He grabbed her leg, holding her still. "I was thinking our wedding night might be appropriate."

She sucked in her breath. "Who said we were going to wed?"

"Who said we were not?"

Was there anyone more stubborn than this man? "You never answered my question. Why?"

Before she could take another breath, Gareth rolled her onto her back. She could feel him looming above her. Even though the weight of his body rested on his elbows, she knew that if she so much as lifted her head a hair's breadth that she'd meet his lips.

"Why?"

"Yes, why?" She kept her voice to a whisper.

He slid one hand to her breast. To her surprise, the flesh came alive at his touch. To her greater surprise, she leaned into his caress.

"Why?" His voice was little more than a rough growl.

She remained silent. Lost in the wonder of this new development. Never before had her body acted without her mind telling it what to do.

He shifted so that half of his body was along her side before trailing his hand down her leg and up under her gown.

Before she could think to grab his wrist, his fingers brushed the wetness between her legs.

Rhian gasped as her thighs quivered and her flesh throbbed, aching for more.

"Because, Rhian of Gervaise, no man will ever touch you like this except me."

Her gasp turned to a moan of need and she reached for his shoulders in the darkness.

"Please."

He swallowed her whispered plea with his lips.

* * *

"You let them escape."

It had not been voiced as a question, so the hooded man kneeling on the ground remained silent. He knew that words would only increase his brother's anger.

"Escape. When we were just heartbeats away from attaining the grand future we have so long sought."

Rocks on the hard ground bit into his knees, but he did not move away from the pain. In a way it was welcome. The sharp, cutting pain helped to ease the pain of failure.

"Have you no remorse? No words of sorrow for what you have cost us with your stupidity?"

"Aye. Of course I have great sorrow, Brother. I, too, have searched long and hard for the key to our future. Bitterly do I regret all of our failures." He spread his arms in supplication before continuing, "Will not our success be even greater after the failures we have endured?"

He flinched as the man standing before him roared. But as usual, the roar seemed to rid him of his anger.

Relief sped through him, wiping out the agony of the rocks cutting into his knees. A gentle touch on the top of his head let him know that his brother had forgiven him. Grateful, he looked up.

His scream of fear and pain died as blood filled his throat. He crumpled to the cold ground, his brother's one hand still on his head. The other hand gripped the handle of the small sickle that drew his lifeblood from him.

"You will never fail me again."

Chapter Thirteen

Rhian awoke slowly. She stretched lazily, savoring the last remnants of sleep.

The cold and damp of the hard floor seeped through the woolen mantle Gareth had spread for them to sleep on—when they finally slept. A smile curved her lips as she reached out to touch the man sleeping next to her.

Only empty air met her fingertips. Rhian quickly opened her eyes and rolled toward the spot Gareth had occupied. Instead of darkness, a thin sliver of sunlight illuminated the cave.

She squinted against the welcome brightness coming through the narrow entrance. Gareth was nowhere to be seen. She held her breath and for a moment her heart raced before slamming against her ribs. Fear sent her toward the sunlit opening.

He wouldn't have left her alone. She glanced about only to realize his sword was not among the small pile of supplies.

What if he'd gone out and had been captured? Rhian

shook that fear away. Nay. Had the oddly adorned men captured Gareth, they'd have come for her. At the very least she would hear them scrambling about on the rocks.

She paused at the mouth of the cave. What if they were out there, just waiting for her to appear? She took a deep breath and stuck her head outside.

The warmth of the sun drew her a little farther onto the ledge at the cave's opening.

"Finally. I thought perhaps you would sleep all day."

Rhian crawled past the short outcrop above her and rose. Muscles that had been cramped for the night screamed at the effort. She rubbed her back, stretched, then groaned, "One would think I have lived on my hands and knees forever instead of one night."

Gareth chuckled. "Are you sure the pain is from crawling?"

The heat building on her cheeks could have started a fire. She looked down the mountain, ignoring his question. "Is it safe to be out here in the open?"

"If your cries last night did not lead them back to our hiding place, nothing will."

The heat grew. "I am certain your snores were much louder."

"With good reason." He feigned a look of innocence. "I was exhausted from—"

"Faucon!"

He shrugged. "If any snoring awoke you, it was not from me. I stood guard while you slept."

Rhian looked up at him, trying her best to glare. But he stared back at her with a look of such hunger in his eyes, it took her breath away.

Had his eyes held that same look last night? She'd

felt the heat in his hands and tasted the fire on his lips, but in the dark it'd been impossible to see his eyes.

Her heart fluttered. They were more than an arm's length apart and his steady hot gaze touched her intimately, flowing over her like warm honey.

Her skin tingled as if he'd touched her. She could nearly feel his hands brushing against her arm, cupping a breast, trailing a path down her belly.

Rhian dropped her gaze in a mixture of embarrassment and confusion. Perhaps not seeing that smoldering stare had been a blessing.

Gareth cleared his throat. "Are you hungry?"

Did he mean for food, or for him? Rhian swallowed the thickness in her own throat before answering, "Yes."

Only stones rushing past her feet gave warning of his approach. He lightly touched her cheek, tracing a fingertip along her jawline, coming to rest behind her ear. "I will ready something to break our fast."

She watched his tall form walk away from her. The morning sun cast a glow about him, making him look like some type of invincible hero from a troubadour's tale.

Rhian shook her head. What was she thinking? Worse, what had she done?

Gareth ducked into the cave, grateful for the sunlight streaming into the mostly darkened hiding spot. While damp and dreary, it had served its purpose well.

Not only had they eluded the enemy and survived the night, they'd awakened a shared passion. They hadn't needed light to see desire. It had been like a thing alive. Something they could touch and taste. And it had lit the darkness brighter than any fire.

Just the memory of the night filled him with a longing, a need for more. He hadn't intended to do anything more than hold Rhian and perhaps steal a kiss or two. But once he'd touched her and felt her answering need, he'd been unable to resist the urgent desire to fulfill her silent plea.

A smile curved his lips. Perhaps not so silent. If her frenzied cries were any indication of what the future might hold, Gareth knew he needed to somehow keep a little distance between them. At least for now.

It'd been all he could do not to consummate their love play last night. As much as he wanted to make her his, he was still honor bound to deliver her to her mother's family.

And to her betrothed.

Gareth frowned as he took the remaining rations out of his pack. There was no other choice—he simply had to find a way around this proposed betrothal and marry her himself.

He'd have it no other way. Be it by battle or surrender, Rhian of Gervaise would be his wife.

Granted, she'd given him no answer to his proposal. But that mattered little. In the end, he would have his way.

By the time Rhian entered the cave, Gareth had his racing heart and thoughts in control.

"Our meal awaits, milady." He patted a spot next to him on the mantle that had served as their bed and handed her an apple.

While she took the proffered fruit, she sat on the far end of the woolen cloak.

A quick assessing glance let him know that building some distance between them would not be a hard task. Whatever heat she had felt last night had sputtered to ashes.

He ripped a chunk of bread from the loaf and offered it to her.

"No, thank you." She waved the bread away.

Gareth leaned back against the clammy wall. Sometimes a direct frontal attack did not win the battle. On occasion, victory required many strategic advances and retreats.

Unfortunately, he did not know Rhian well enough to determine what was required at this moment. But he'd never backed away from any battle or game of chance. He'd not start now.

With a chunk of bread halfway to his mouth, he stopped and apologized. "Forgive me. My manners are woefully lacking this fine morn. How are you feeling?"

After a slight widening of her eyes, she narrowed them by frowning. "Why do you ask?" Her tone was as leery as her posture. She'd crossed one arm in front of her and leaned away.

He popped the bread into his mouth, brushed the crumbs from his fingertips and after thoroughly chewing, he swallowed the food. Then, he took a long drink of water from the wineskin and offered it to her.

Rhian reached for it, but when her fingers touched his, she pulled back as if burned.

Gareth stilled his twitching lips and placed the container next to her on the cloak.

He glanced at her, only to find her still frowning. Finally, he answered, "Two reasons. One, I was seeking to make polite conversation."

Her eyebrows momentarily disappeared beneath the tousled hair covering her forehead.

"And two, I know that you fell a time or two on the way up here. Combined with our activities of last night, I was concerned for your well-being."

She made a noise that sounded like a snort of disbelief. Gareth matched her stare, refusing to back away from the silent challenge until her face flushed red and she lowered her gaze to her lap.

"I am well enough." Her mumbled response made him pause.

Retreat.

He bent his knees, propping his legs up to give her the image of a wall between them. Perhaps it would help her feel a small measure of safety.

"What precisely does well enough mean?"

Rhian shrugged. "I am bruised and sore. But nothing appears to be broken."

"Perhaps we should spend another day or two here, until you feel able to continue."

"No." She snapped her head up. "No, I am well able to travel." Rising to her knees, she headed toward the mouth of the cave. "We can leave now."

Advance.

Gareth reached out and grasped her arm as she crawled by him. "Stop."

"Why?" She tried to shake off his hold. "Do you not have a mission to complete for your king?"

The anger and confusion in her voice could have been heard by someone without ears. Gareth winced at her long shuddering breath.

Before he could say anything, she continued, "We only delay this journey by sitting here."

With a gentle tug, he sought to pull her to him. Rhian stiffened, making the simple task harder.

Finally, he released her and asked, "What is wrong?"

She shook her head, saying nothing.

"Rhian, talk to me."

"There is nothing to discuss."

His short laugh of disbelief echoed back at him and stiffened her muscles in preparation for flight. Gareth stretched out his legs, as if to relax. "Are you embarrassed or angry about last night?"

"Neither." Her shoulders bunched. "You fool." The last was a soft whisper as she darted toward the opening of the cave.

Quicker, Gareth lunged and grabbed her around the waist. He ignored her curses and flailing limbs. Instead he dragged her across his lap and wrapped his arms tightly around her.

"Rhian, cease this." While he did not understand her sudden anger, he did understand the confusion.

He slid one hand up the back of her head, threading his fingers through her hair and drew her forward.

She closed her eyes. "Please, do not."

Gareth ignored her and covered her face with light kisses. Her forehead, closed eyes, cheeks, chin—anywhere his lips wanted to stop. All the while whispering, "I know. It is all right."

Finally, she relaxed against him and he brought her head to rest against his shoulder before sliding his fingers from her hair.

"It is not all right." She slipped an arm around his neck. "It is wrong. This is all wrong."

He rubbed her back, easing the tension he found there. "What is wrong?"

For a few long moments she remained silent. Just about the time he thought she'd intentionally chosen to ignore his question, she said, "What we did last night." Rhian pressed her breasts against his chest, drew her other arm around him and whispered into his ear, "What I want you to do now."

Had his very life depended on it, Gareth couldn't have stopped the smile from curving his lips. He returned her embrace. "And what is wrong with that?"

"If I remember correctly, I am to be married to another."

"Hmm…" He did his best to ignore the feel of her lips brushing against his neck. It would have been easier to ignore a sword piercing his side than the intense desire rippling down his spine to his groin.

"I thought you wished not to marry this man." He nearly laughed at the crackling tone of his own voice.

"I don't. Perhaps now I will not have to." She twirled her fingers through the hair at the nape of his neck sending another ripple down his back.

Gareth swallowed. All she had to do was accept his proposal. Then he could end this game he started before he was unable to think past the growing haze. "Why not?"

"After last night, you have to ask?"

The idea of seducing her into marrying him suddenly seemed very wrong. And more of a risk than he'd first imagined. He pulled her arms from around his neck and looked at her. "Call me thickheaded, but yes, I have to ask."

Sapphire eyes stared at him unblinking. A smile tilted the corners of her mouth, drawing his gaze to the fullness of her bottom lip. "We are alone. I would surrender all to you and you know that." She ran a finger across his lips and arched one eyebrow. "So why are we talking?"

His racing heart tripped over itself, then slowed. The haze began to lift. "Answer me. Why might you not have to marry this man?"

She shrugged one shoulder. "Another time or two like last night and I will be ruined beyond redemption."

The haze of desire cleared in the blink of an eye. Gareth swore he heard his heart scream, *Retreat!* at the same time Melwyn's words echoed in his head. *Take her.*

He narrowed his eyes and stared at her. A dull flush of red coursed up her neck and tinted her cheeks. She dropped her gaze and pulled her hands into her lap. "What game do you play, Lady Gervaise?"

The man's mind worked fast. Rhian closed her eyes. She deserved the coldness she heard in his voice. She'd truly not expected him to see through her ploy.

Obviously, she'd overdone the mummery. Now what? He'd think her a whore, or worse—heartless. She knew what he wanted. Gareth wanted her to accept his proposal of marriage.

While it would save her from marrying this stranger awaiting her arrival, it would do nothing to protect her heart.

She did not want to care for this man as much as she already did. If she surrendered all to him and became his wife he would have complete and total control of her heart.

How could she be certain he would do nothing to bring it harm?

She swallowed the painful lump growing in her throat, lifted her head and returned his hard stare. After forcing that sickening smile back onto her lips, she played dumb, "Game? I play no game." To add emphasis to her words, she ran a hand up his chest and let her fingers come to rest against the side of his neck.

She kissed his chin, hating the way he drew his head back. "Is that not what I always wanted? Did I not ask you to ruin me just a few days ago?"

"Yes, you did. But—"

"But what, Faucon?" She narrowed her eyes. "You thought perhaps that a few heated kisses and a journey or two among the stars would change my mind?"

Before she could form another stinging question in her mind she found herself on her back on the floor of the cave with him looming above her. She'd gone too far. Rhian knew a moment of terror when she saw the rage in his eyes mirrored in the tick on his cheek.

"A few heated kisses?" He spat the question directly into her face. "A journey or two?"

"Stop it." When she tried to push him off of her, he grabbed her wrists and pinned them to the floor. Rhian stopped struggling and stared up at him.

"You want to act the whore to avoid marriage?" He lowered his head. Before she could turn away, he captured her lips with his.

She'd expected him to punish her with his mouth, but to her surprise his kiss was filled with passion, not anger. Amazed, she realized that the passion carried with it a tinge of sadness that tore at her heart.

What was wrong with her? She wanted this man. Now. Always. What did she fear? To her complete horror, tears slipped free from behind her closed eyes.

Gareth rolled away from her and with a choked curse left her alone in the cave.

Unable to stop the tears from falling, Rhian turned over and buried her face in her crossed arms. Not knowing where else to turn, she prayed softly, "Dear Lord, I wish not to love this man. Help me."

As quickly as the anger had flared, it dissipated. Gareth got no farther than the entrance before he turned back to the cave.

He'd felt her tears and in her answering kiss he'd tasted the truth. While she played a game with him, he knew Rhian was no whore.

He paused in the archway into the cave and stopped dead at her heart-wrenching prayer.

He backed away to give himself time to think, to sort out the swirling emotions and thoughts flying through his heart and mind.

Gareth climbed back up onto his earlier perch on the top of the mountain. The warmth of the sun drove away any lingering anger.

She didn't want to love him? Did that mean she already did? Or that she was close to the emotion she wanted to avoid?

He resisted the urge to race back into the cave and force her to admit what she felt. How could he do that to her when he wasn't certain himself what was happening inside his own head?

He also resisted the urge to laugh at both of them. At himself for mooning about like a lovesick youth.

And at her for fighting something that could not be controlled.

Ridiculous.

What he should do is simply find the nearest clergy and marry the woman. It would put both of them out of the insanity that seemed to hover about them at the moment.

What did she fear?

He sighed. She was afraid of loving him.

Love?

He would not describe what he felt in quite that way.

While it was much stronger, and went deeper than the simple lust he'd experienced with other women, he did not think it could be love.

Gareth tossed a stone over the side of the mountain. It sailed into the air, then disappeared. Not even a sound marked its landing.

A wry smile quirked at his mouth. He felt much like the stone—lost.

"Have you nothing better to occupy your time than tossing stones at those coming to your rescue?" Melwyn appeared at the crest of the mountain, tossing the stone up and down in his hand.

Gareth laughed at the absurdity of his thoughts and Melwyn's timely appearance. Would that his brother's captain could so easily catch him as he fell through the empty air into insanity.

The captain stared at him as if he'd already reached that point. "Milord?" He looked around. "You see something humorous?"

Gareth waved off Melwyn's concerns. "Nay. It is just that type of day." He gestured toward the blue sky. "A fine day in which to laugh."

Melwyn's eyebrows rose briefly in question before smoothing back into the familiar single line above his eyes. "You took my advice."

"No." Oddly enough, Gareth had no wish to discuss his and Rhian's relationship with Melwyn. To keep the man's avid curiosity at bay, he added, "But not for lack of trying."

Never one to give up easily, Melwyn asked, "And the Lady Rhian, she is about somewhere?"

In mock despair, Gareth slumped his shoulders and sighed loudly before admitting in a low voice, "Nay. I fear the rigors of the night were such that I had to toss her over the mountainside, too."

"Damn shame about that. I thought she would make you a grand wife. One who might keep your mouth occupied with something other than sarcasm."

Gareth choked at the vision flashing through his mind. "You win."

Melwyn smirked. "Of course."

With a shake of his head, Gareth wondered out loud, "How you remain alive is baffling. I am always amazed that Rhys does not cut you down where you stand at times."

The captain laughed. "We have a simple agreement. I will not speak out of turn in public and he will not be forced to kill me."

"Good plan."

"One you cannot put to use." Melwyn's voice cracked with humor.

"Meaning, I must just deal with it?"

Melwyn nodded. "You are quick."

Gareth gave up and asked, "You had no difficulty following my trail?"

"No. Your markings were obvious. We caught up as you and the lady headed up the side of this mountain."

"The men following us. Where are they?"

Melwyn pointed down toward what in the daylight appeared to be a well-trod path. "Those who remain are long gone."

"Those who remain?" Gareth knew that one had fallen before reaching the top. "Another accident?"

"Not hardly accidental. The one wearing the black hood lies at the next bluff. His neck was punctured in the same manner as those at Browan."

Gareth sucked in a breath, before muttering, "By all that's holy."

"And unholy," Melwyn added.

"So the hooded man was not the leader of this group of murderers. Did you discover anything else?"

"An interesting discovery to be sure." Melwyn frowned before shaking his head and stating, "This one is nearly identical to the one you killed."

Gareth closed his eyes for a heartbeat. "One who looks like Rhian is a possibility. But two?"

"I understand it not, milord. Brothers? Cousins? Other kin? I am sure we will find the answer soon."

"Soon?"

"Aye. They have given up trailing you and have headed toward the lady's home."

A quick, sharp burst of pain raced between Gareth's eyes and fled as quickly as it had appeared. "We must discover the secret of that blasted pendant before we deliver her into her family's hands."

"I agree. Did you find anything out from her?"

Gareth held back a smile and hoped that the fire heating his cheeks did not show. "I did not ask."

"Forgive me for saying so, but perhaps it would be wise if you set your mind on the initial task at hand and dwell on…other activities later."

At first Gareth was taken aback that Melwyn had asked pardon before suggesting what should have been an obvious course of action. Then he realized that his brother's captain only followed a loose form of protocol when he was dead earnest.

He rose and motioned toward the cave. "Lady Rhian is inside. Give me a few moments to inform her that the time has come to continue our journey."

Melwyn took a seat on the slab Gareth had occupied and nodded. "Aye, milord."

Gareth left the captain and turned his attention to Rhian. Not normally a coward, he prayed she'd had enough time to find a measure of composure. Her tears would only rip the heart from his chest.

He paused at the entrance and chanced a glance inside, breathing a sigh of relief when he saw her sitting cross-legged against the wall of the cave.

Her eyes were closed and she appeared to be sleeping. So he slipped in as quietly as possible and sat next to her.

Startled, Rhian jumped when he took her hand between his. Unsure of what he was about to do, she did not attempt to pull it away from him as he lifted it to his mouth and kissed her fingertips.

One by one. Each light kiss sending tremors up her arm. She held his steady gaze and ached for what she had said and done.

When she opened her mouth to apologize, he shook his head and placed a kiss on her palm before reaching out to draw her to his side.

She leaned into him and found the position comfortable. Her heart did not race as it did when he held her on his lap. Instead, it beat at a more steady, content pace.

He kissed the top of her head. "If you think to apologize to me, I will leave you here to fend for yourself."

Rhian rolled her eyes up, then back down. Someday she would discover how he did that. How he sometimes knew exactly what she was thinking or feeling.

He continued, "It is I who owes the apology." He tightened the arm he'd draped around her shoulder. "I am sorry for acting like a half-crazed youth who cannot control his temper. It will not happen again."

She glanced up at him. "It was not your fault. I—"

Gareth placed a finger over her lips to cut off her words. "Hear me well, Rhian. I want you. For my wife. I will not harm you. I will do all I can to not frighten you. But I will not cease the chase until you bear my name. Do you understand me?"

Speechless, she nodded.

"You are free to try fending off my advances, but you will not win." He lowered his lips to her open mouth and gently, surely swept away the niggling fear building in the pit of her stomach.

She sighed softly when he pulled away. A thin veil would not have fit between their lips.

"What I feel for you is more than simple lust. But I cannot claim it to be love." When he spoke his lips brushed lightly against hers. "All I know is that this is right. If you do not agree, say so now before it is too late."

She could not deny his claim. She felt it, too. And while it frightened her clear to her bones, she had to admit, even if just to herself, that it also fired her blood, set wings loose in her stomach and filled her heart with joy.

At her silence, Gareth slipped his other arm around her and drew her up against his chest. Before claiming her lips with his own, he whispered, "Come, journey with me, my sweet."

Chapter Fourteen

Why did the hike down the mountain seem more difficult that the one up? Rhian swore that if she tripped once more, she'd remain where she landed and they could continue on without her.

She looked up from the path to cast a glance at Melwyn. Comte Faucon's captain did not help matters. If a frown did not furrow his forehead, a scowl did.

The toe of her boot caught a tree root. "Blast." Rhian hit the stone-littered ground with a curse.

Gareth's hands were beneath her arms instantly, lifting her back on her feet. She swatted at him. "Go. Just leave me alone."

He ignored her and bent over to run his hands down her ankle. "Are you hurt?"

"No. I am just sick of this journey. It will be the death of me." The whine in her voice set her own teeth on edge.

Melwyn turned to look back at her. "Aye. At this rate it will be."

"Melwyn. Enough."

At Gareth's near growl the captain tugged on his forelock and shot back, "I will await you by the body." He then marched off down the path.

"Body?" Her heart raced. "Who is dead?"

Gareth glared at Melwyn's disappearing back before answering, "There has been another killing."

She gasped and lifted a hand to cover her throat. "Who?"

"One of them."

"What? Why would…" She bit her lower lip and answered her own half-asked question. "Because I escaped?"

"That would be my guess, yes."

Rhian clutched his leg. "Can we not just stay here and rest until we are certain they are long gone? Would that not be safer?" She'd do anything to avoid those seeking her. Even if it included acting the coward and hiding.

Gareth knelt next to her. "Rhian, it cannot be much farther to my men. You will be safer in their company."

She agreed with his logic, but slapping at the skirt of her gown, she pointed out, "It matters not how short the distance is when I can do nothing but trip over fabric at every other step."

He rose and looked down at her before pulling his knife from its sheath. "Stand up."

Rhian narrowed her eyes. "What are you thinking?"

Gareth grasped her hand and pulled her unceremoniously to her feet.

"Faucon." When he ignored the warning tone in her voice and just stared at her long gown, she took a step away.

He dropped to his knees before her. Before she could

back away farther, he caught the front of her gown and pulled her forward.

"What are you—" She gasped as he tucked the front of her gown between her knees and pushed her legs together.

"Hold just like that and do not move."

Rhian flinched and closed her eyes as he held out the side of her gown and under gown. Then he proceeded to cut and rip the fabric straight down from just below her hip. He then did the same to the other side before cutting across the front just below her knees.

"Take a step."

She looked down at what used to be her gown and saw a rather shabbily made tunic that hung nearly straight down with slits on each side. After a step or two, she realized that in truth this strange garment would make it easier to walk.

There was only one slight problem. "I cannot go about in this manner." She stuck her leg out. The side openings bared her flesh for all to see.

Gareth ran a finger down the display of skin, then quickly stood up, jammed his knife back into the sheath and took her hand. "We will find you something more suitable when we reach camp." He ignored her hissed intake of breath and headed down the path Melwyn had just taken, tugging her along.

"Gareth!"

He shot her a wicked grin from over his shoulder. "Rhian!"

Short of screaming like a banshee, Rhian had little choice but to swallow her humiliation and trudge after him.

Thankfully, he'd been correct. After what seemed to be a short downward hike, the ground leveled out a little and soon they walked into a glen.

Melwyn rose from his seat against a tree and looked at her. The ever present frown left his face. In its place was utter surprise.

Rhian blushed. It was all she could do to not laugh at the shock on his face before he drew his scowl back in place.

Gareth directed her attention to a body lying in the center of the glen. "Do you know him?"

Her amusement fled. She bent over the body to get a better look. "No."

"Does he look familiar to you at all?" Melwyn asked, walking up to join them.

Rhian studied the man. His overlong, raven-black hair lay in matted waves against his head. Sapphire-blue eyes stared unseeingly up at the sky.

Her heart jumped. She touched her nose, running a finger along the curved bridge, then did the same to her chin and cheekbones. The breath whooshed out of her body as if someone hit her in the stomach.

She turned to Gareth, whispering, "Upon my honor, I do not know him."

He pulled her against his side. "I believe you."

"How can he look like me?" She shook her head, trying to rid herself of the questions running through her mind.

Melwyn answered, "He was not the only one."

"Was?" She closed her eyes and leaned into Gareth. "How many more have you found?"

"Just the one who attacked you back at Browan."

She blew out a long breath. "He looked like this one here? Like me?"

Melwyn reached inside his tunic and pulled her pendant out. "Just like you, except his eyes were the color of this bauble."

Rhian reached out and he tossed it to her. Gareth snatched it from the air, turned it over in his hand and frowned before placing it in her open palm.

She closed her fingers around the amethyst dragon, letting the heat of the pendant grow until it warmed her hand. Rhian slipped the ribbon over her head, asking, "What do you think this is worth?"

With the toe of his boot, Gareth tapped the dead man's leg. "Obviously, more than we can imagine."

She slipped the dragon inside her gown and held her breath as it came to life against the skin between her breasts. The inanimate stone pulsed warmth into her flesh and reached out to wrap its talons around her heart.

She laughed softly at the direction of her thoughts and turned to Gareth. "Shall we complete this mission?"

He looked down at her and she reached for his hand, lacing her fingers through his. "I would like to finish whatever must be done before starting the journey to the rest of my life."

A smile curved up the corners of his mouth. He leaned down and kissed her.

"Oh, Lord, yet another falcon will fly blindly into a net."

Rhian laughed at Melwyn's dire proclamation. Gareth caught her bottom lip between his teeth and gently drew her back into a kiss that tasted of promise.

She vaguely heard Melwyn snort before he said, "When you two are finished here, feel free to join us."

With a sigh of regret, Gareth broke away from Rhian. "There will be time for this later." After one last caress of her cheek, he headed toward Melwyn's retreating back.

Rhian followed, savoring the unfamiliar brush of the forest air against her legs and the freedom of movement the odd manner of dress provided.

In public she would prefer a more normal mode of clothing. But in her mind she conjured a great many ideas to try with cloth for more private moments.

Of course in her thoughts these moments were shared with Gareth. She could not envision sharing them with anyone else.

A sudden chill numbed her arms. She refused to allow this unwelcome foreboding to dictate her thoughts—or her fate.

Another man, a stranger, would not be foisted upon her as a husband.

Somehow she and Gareth would discover the true worth of the pendant and the identity of those willing to kill to possess the dragon. They would find the truth—together.

Then, and only then, would they be free to explore this inexplicable attraction growing between them. If nothing more than lust lay behind their feelings, so be it. And if Gareth was correct, and it was nothing more than the heady thrill of victory, again, so be it.

But what if these emotions racing through her veins and unsettling her heart proved to be something else— something stronger?

Still lost in thought, Rhian stepped into the small clearing where Gareth's men had gathered. Their collective gasp at her appearance drew her attention back to her clothing and exposed legs.

Before she could dart behind a tree to hide, Gareth grasped her arm, issued a sharp order for the men to return to their tasks and led her into the only tent still standing.

He unrolled a small bundle and tossed her a gown and shift. "Here, you can wear these." At her hesitation, he added, "They were for my sister."

Rhian handed them back. "I cannot take your sister's clothes."

Gareth waved off her concerns. "Marianne has more than enough gowns. She will not miss this one."

As he headed toward the flap of the tent he paused and looked at her legs. "You might consider keeping that gown, though." With a broad grin twitching his lips, he added, "I am certain it will prove useful in the future."

He ducked out of the tent laughing before Rhian could respond.

Through the falling mist, Gareth, Rhian, Melwyn and the others stared across the open field at the tower keep on top of what appeared to be a man-made hill.

Melwyn broke the silence. "Do you think that is Dougal's Keep?"

"Unless you see another one about, then this must be our destination." Gareth rode forward. "There is only one way to be certain."

"Wait." Melwyn spurred his horse ahead, stopping in front of Gareth. "Let me, milord."

"No." Gareth led his horse around his brother's captain. "It is not you Sir Dougal expects."

The two men volleyed back and forth for the lead position. Until, out of patience, Gareth ordered, "Cease this."

Melwyn opened his mouth, only to close it at Gareth's uncompromising stare.

Finally, the captain moved his horse alongside Gareth's. "I would apologize, milord, but I am only attempting to perform my required duties."

"Apologize?" Gareth's voice rose in surprise. "And if you did, I would perish from shock."

Rhian slid her beast between the two men. "I have an idea, let us all three ride forward." Her knee bumped against Melwyn's and she sidestepped her horse into Gareth's. Fighting to ignore the closeness, she reasoned aloud. "Then none will need to argue the honor and we can perhaps find dry lodgings quicker."

"No!" Both men shouted at her in unison. She shook her head to clear the ringing in her ears.

"Excellent." With a flick of the reins, she urged her animal forward. "The two of you stay here and argue. I will seek shelter with…" She glanced over her shoulder at Gareth and nearly choked on a laugh at the look of dismay on his face. "You said his name was Sir Dougal?"

Mutely, Gareth only nodded.

Rhian counted to herself as she turned back around and headed toward the keep. *One. Two. Three—*

"Like hell you will." He grabbed the reins from her hand.

She smiled up at him. "My, my, that did not take long."

From behind them, Melwyn muttered, "It will be a fine thing if all of us end up dead. I am certain Comte Faucon will not be pleased."

Gareth laughed. "And if we are all three dead, exactly what do you fear he might do?"

"Feed my rotting corpse to the vultures."

"A possibility, I am sure." Gareth glanced back at Melwyn. "Do you think it matters greatly?"

"My wife would follow me into Hades just to make my life miserable."

Curious, Rhian asked, "And this notion bothers you?"

"Of course it bothers me. No man wants to listen to his wife's wrath for an eternity. A mortal lifetime is enough."

She tried to listen to the tone of his voice, but Gareth's laughter drowned out the inflection.

When Gareth finally ceased his outburst, he leaned closer to Rhian and said, "Melwyn here wants all to think his wife is an unwanted stone about his neck."

Rhian chanced a quick look back and nearly burst into laughter herself. A red-faced Melwyn glanced everywhere except before him, as if he wished he were anywhere but here.

Gareth continued, "If truth be told, yon grousey man here chased the fair maiden for years before she finally consented to be his bride."

"Sir Melwyn?"

"Aye. The very same Sir Melwyn. The love-struck swain was nigh unbearable to live with during that time."

"I am sorry." Rhian's laugh escaped. Finally gaining control, she admitted, "I find that very hard to believe."

Gareth shrugged. "So did those who knew him well."

"It is amazing what havoc the heart can wreak with one's brain." Melwyn spurred his horse past them, adding, "As witnessed by the two of you now."

He raced toward the keep ahead of them, hailing the gate guards as soon as he was within shouting distance.

A brisk wind whipped about him, beating the driving rain into his flesh. Gareth looked out across the water. White-capped waves raced toward the rocky shoreline. This was not a fit place for any breathing beast. How anyone could live here baffled him. Why anyone would do so willingly was beyond his comprehension.

But their current host, Sir Dougal, seemed to enjoy the ever changing elements this far-flung outpost provided.

Gareth leaned against the keep's wall. The water-logged wooden structure was nothing more than an old palisade.

It leaned under his weight. Obviously built, not for defense, but more to keep the wild animals out. He turned and glanced up at the tower. Again, of older design, the wooden donjon was generally not used for living quarters, but as the last defense against an attack.

This day, however, Dougal deemed it appropriate to open the Great Hall for his visitors.

Suddenly grateful for the gold his father poured into improving Faucon, he wondered idly how long Sir Dougal and his men could fend off a well-armed force.

The sound of someone climbing the ladder to join him on the wall halted his musings.

Two steps took him to the top of the ladder; he arrived at the same time Rhian's head cleared the wallwalk.

He assisted her onto the wall. "What are you doing out here?"

She gazed out across the stormy water. "Do you think my escorts will arrive anytime soon?"

"Anxious to leave?" He could not stop the end of the journey from arriving, but he wished it'd not arrive too soon.

"No. I simply want the waiting over."

Gareth stood behind her, his hands on her shoulders. Even through the layers of clothing, he felt the tenseness in her muscles.

"How can you be so certain you will not like life on Ynys Môn?" He tightened his fingers when she tried to move away. Waiting until she stopped her brief, half-hearted struggle, he kneaded her shoulders and neck while continuing, "You have judged and condemned your family without having first come to know them."

"I do not need to see the devil to know of his evil."

"That is absurd, Rhian. It is a comparison with no basis."

This time when she pulled away, he released her. "We have had this conversation before, have we not?"

Gareth nodded. "We did. If I am not mistaken in my memory, I thought you agreed to give them a fair chance before making any decision."

"And I thought you asked me to be your wife."

"Even had you graced me with an answer, you would still make this journey." She would not use him to shirk her responsibility. He would not permit it to happen.

He watched in amused amazement when Rhian crossed her arms in front of her, tossed her head and huffed away along the wall. "Aye, Lady Gervaise, employing tactics learned in the nursery will go far in assuring you are given your own way."

She said nothing. Simply stood with her back to him. Gareth headed for the ladder. "Feel free to stew alone."

Rhian spun around. "Wait."

He paused and leaned his elbows on the top rung. "Yes?"

She reached up and toyed with the pendant. "Do you think these men may be from my family?"

"No." Gareth shook his head. "Would it not have made more sense and perhaps been easier for your family to cry foul when you were given the pendant and demand its return?"

A frown crinkled her forehead as she contemplated his answer. Finally, she nodded in agreement. "I suppose you could be correct. But that man, he looked nearly like me."

"Aye. And so did the one back at Browan. But as far as King Stephen knows, you have no siblings." Now Gareth frowned in thought. "Perhaps that was why these men were chosen—their likeness to you."

"Then the person in charge must be someone who knows me."

"Not necessarily. It could be one who has done his research well. Perhaps he saw you once, or had others describe you to him."

She gasped. "If he has investigated me that thoroughly, then he knows where I am headed."

Gareth climbed back up on the wallwalk and pulled her easily into his arms. "Worry not. Have I not vowed to protect you?"

She burrowed into the folds of his mantle, snuggling against his chest. "You will cross the water with me?"

"Of course I will. To keep my promise, I must."

"What if you are not welcome?"

He chuckled against the top of her head. "It would not be the first time. Nor the last, I am sure."

"Do you think the man seeking the pendant will be there?"

"I am sure of it." Her shivers trembled against his chest and he pulled her closer. "I imagine they are mired in the same danger."

She backed away slightly. "I wish I had never beheld this amethyst dragon." With a quick yank she pulled it from around her neck.

"What are you doing?"

Rhian held the pendant in her hand and lifted her arm. "It deserves a watery grave."

Without thinking, Gareth grabbed her hand before she flung the dragon into the sea. "No."

"What are you doing?" She struggled to free her hand from his grasp. "Do not stop me. It is mine to do with as I wish."

"Think, Rhian. If it is so important to others that they will kill for ownership, it must be important to you, too."

"How?" She lowered her arm.

"I know not the how's or why's—yet. It might prove an interesting thing to discover." Gareth flashed her a small smile. "All I do know for certain is that the thing is somehow alive."

Her eyes widened. "You do feel it." She slipped the dragon back over her head, then lowered her voice. "I feared only I knew of its secrets."

Gareth stepped back and lifted his hands. "Stop. I care not to learn its secrets, only its purpose." He stroked her cheek, tucking a wayward strand of hair behind her ear. "I know only that it warms beneath my touch... much like you do."

Rhian's face reddened as she rubbed her cheek against his lingering palm. "Gareth, I—"

"Milord!" Melwyn's shout broke into their shared moment.

Gareth rolled his eyes skyward before moving away to look down. "Aye?"

The captain pointed toward the opposite side of the keep. "A party approaches. One I think you should see."

"Is it them?" Rhian's whispered question carried all her fears, prompting Gareth to take her hand in his own.

"Come." He led her around the sometimes rickety walkway to the twin gate towers where they joined Sir Dougal and Melwyn.

Gareth had foolishly hoped the new visitors would be nothing more than merchants or perhaps a troop of men looking for a night's shelter.

But as he stared out at the open field between the forest and the keep, he realized his hopes had been for naught.

Chapter Fifteen

Rhian peered out over the wall. The wild tumbling of her heart to her toes sent her head spinning and she grabbed Gareth's arm for support.

What was this? A sick joke the fates played for amusement?

A troop of men approached the keep on foot. They appeared to be led by two dressed in long black robes and white tunics.

Emblazoned on each of the tunics was a crudely formed dragon—like the one etched on her pendant. One man sported an amethyst beast, the other was sapphire.

Rhian grasped her pendant. She stared down at it, then back to the men. "What is the meaning of this?"

Gareth answered her whispered question. "It appears we will make that discovery soon."

The men drew closer. A shiver lifted the hairs on the back of her neck.

When they reached the base of the wall, one of the leaders lowered the hood of his robe exposing a head of long silver hair and stared up at Rhian. He knelt and the others followed suit.

Rhian backed away from the wall. Gareth moved behind her stopping her retreat. "Well, Princess." His soft voice held a note of humor Rhian did not share. "I think your subjects await."

She glared at him from over her shoulder. "That is not funny."

"For good reason." He nodded toward the men outside the wall. "It was not meant to be."

Dougal called out to Gareth from the opposite gate tower, "M'lord, shall I open the gates?"

Gareth nudged Rhian forward. *What was she supposed to do?* These men knelt in the mud with the steady mist of rain falling down on them. They came looking for a princess. How disappointed would they be to discover only her?

For a heartbeat or two, she studied the men, then asked Gareth, "Can you control these eight men?"

Melwyn drew back as if insulted. Guilt gnawed at her. She'd no reason to ask so foolish a question. Before Gareth could answer, Rhian asked another, "Can we be certain these men are not in league with those who have caused such havoc of late?"

Gareth gently caressed her back. "We cannot be certain. But I can promise you that they will bring you no harm." He paused, lifted his hand to her shoulder and urged, "Get them out of the mud and rain, Rhian."

Dreading the moment of their entry into the keep, she called out, "Rise and state your reason for approaching this keep."

All eight men rose. The one with the amethyst dragon

on his tunic stepped forward. "We have arrived to escort you to your mother's family." He held out a scroll. "We have safe passage from King Stephen."

She motioned to Sir Dougal to open the gates. While he did her bidding, Rhian, Gareth and Melwyn descended the ladder to meet the men as they entered the bailey.

There was nothing about these men that could be considered strange, or out of the ordinary. Yet Rhian looked at them and felt an overwhelming fear. Without thinking, she grasped Gareth's hand, seeking the physical sense of safety his touch offered.

Gareth beckoned Melwyn closer. "See that the men are ready to leave at a moment's notice."

After Melwyn left to do Gareth's bidding, Rhian asked, "What do you expect to happen?"

"Nothing at all." He avoided meeting her stare. Before Rhian could pursue the matter, he led her across the bailey to the center of the yard.

When the two groups met, Sir Dougal stepped forward, "Please, let us retire to the keep. The comforts will be few, but it will be dry."

Without releasing her hand, Gareth fell in behind their host and followed him up to the tower keep.

Once they entered the keep, Dougal's servants attended to the newest visitors, divesting them of their wet robes, then leading them away to clean up the mud and dry off. Hopefully, they would be made comfortable before sharing a meal.

Gareth released her hand. He glanced around the hall. "I need to confer with Melwyn. Would you care to join me, or stay here?"

She nodded toward the lit fire pit in the center of the hall. "There are plenty of servants and guards about, I would prefer to sit by the fire awhile."

"I will return before any realize you are alone. Do not leave this room."

Rhian shooed him away. "Go. I will be safe."

Sir Dougal left to attend to other matters. Rhian guessed by his scowl and brusque voice when they entered the keep that something was amiss. A quick survey of the Great Hall revealed plenty amiss in her opinion.

Granted, this was little more than a dank outpost, a long way from any social niceties. Still, it would not hurt to slap a fresh coat of whitewash on the walls, or to scatter some herbs among the reeds on the floor occasionally.

Rhian silently blessed the older couple who'd offered to share their hut with her this evening. Even though the dwelling was small and humble, at least it was clean, free of vermin and smelled of freshly cut lemon balm and mint.

She sat by the fire. The heat warmed her flesh, but not her heart. She'd no desire to complete this journey to Ynys Môn—Anglesey, or whatever name they wished to use. In her mind it was Druid's Isle and there would be no place for her there.

But, in truth, there was no longer a place for her anywhere.

Rhian knew not whether to lay the blame for this ill-gotten fate at her father's feet, or her own. Why had he not told her of her mother? If not while she was a child, then when she'd left childhood behind. She could have benefited from a little more information than his "we did what was best" explanation.

Did he know they'd send for her upon his death? Had he been aware of this arranged marriage? Was that why finding her a husband had not been of any great concern to him?

Why had she simply not accepted Faucon's offer of marriage? She could have said yes and perhaps ended this uncertainty. While he'd already stated that, even had she agreed to marry him, she would still have to complete this journey.

But at least then she'd have arrived in her family's bosom as a married woman. One not free to be given to another man.

She leaned closer to the fire, staring into the flames. She wondered why she'd not believed that Gareth had asked in earnest. He did not seem the type of man to take marriage lightly. She doubted if he'd ever made the same offer to another woman.

So why had she not accepted?

"It is time."

Shocked by the voice behind her, Rhian jumped up from her seat, knocking the small three-legged stool over in her surprise. She backed away from the man and quickly searched for someone who would come to her aid if need be.

The hall was surprisingly empty save her, a few servants and the tall, older visitor from Anglesey. She took another step backward, mentally searching for a way to stall until Gareth returned. "Time for what?"

He smiled as if seeking to banish her fears. "Why, to take you home to your family. They have awaited this day for a long time and are anxious for your return."

Even had his calm manner succeeded in putting her

at ease, his words did not. "It will be dark soon and I have no wish to travel at night. They have waited this long. What will another day matter?"

"We will be upon our shores before the sun sets." He spread his arms in a beseeching manner. "My good lady, your family loves you and wishes only to finally welcome you home."

Rhian stared at the dragon on his tunic. With his arms spread, the amethyst beast seemed to come alive. Each time the man moved his arms, the dragon's wings flapped. With every breath, the dragon's chest rose as if it, too, breathed.

"Lady Rhian?" He touched her arm, jolting her out of her strange fit of fancy. "Are you well?"

She jerked away from his touch. "I am fine."

"You do not appear to be fine." He reached out to feel her forehead. "If you are fevered, the herbalists can help you."

Rhian knocked his arm away. "Do not touch me."

The man folded his arms against his chest and stepped away from her toward the fire. He righted the stool and offered, "Please, sit down and let us begin again."

She declined the seat. "I will stand."

"Milady Rhian, I am Aelthed. I come to offer you safe escort to your family."

"Well, Sir Aelthed—"

"Nay. Not *Sir*." He shook his head. "Simply Aelthed."

Rhian started over. "Well, Aelthed, while I truly appreciate the offer, I already have an escort."

He stared hard at her, hazel eyes widened briefly then narrowed beneath a wild shock of graying brows. "From what I have seen, a very unsuitable escort."

"Unsuitable? How so?" She was certain Gareth would laugh at the description.

"This man was touching you in a manner suited to only family or husband. You will be better off when you are separated from this cur."

"He is not a cur." She was surprised by the level of defensiveness fueling her blood. "I happen to have strong feelings for this man."

"I think not. You will forget this notion when we leave this place."

"I will not leave here without Gareth."

"What has this man done to you? Has he tried to claim what is not his?" He leaned forward. When she would not meet his forthright stare he snorted, then said, "Had your lady's maid been more attentive to her charge these unseemly emotions would not exist."

"Lady's maid? There were no servants left at Gervaise who would accompany me on this journey. The lady's maid that Gareth arranged for me tried to have me killed." Rhian refrained from slapping a hand over her mouth.

"Killed? Explain."

She shrugged as if the matter were of no importance. "There is nothing to explain."

"Lady Rhian." His tone was that of a father lecturing a child. "Whether you like it or not, I am your current guardian, and if I see fit, I will have you bound and tied and force you to leave this place."

"You would not dare."

"That is where you are wrong. I will dare much to complete my given task."

Rhian paused. He sounded like Gareth. Were all men

the same? Did the task, the quest, the mission always come before any of the people involved?

She studied this Aelthed for a few moments. Even though he looked like the men who'd been trying to gain possession of the pendant, he hadn't made a move to harm her. She glanced about the hall. Still empty save for the two of them and a few servants, he'd had every opportunity to kill her and steal the dragon.

Even if she only stayed with her family for a short while, she'd have to trust someone at some point in time. Perhaps she could start with Aelthed. *Dear Lord, let me be right.*

She pointed at his chest. "That dragon you wear, is it some type of family crest?"

"From ancient times, yes."

"I have a pendant—"

He nodded. "The amethyst one."

Rhian tipped her head back in surprise. "The amethyst one? There are more?"

Aelthed only smiled. "You will see." He then urged, "Please, continue."

"There have been men seeking to possess it by any means. Even murder."

Aelthed paled. His mouth fell open. He looked as if someone had punched him in the stomach. Rhian rushed forward and grasped his arm. If the bony limb beneath her hold was any indication, he was much older than he appeared. She guided him down onto the stool. She could feel him tremble beneath her touch.

"Aelthed? What is it? Shall I call for help?"

"Nay." He croaked and waved a hand in the air. "Give me but a moment."

Rhian spied a pitcher and goblets on a side table and retrieved them. She poured half a goblet of water and handed it to the man.

After downing the contents, he looked up at her. "Forgive me. I do not normally act the old fool."

"Then obviously you have good reason to act so."

"Aye. These men, have you seen them?"

"Yes. Oddly enough the two dead ones look like me."

"Dead?" His voice cracked. "How did they die?"

"Gareth killed one who sought to attack me in my chamber at Browan. The other one kidnapped me and after Gareth rescued me, we found him dead on the mountain trail."

Aelthed's hand visibly shook as he lifted it to rub his forehead. "This Gareth is in grave danger then."

"What are they after?"

"Child, they need your pendant for reasons dark and dangerous. Now they will also seek revenge on your former escort." He frowned, then looked up at her. "Gareth is a good fighter?"

Gareth crossed the room and joined them. "I am still alive."

Aelthed smiled before masking the expression with a glower and turning toward Gareth. "Aye. That is obvious and is not what I asked." He lowered his head and looked up at Gareth from beneath his bushy eyebrows. "Are you a good fighter?"

"Depending on your definition of good, I would say again, I am still alive."

Rhian went to Gareth's side and addressed Aelthed, "Aye, he is a good fighter. Cunning, quick and with deadly accuracy."

Gareth looked down at her and nodded toward the older man. "Normally, I have manners, too. Which you seem to lack."

She ignored his sarcasm. "This is Aelthed. The escort sent from my family."

"Sir—"

Rhian tugged at his earlobe. "Did you hear me say Sir? He is simply Aelthed."

Gareth stepped away from her, rubbing his ear. "Simply Aelthed, I am Gareth of Faucon."

Aelthed mumbled something in a tone that made Rhian realize she didn't want to hear his words. When he was finished, he rose and beckoned to Gareth. "It is apparent we need to have a discussion. Is there someplace more private?"

Gareth pointed toward a deep-set alcove at the other end of the hall. "I do believe that will have to suffice, unless you wish to go outside."

The older man gave it half a heartbeat of thought before he turned toward that end of the hall. "The alcove will do if there is someone about to stand guard."

Gareth shouted for David, then led Aelthed toward the alcove.

Rhian followed. When the men paused at the open doorway, Aelthed reached out and grasped her arm. "Not you, milady. This is men's talk. We need no women to hear what needs to be said."

"I beg your pardon?" What could they have to discuss that did not include her?

"Do not argue, child."

"Stop calling me child. I am not a child." It was all she could do not to stomp her feet.

Gareth stared down at her. "Then do not start acting like one."

There were times when his manner begged for a tongue-lashing. This was one of those times. But Rhian did not care to dress him down in public. That would require someone with more practice than she possessed.

Instead of saying anything, she just glared up at him, hoping he could read the fire in her eyes.

"Milord, you needed me?" David came to a breathless halt in front of Gareth.

"Make certain no one gets within hearing of this alcove." He nodded toward Rhian. "And that includes her."

David looked at the floor and groaned. "Milord Faucon…"

Rhian bit back her laugh. "I swear, David, I will leave the hall. So you need not worry."

The boy looked up and smiled in relief before squaring his shoulders in preparation to do his lord's bidding.

"While you men decide who is in charge, I will go see what is holding up the food."

In unison, they both replied, "I am."

Rhian didn't even try to hold back her laughter. Instead, she let it loose, turned on her heels and waved over her shoulder as she left them alone.

Gareth stood on the shoreline and looked across the narrow channel of water separating them from Anglesey. Somewhere through the ever-thickening fog lay Rhian's new home.

The thought made him ill. He curled his fingers into tight fists at his sides, fighting the overpowering need to lash out in anger and pain.

But he'd spoken a promise that forbade him from acting on, or even speaking, his emotions. A vow given in exchange for one more day in Rhian's company.

A day where he could do nothing to further tie her heart to his.

With the sunset tomorrow, she'd be safe in the arms of her family, preparing for a wedding—her own. And he'd be headed back to King Stephen's court—alone.

Let her be, Faucon. If you care for her as you say, leave her free to live her fate without regrets.

In the shadowed alcove, Aelthed had made sense. His logic was flawless and Gareth had been unable to find the slightest chink to slip through.

But now, with the damp, cool wind blowing his hair across his face and the sound of gentle waves lapping at the shore, nothing made sense. The only things Gareth was certain of were his anger and the heaviness of his heart.

A heaviness he feared would never leave him.

"Milord?" Melwyn laid a hand on his shoulder. "Gareth, what is amiss?"

Gareth shook his head, unclenched his fists and brushed the hair from his face. He noted the dampness on his fingers, but refused to acknowledge it as anything more than the sea's mist.

Finally, he answered Faucon's captain, "Nothing is amiss."

"Oh, aye. And I am suddenly blind and bereft of thought." Melwyn stepped before him. "Your silence has unsettled the entire camp. The men are as skittish as their horses. What is amiss?"

Gareth bit the inside of his cheek. When he was certain he could open his mouth without breaking his vow, he answered, "Ask me again tomorrow night."

Melwyn made a noise that sounded more like a snort of impatience. "You did not ride beside Lady Rhian. Have you two had a quarrel already?"

No. He had not ridden alongside Rhian. It would have been impossible to ride beside her and not touch her, not take her hand, not gaze upon her with desire.

But to tell Melwyn that would only reduce the man to hysterical laughter. "Would you find it odd if we had?"

"Not at all. But the lady appeared hurt, not angry."

Fresh pain flicked at Gareth's heart. He'd not meant to cause Rhian pain. How could he avoid her without making her wonder what was wrong?

Melwyn continued his pestering. "For days on end I have observed you watching her. It has been nigh embarrassing the way you appear to make love to her with your eyes. Yet today you have not so much as glanced at her. Have you tired of her delights already?"

Tire of her? Never. Not even when the world came to an end would he tire of Rhian. "Perhaps I have. Would that also be considered odd?" The lie nearly scorched his tongue.

The captain narrowed his eyes. "I find it odd that you answer questions with questions."

Gareth shrugged and turned away from the channel. "The barge should arrive soon."

Melwyn grabbed his arm. "Why do you seek to avoid my questions?"

In less than the blink of an eye, Gareth reached out, grabbed the front of Melwyn's tunic, lifted the captain from his feet and yanked him up so they were face-to-face. "When I desire your questions, I will ask for them. Until then, leave me be."

To his amazement, his snarl had the wrong effect. Instead of agreeing to follow orders, Melwyn smiled. "What is the matter, little man, are they taking your lady away from you?"

Gareth dropped Melwyn as if he'd suddenly turned to fire. The captain instantly sprang back up to his feet and slammed his fist into Gareth's shoulder.

Without thinking, Gareth swung back and cuffed the side of Melwyn's head. The contact of flesh on flesh and the flow of outraged blood fueled the need for more of both.

Melwyn danced before him, blocking each blow. The men gathered in a circle around them, cheering the two combatants on.

Gareth finally got one hand on Melwyn's tunic again. He pulled the man toward him and at the same time reared back his fist.

When he hesitated, the captain urged, "Come on, little man, let me see you do your best."

Little man.

It was a jest. He had towered over his sire and brothers by the time he'd reached his twelfth year. Just a jest his father had used whenever he wanted to cajole Gareth into doing something the then young boy feared.

Melwyn was using the same tactic to get him to spend his anger.

Gareth dropped his raised fist and released the captain. They stared at each other. When the circle of men around them broke up, Gareth closed his eyes. "Yes. Yes, they are and I can do nothing to stop them."

Melwyn called for a wineskin, then pointed toward a nearby copse of trees. "Come. Let me tell you the worth of a wife you love."

"I already know the worth."

The captain headed toward the trees. "Then let us find a way out of this dire fate you seem to fear."

Gareth followed. "There is no way out."

Melwyn's laugh echoed in the fog. "And you call yourself a Faucon?"

Chapter Sixteen

Rhian, Aelthed and his companions rode into the makeshift camp Gareth's men had hastily erected alongside the channel. A fire blazed and an awning was stretched between a couple of trees. She welcomed both the warmth and the shelter from the mist while awaiting the barge that would carry them across the water.

Without turning away from Aelthed's rather boring description of her new home, she searched the camp for Gareth. Rhian fought the urge to rush to his side once she'd spotted him standing with Melwyn along the shoreline.

As much as she wanted to be near him, he'd made it plain he did not share the desire. Not one word, or even a single glance had passed between them on the ride from Dougal's Keep.

A happening that was so far out of the ordinary when compared to the last few days that Rhian knew something was wrong. She'd queried Aelthed and had received nothing more than some mumbled reply about Gareth knowing his place.

She knew that she hadn't done anything to anger him. Even if she had, Gareth was not one to sulk. No, just the opposite—he seemed to take great pleasure in scolding her whenever she'd tried pouting to gain her way.

Everything had been fine until Aelthed and Gareth had their little man-to-man talk. She shot a quelling look at Aelthed, wishing she could somehow read the man's mind.

What had the old fool said to Gareth?

She reined in her horse, dismounted and tossed the reins to a waiting David. "Tell your master I wish a word with him."

Aelthed was immediately at her side. "I do not think that wise or necessary."

Rhian cocked her eyebrows and stared at him. When he did not appear willing to back down, she asked, "Do you have some sort of control over me that I know nothing about? Are you my father? My husband?" She snapped her fingers. "Perhaps *you* are my betrothed?"

He returned her stare with a hard one of his own. "I am your guardian. Your mother's brother."

Rhian laughed. "My guardian. How nice. I have slipped away from guardians more spry than you, Uncle dearest."

Aelthed blinked rapidly before finding his tongue. "See here, milady—"

"No." She cut him off with a wave of her hand. "You see here. I am going over to that shelter." She pointed toward the awning. "And Gareth is going with me." Rhian then nodded toward the approaching men.

"And if you try to stop me, Faucon's captain will be my champion." She turned a smile on Melwyn. "Will you not?"

Melwyn bent into an exaggerated half bow. "I would be honored, Lady Rhian."

Aelthed nodded, backing down, but she did not miss the look he shot at Gareth. Thankfully, his warning glare was not able to loose arrows.

Rhian marched to the shelter, stopping only when she was beneath the stretched fabric. She turned and waited for Gareth to join her.

He stopped just beneath the awning with his back to the men gathered on the shoreline and his hands clasped behind him.

Rhian swore and did her best not to glare up at him. Instead, she smiled as sweetly as she could before asking, "Would you care to explain yourself?"

"Ladies do not curse, Rhian."

"At the moment, I am no lady. Answer me, Faucon."

He looked everywhere but at her. "We are here to meet the barge that will carry you to your mother's family."

Rhian stepped toward him. He stepped away.

She swallowed a vile curse. "What did he say to you?"

"Who?"

"Good God, Faucon, you will have me screaming like a banshee in a moment."

"Nothing. He said nothing I did not already know."

"Oh. Then having him repeat something you already knew caused you to decide you no longer desired my company?"

Gareth said nothing, but she saw his throat convulse as he swallowed hard.

She stepped toward him again and when he moved his foot to take another step back, she warned, "If you move from that spot, I will throw myself at you, tear your clothes from your body and have my wicked way with you before all."

He moved his foot forward and stood still. But she saw his chest shake with restrained laughter.

She narrowed her eyes and took the last step that brought her within arm's reach. Rhian extended her hand and placed her palm on his chest. "I can feel your heart pounding beneath my touch."

She placed her other hand on his stomach. His heart beat faster.

"Rhian." Gareth's voice was but a choked whisper.

The deep, one-word warning only fueled her desire to obtain an honest answer from him. If he would not voice that answer, then she'd listen instead to his body.

She slid her hand lower, until she brushed the edge of his sword belt and smiled. "Tell me, Gareth, do you no longer desire me?"

He remained silent.

"Oh, Gareth, did you not realize that I am an excellent student?" She slid her palm down over the leather of his belt and splayed her fingers. "And that you were such a good teacher."

His throat constricted. His chest muscles tightened beneath her palm. And his heart raced so fast that she would not have been surprised had it burst forth from its confinement. But still, he did not respond.

Rhian kept her gaze trained on his averted face and slowly inched her fingers lower.

"Yes." Gareth closed his eyes, then looked down at

her. "Yes, I still desire you. Must you play the whore to discover that?"

Anger blazed in her heart, but Rhian forced herself to remain calm. She studied his gaze. To her complete amazement, no anger shimmered in the emerald orbs.

She easily interpreted barely restrained lust and need. But beyond the desire beat something else. Something more. Fierce possession and longing flickered along-side pain.

Her anger fled as quickly as it had appeared. She accepted his lust—it only rivaled her own. He wanted to possess her in the same manner she wished to possess him—completely, body and soul. But she could not bear his silent pain.

"Gareth, what are you doing?" She slid both hands up to his cheeks and held his head steady. "I can with-stand your coldness if I know the reason."

When she brushed a thumb across his lower lip, he grabbed it with his teeth, pulling it into his mouth.

Rhian gasped softly at the sensation of his tongue circling her thumb, reminding her of the things he did that night in the cave. "Heavens. Tell me, do all men possess the ability to make love with only their mouths?"

He laughed softly, released her thumb and answered, "No, it is an art only I know."

She tapped his chin with a finger. "Somehow I think you lie."

Gareth lifted one eyebrow. "Do you plan to discover if I do or not?"

"That depends on you." She leaned against his chest. "Do you plan on letting me?"

A frown marred his features. "That choice may be out of my hands."

"Ah, so now the truth finally emerges." Rhian backed away. "Hear me well, Faucon. I care not who this man they have chosen may be. I will not marry him. My heart belongs to another."

"What if—"

She placed a finger over his lips. "What if nothing. He could be the king of some great country, yet I will not be his queen."

He shook off her finger. "But—"

Rhian covered her ears and shook her head. "I will hear none of it."

"You—"

"Nay. None of it."

When his shoulders sagged, she lowered her hands and whispered, "I know it is impossible right now, but I need to feel your arms about me, your lips on mine. I need to know that you will not forsake me, Faucon."

"Close your eyes, Rhian."

She did as he bid and he continued, "My arms will always keep you safe and warm. I will hold you to my heart until the day I die and after. My lips will ply yours with kisses that will never end. You will taste my love and I will swallow yours. Never will I forsake you, Rhian. Never. I have vowed to deliver you safely to your family and I will honor that vow even from the grave if need be."

Rhian's heart beat with such force of emotion that she thought she'd die. She nearly drowned in the love reflected in his eyes. If she did, she would go content. She had to ask, "What about after, Gareth? After you have delivered me to my family, what then?"

He shook his head. "I do not know, Rhian."

She gasped at his answer. "I...I thought we would marry."

He closed his eyes. "If we do not, you will always be the wife I carry in my heart. You will be the one I honor. The one I await in the next life."

He stared at her. Through her unshed tears she thought she saw the same moisture shimmering in his eyes.

"Lord Faucon, the barge has arrived."

Aelthed's shout brought Gareth to action. He gazed down at her one last time, then abruptly turned away.

"Gareth. Please, not like this."

Her cry did not halt his footsteps. Rhian wanted to run after him, but her legs refused to obey. She stood rooted to the ground beneath her, wishing it would open and swallow her.

She thought she knew the depths of anguish when her father died and she'd lost everything of value. The hurt and agony had been nearly unbearable. Yet, she'd lived on.

Gareth barked orders at his men. His hoarse voice echoed back to her against the thick fog. His pain, raw and heavy, carried clearly to her heart. She realized that not even her beloved father's death had prepared her for this loss.

How could she simply go on? Where would she find the strength to live without Faucon, knowing his anguish was as great?

Aelthed took her arm gently. "Child, come. What must be, must be."

"No." She shook her head. This was not happening. "No. He asked me to marry him."

"You have a husband waiting for you already. What need you of two?"

"I do not need two. Nor do I need the one you have waiting for me. My very heartbeat and breath depend on the one already before me."

To her horror her voice broke. Rhian gulped. She'd not cry. If she permitted one tear to fall, she'd be powerless to ever stop them.

Aelthed shook her. "Stop this. You have known this man less than the cycle of one moon. You will forget him. Soon, he will become nothing more than a fond memory from your youth."

Rhian tore her arm from his grasp and shouted, "Never, old man. Never in this lifetime."

"Lady Rhian." Sir Melwyn gently touched her shoulder. "Please, milady, you only make it worse."

She looked toward Gareth. He held himself as rigid as an unyielding tree. But she saw the tick in his cheek, the lines furrowing his forehead and the slight paleness of his sun-darkened face.

Rhian forced herself to look to Melwyn instead. The sympathy she found there nearly caused her to lose what little control she clung to with all her might.

Melwyn turned her around to face him. "Lady, there are other things in life as important as love."

She laughed, before asking, "Such as?"

"Honor to yourself, your liege and your family. Duty to your God, your husband and your children."

"So honor and duty can take the place of desire and love?"

He ignored her question and finished, "Trust and faith that all will end as it should."

Rhian frowned. The man who'd not spoken ten words to her since he'd arrived to assist Gareth was obviously trying to tell her something.

Before she could form her thoughts into a question, he leaned forward, placed a kiss on her forehead and quickly whispered, "Love and trust will ever win."

Melwyn stood back and nudged her toward Aelthed. "I will bid you farewell here, Lady Rhian." He bowed, then rose and took her hand. "It has been a pleasure to serve you." After placing a kiss on the top of her hand, he left her standing in openmouthed surprise alongside Aelthed.

She blinked. "Where is Sir Melwyn going?"

Aelthed directed her toward the waiting barge. "Lord Faucon and I decided that he need not take any more men than absolutely necessary across the water."

Rhian fought to keep her surprise in check. "I will sorely miss him. Sir Melwyn has a strong arm and a level head that has served me well."

"He has been well compensated for his efforts."

Rhian remained silent as they crossed the small clearing. Before stepping onto the plank that led her to the barge, she turned and found Gareth watching her. She bit her lower lip and nodded. *Please, my love, be safe. Be happy. Do not forget me.* As if answering her voiceless plea, he returned her nod.

A small silk tent had been erected on the barge. Each of the double flaps was adorned with a dragon; Rhian was not at all surprised to note one beast was amethyst and the other sapphire.

She fingered the fine embroidery work as she brushed through the flaps into the seclusion of the tent.

Someday she'd learn the story behind not only the twin dragons, but the color choice.

Inside the silken enclosure was an elaborate cushion large enough to recline upon if she desired. There was a small table laden with bread, an array of fruit, cheese, a jug and a jewel-encrusted goblet. She didn't need to give the drinking vessel more than a cursory glance to know what gems adorned the rim.

Her stomach churned at the mere thought of food or drink, so she let the repast sit untouched. She turned around and spied a chest in the other corner.

The barge tilted, creaked and groaned as Gareth and his men boarded. Their friendly banter with each other made her smile.

Aelthed ducked into the tent. "You have not touched your food."

"I am not hungry."

"You should try to eat something, even if just a taste."

Out of all patience with the man, Rhian snapped at him, "Do not fuss like an old woman."

He moved away from the table, crossed to the chest and opened the lid. "These items are yours." He pulled out a brilliant green gown that reminded her of Gareth's eyes. "If it pleases you, feel free to make use of anything this chest contains." He handed her a leather pouch. "These were your mother's. Now they are yours."

Rhian emptied the contents into her hand. Exquisite gold jewelry shimmered in the candle's glow. A torque, armillae, several bracelets and rings were all finely made pieces with emerald settings.

She held the jewelry to her chest. "I do not understand. I would have expected amethyst, not emeralds."

"You do not like them?" Aelthed sounded incredulous at her statement.

"No. They are beautiful. I just thought my mother favored amethyst."

Aelthed smiled. A sad, remembering type of smile. "Nay. Amethyst was only one of her favorites."

"And her others?"

"Sapphires and emeralds." He headed toward the tent flaps. "If you wish to change, do so quickly. This is but a short trip across the water."

Left alone Rhian sifted through the chest, pulling out an undergown of thin golden cotton so tightly woven that it felt like smooth silk beneath her fingers. Everything she would need to dress like a queen was inside the chest. Belt, shoes, stockings and even a fine mesh net made of gold for her hair. Tiny emeralds winked at her from the mesh.

As quickly as she could manage alone, Rhian changed into the clothing. Everything fit as if it had been made just for her; an impossibility to be sure. She hooked the torque around her neck, slid the armillae up her arm to settle just above her elbow. Studying the remaining pieces, she chose one bracelet and a ring with winged engravings that reminded her of Faucon.

Rhian twirled the ring around her finger. She should have felt as beautiful as a princess or a bride. Instead, she felt only empty and cold. She paused. *A bride?* "Oh, no," she groaned.

She reached up to remove the jewels from around her neck. She'd not leave this barge to immediately attend her wedding. Her fingers shook in her haste to change back into her own clothes.

The barge hit land with a sudden lurch, sending her to her knees. *Not yet. Dear Lord, help me.*

A heavy thud of the plank being dropped into place warned her that time grew shorter. She scrambled to her feet.

The barge swayed, creaked and groaned as Gareth and his men departed. Rhian jerked the armillae from her arm and tossed it into the chest.

Aelthed's companions crossed the plank. She bit back a cry of despair. *Please, no. I wish not to be torn from my hopes this quickly.* As long as Gareth was nearby, she had hope. But once she left this barge and stepped into her new home, he would leave, taking hope with him.

"Lady Rhian, come. It is time." Aelthed's call turned her blood to ice.

Rhian closed her eyes and took a shaking breath. Not knowing who to turn to for help, she begged, *"Please, Mother, hear me. Help me. I knew not your touch, or your love. I love Faucon and I know it is returned. Let me not live without his touch or his love."*

A breeze parted the tent flaps and a warmth stole over her, calming her racing heart and easing her fears. A strange haunting melody soothed her mind of worries.

Rhian opened her eyes, straightened her spine and left the tent. She followed Aelthed across the deserted barge and to the end of the plank.

Once he was on land, Aelthed turned to face her, then dropped to one knee in the sand. "Your highness, may I be the first to welcome you home."

Rhian choked. "What the…" She stepped forward to pull the fool to his feet. The moment she stepped off the plank, the men gathered on the beach knelt as one.

She froze, then searched for Gareth. His men flanked the well-marked path leading from the barge to the forest. She found him—kneeling at the head of the line.

"Get up." Rhian directed her whispered order to Aelthed.

When he rose and faced her, she spoke as calmly as she could manage. "What is the meaning of this?"

"All will be explained soon." He extended his arm, waiting for her to place her hand on his wrist.

She did so and he led her down the path. Rhian stared at Gareth as she walked by him, hoping he'd laugh and admit this was all some sort of odd ruse. But he didn't move. He didn't so much as blink.

Just before they reached the end of the path, another party emerged from the forest. All but one knelt before her. Rhian ignored the heat rushing to her face and stared at the woman standing before her.

She trailed her gaze up past the golden undertunic peeking from beneath the emerald gown.

She paused briefly as she took in the gold and emerald jewelry—bracelet, armillae and torque. Rhian shifted her perusal higher and her heart momentarily stood still. Her breath caught in her throat.

She moved her lips but no sound came forth. Rhian found her breath and used it to shout, "Gareth!"

Gareth could not mistake the fear in her voice. Regardless of protocol, or vows, he stood and rushed to her side, catching her as she literally fell into his arms.

Certain she had only fainted, he lifted his head to see what had brought about this fear.

His questioning look met and held a surprised one.

Gareth blinked, hoping the motion would clear his confused vision.

No. He looked down at the woman he held, then back at the one stepping closer.

They were identical. Features, size, clothing, even the way they moved were identical. The two were a perfect pair in all ways except the eyes.

Where Rhian's were sapphire, this woman's eyes were amethyst.

Chapter Seventeen

As the parties entered the great Mirabilus Keep, one man watched in glee from the tower. The twins were together in one place. He could never have envisioned this amount of luck even in his wildest dreams.

The fact that Faucon carried the one sister made little difference. His informants had already explained that she'd only fainted and her hero had rushed to her aid.

What a waste of his energy. The elders would not permit this man to remain here, by her side, for long. Faucon was not of the right bloodline. They would never permit him to forge a lasting relationship with the woman.

Nay. Her fate had been laid out many moons ago and nothing would change it. He would see to that personally. Now that the family had all gathered together at "home" it would be a simple task to destroy them.

Why had he not thought of this before? He'd not needed to send simpletons across the water to do his bidding. He could have simply waited for the dragons to come to him.

He waved the thought aside. It mattered not that a

*few of the men had died. Their lives had been given for
a cause, lost during a quest for eternal power.*

*His only regret was that he'd had to leave Mirabilus
for a day just to send one of the simpletons to his grave.
For what seemed the hundredth time, he scraped his hands
down his black robe. Would the blood ever leave his flesh?*

*Again, he studied the arrivals. Aye. The blood would
leave. As soon as the dragons served him.*

*Backing away from the high tower's window, he
straightened his clothing, then smoothed back his hair.
He must look his best when he paid homage to the newly
reunited family.*

Rhian tossed on the bed, mumbling in her sleep,
"Nay. It cannot be."

Gareth and the woman claiming to be Rhian's sister,
reached opposite sides of the bed at the same time.

They stared at each other across the narrow expanse.
A silent battle of wills ensued, each wanting victory. Not
yet ready to give Rhian over to a stranger, Gareth held the
amethyst gaze and reached down to smooth Rhian's raven
tresses from her face. She calmed beneath his touch.

The woman nodded and backed away. "I will permit
you this, but no more." She turned on her heels and
moving as if she owned the world, returned to her seat
across the chamber.

Gareth sat on the edge of the bed. The leather straps
whined against the wooden frame. "Rhian, wake up."
He leaned over her, searching for any sign that she'd
soon return to normal.

He was quickly rewarded. Her eyes flickered beneath her lids. Her lips moved with voiceless words.

He wondered what she dreamed and worried that her dreams were not the kind he desired for her. He wanted her to always have nothing but good dreams. Ones that sometimes included him.

Gareth memorized her face, knowing full well that dreams would be all they could share in the future. The plans he and Melwyn made to steal her away in the dark of night had to be stopped. They'd made their bold plot before he'd known who, or what, Rhian was.

Enough gold in the king's palm would make the crime of kidnapping a woman disappear. However, kidnapping this woman would only be forgiven by his death.

He'd willingly accepted this mission with the intent of restoring his honor. In a few short weeks he'd tossed honor into a deep grave all for the sake of desire. The only way to bring it back from the dead was to walk away from his desire.

He wanted to laugh at himself. Desire? No. This gut-wrenching emotion was more than simple desire.

Rhian opened her eyes, smiled and touched his arm. "Was it all naught but a nightmare?"

Gareth breathed a sigh of relief. "You are awake."

"I hope so." She turned her head, looking at the chamber. "Where am I?"

Her breath hitched and he knew she'd spied her sister.

Gareth touched her cheek, gently turning her face back to his. He held her hand. "Rhian, nothing you remember was a dream. You are home, on Anglesey at Mirabilus Keep." He nodded his head toward the far side of the room, beckoning the woman to come forward. "And this is your sister, the Princess Evonne."

Rhian sprang upright. "My *what?*"

He glanced from one woman to the other before settling on Rhian. "Look at her. How could any believe you are not sisters?"

"This is not possible." Rhian's eyebrows met as she scooted up into a comfortable position. "Why did I know nothing about this?"

Evonne sat on the other side of the bed. "For the same reason I knew nothing of you until quite recently." She shrugged her shoulders. "Our parents did not see fit to tell us."

"How many other things did they fail to impart?"

Gareth stood. "The two of you need to talk." He squeezed Rhian's fingers, reluctant to release her hand.

Evonne sighed before saying, "And so do the two of you."

"No." He shook his head. If he stayed in this chamber much longer he would never be able to leave. "We have said all that needs to be said." He released Rhian's hand and stepped away. "Nothing has changed."

"Gareth." Everything she felt resounded in his name upon her lips. She reached toward him. "Stay."

He gritted his teeth. He needed to find and stop Melwyn. "I cannot stay." When she opened her mouth, he hardened his voice. "Nay. Do not keep me from my duty." Guilt at the stricken look on her face caused him to soften his tone. "I will seek your farewell before I leave."

Quickly, before she could talk him out of it, and before he could change his own mind, he bowed to both women and escaped the bedchamber.

The women watched his hasty exit, then turned to study each other.

Rhian broke the uneasy silence. "Sisters?"

"Twins," Evonne corrected.

"Ah." Rhian wondered, what do you say to someone who looks like your reflection?

She pulled her pendant from beneath her gown and held it out. "And I imagine yours is sapphire?"

Evonne laughed as she retrieved her dragon from beneath her own gown. "Of course."

"And the emerald?"

"Now, that one I have not yet deduced." Evonne furrowed her forehead in thought. "What color were our father's eyes?"

Rhian slapped a hand to her forehead. "Oh, for the love of the saints." She lowered her hand and laughed. "Why, they were emerald."

"Of course. What a unique way for mother to keep her family together."

Rhian drew her legs up and wrapped her arms around her knees. "Tell me, are you as nervous as I?"

Evonne crawled farther onto the bed and sat opposite Rhian in the same position. She rested her chin atop her knees. "Yes. And rather angry, too."

"What do you think it would have been like…" Rhian began.

"…had we been raised together?" Evonne finished the question.

Both stared at each other before breaking out into laughter.

When they regained their composure, Rhian asked, "So you are a princess?"

Evonne kicked her. "So are you."

"Yes, well, forgive me. This new title does not sit easily upon my head."

"Yes, well, get used to it."

Rhian rolled her eyes toward the ceiling. "A sister with a sharp tongue and wit. Thank you."

"Oh, and I am certain *you* are never the sarcastic wench."

"Me?" Rhian felt the heat steal across her cheeks. To banish her flush, she asked, "Now what?"

Evonne scrambled off the bed. "Now we discover the use for these pendants."

Rhian quickly followed. "They have a use?"

"So I am told." Evonne opened a small bejeweled wooden chest. "Mother left us a letter." She pulled a ribbon-tied scroll out of the chest. "I was ordered not to read it until you arrived."

Rhian stood by her side as she slipped the ribbon off the missive. Evonne handed it to her, then suggested they sit by the fire and read it together.

When they were seated, Rhian unrolled the parchment, amazed that her hands shook as she did so. Smoothing out the note, she felt a sudden warmth flow through her fingertips.

After clearing her voice, she began to read the words their mother had left for them.

"My dearest daughters. I pray that the two of you are together, perhaps before a warm blazing fire, sitting side by side as you read of my love for you. I will be as brief as possible—"

Evonne's soft chuckle made Rhian pause and look at her.

"Mother could not welcome someone into the keep

without it taking half a day. Brief is something she knew nothing about."

Rhian smiled. "And Father knew few words. His welcoming grunt was over before the guest knew it had happened."

"A fine pair, I'd say."

Rhian nodded in agreement before she continued reading.

"Business first. You each possess a dragon, crafted specifically for you. As you have already discovered, they match the color of your eyes. I gave you each the opposite color so it would become familiar to you. I hope that it has worked. These pendants, in truth, are dual keys. Keys that open a lock concealing more power than our world can hold safe."

Her heart raced as she read faster.

"Rhian, I am certain by now you have heard the rumors. Know that they are true. I mean not to frighten you, or turn you away from your remaining family. But I am, I was in fact a Druid priestess. Guardian of a sacred trust. A trust I leave to Evonne to do with as she sees fit."

"We are the end of our line, my dearest loves. It is time to let some of the old ways die. Our world has seen much darkness, death and destruction of late."

None could deny that simple truth. With Stephen and Matilda's ongoing war for the throne many had fallen into despair. There was no telling how long this madness would continue.

"Let the future come into our lives with hope, light and love. The first step toward this end is to destroy what evil men seek to control most of all—power."

Rhian's dragon grew hot against her skin. She pulled the pendant over her head and glanced at her sister. She had also removed her pendant.

Evonne took the letter and continued reading.

"Use your dragons together to open the bottom of this chest. Inside you will find a book. A record of ancient spells that could mean the end of the world if possessed by one weak and greedy."

"My daughters, know in your hearts that you were not separated out of spite, or lack of love. Your father and I loved each other heart and soul. And will continue to do so through all eternity. I know without a single doubt that he lived the rest of his life as I did—alone and lonely, the only proof of our love was each of you. Looking upon your faces each day kept that love alive."

When Evonne's voice broke, Rhian put an arm about her sister's shoulder and continued to read.

"Rhian, you are here only because your father is now gone from you. Do not hate me for saying I am glad. You are reading this together because I, too, am no longer there. I am now with my love, his arms about me once more. I am at peace and I wish the same for both of you. Do not grieve overmuch. The number of years is meaningless in eternity. We will be together again in the blink of nature's eye."

Rhian swallowed the thickness in her throat. Her parents knew love. Why then could she not have the same? Tears blurred her vision, but she continued.

"Your father and I had two different lives to live on this earth. I could not leave my people alone. He could not forsake his vow to his king. He was at my side the day the two of you entered this world. His tears of joy mingled with my own. And knowing we would soon part, his tears of regret were as strong. I knew from the moment I held each of you in my arms that you also had separate lives to live in this world."

Evonne joined in.

"There was no denying the paths fate had laid out for you. Nothing I could do to stop what must happen. To do so would only destroy your special gifts to life. Evonne, you were destined to follow in my footsteps at Mirabilus. You and you alone possess the gift of the old ways. Your fate was to remain with me. To learn the things you needed to know to go forward in my place."

Both women stopped and took a steadying breath.

"Rhian, it tore the heart from my breast to place you in your father's arms and watch the two of you ride away forever. Your gift, my child, is love. A love stronger and truer than any power in existence. It is the pure power of a love this great that keeps the world alive. Enjoy this love and all it brings. And know that it is returned to you threefold."

Rhian closed her eyes. Behind her lids appeared Gareth. She saw him tower over her glaring in anger. That vision swiftly melted away, and he stared in surprise, then gazed upon her with desire. Again, this mental image faded and she saw the pain in his eyes as he swore to honor her forever. This was the love fate had in store for her. This one and no other.

Evonne's voice, as she finished their mother's letter, tore Rhian from her daydreams.

"Now, my girls, love one another. Seize the opportunity to know one another. And when you start out on the journey fate has in store for you, carry your love with you. Remember your parents fondly and know their love will always surround you. I bid you farewell—for now."

Evonne rolled the letter into a scroll and retied the ribbon around it. She heaved a heavy breath and wiped the tears from her face before turning to Rhian. "Shall we be good children and do as we were instructed?"

Rhian held out her pendant. "It is your decision to make."

"No. We do this together." Evonne crossed the floor and pushed the chest toward the fire until it rested in front of their bench. She sat next to Rhian. "Where should we start looking for the lock?"

Rhian opened the lid and peered inside. The chest was empty, yet it appeared that the bottom was only halfway down. In fact, the entire inside of the chest appeared to be quite a bit smaller than the outside. She ran her hands along the sides "I feel nothing here."

Evonne reached in and poked her fingernails at the padded bottom until it came loose. She tore out the padding and the fabric, exposing a smooth flat panel. "Nothing here, either."

Rhian frowned. Obviously, there had to be a lock somewhere. She reached out, grasped a handle on the side of the chest and yanked it closer. Her hand slipped as the smooth metal handle came loose on one side.

The sisters looked at each other, then at the chest. Evonne got down on the floor and toyed with the now hanging handle. She twisted it toward the back and gave it a push. The side of the chest moved, exposing another layer beneath.

Rhian joined her on the floor and repeated the same process on the other side. Again, the false side panel slid back.

A deeply carved shape graced the newly exposed sides of the chest. Rhian studied hers for a moment, then smiled. "What color is your side?"

Evonne laughed. "Sapphire. Yours?"

"Amethyst."

In unison they placed their dragons into the carved shapes on the chest. Evonne nodded, asking, "Ready?"

They turned the dragons, but nothing happened. Rhian frowned. Evonne scowled. They removed the pendants from the shapes and switched, Evonne taking the amethyst and Rhian the sapphire.

Quickly inserting the pendants into the sides of the chest, they again turned the dragons in unison and held their breath.

A definite click from the chest brought smiles to their faces. They looked inside and saw a small handle sticking up from the bottom. Evonne reached in and grasped the handle. She easily lifted the panel and removed it from the chest.

"Thank you, my lovelies."

Rhian jumped to her feet and watched in horror as a man cloaked and masked in black grabbed Evonne and threw her across the room. Her sister hit the stone wall and crumpled to the floor.

Without thinking, Rhian reached inside the chest and pulled a leather-bound book into her arms. She raced toward the window screaming for Gareth.

Before she reached the opening, the man tackled her from behind. "You will not keep me from what is mine."

He knocked her to the floor and landed on top of her back. She gasped for breath, fighting to remain alert as the room spun around her.

The book was beneath her and she hung on to it for dear life, refusing to let go. The man rolled off of her and grabbed the braid trailing down her back.

"Come, come, sweeting, give the book over to your uncle."

"My uncle?" Shocked, Rhian denied his claim. "Aelthed would not scheme in this manner."

"Aelthed?" The man laughed. "Nay, my brother would not have the stomach for such grand plans." He rose, trying to yank her to her feet. "I have plotted long and hard to gain what my beloved sister left behind for her worthless daughters. You will not thwart me now."

This crazed murderer claimed to be related to her? With a will she'd not realized she possessed, Rhian pulled away from him, crawling on her belly to protect the book while she sought escape.

Right behind her, he scrambled to recapture her. "My minions may have failed, but I will not be as unlucky."

He grasped at her gown, only to lose his hold when Evonne threw an empty pitcher at him shouting, "You spineless son of Satan, leave her alone."

Rhian had a moment of respite when the man turned to Evonne. "Son of Satan?" He ripped the cover from his head. "If so, then we come from the same seed. And I will prove it, once I have that book in my hands."

Both women sucked in a deep disbelieving breath. None could deny that he did indeed come from the same family. The resemblance between the three of them was more than remarkable, it bordered on unholy.

Not quite as old as Aelthed, the man was of the same generation. This man could have been their father.

Rhian quickly crossed herself, quietly praying, "Dear Lord, let this not be so."

The man swung around toward Rhian, shocking her with harsh, near insane laughter. "No amount of praying to your God will change what is so." He lunged for her, screaming, "Give me that book! Your lives are over either way!"

Rhian turned and ducked, hoping to miss his attack. Something sharp dug into her shoulder. The pain knocked her to her knees. She knew without looking that the weapon was a sickle. Her heart lurched, giving her an extra burst of power. She rolled away from his instrument of death, ignoring the flare of more pain as it tore through her gown and down her back.

He cursed at her and screamed again.

Another scream joined his. Evonne crawled toward the door of the chamber shouting for help.

The man turned and rushed for Evonne, his weapon extended. Rhian pushed herself up from the floor and threw herself at his legs. "No!"

He tumbled to the floor, shouting, "You both will die!"

The door to the chamber banged open against the wall. Men rushed in with drawn swords as the man again lurched toward Evonne.

Gareth and a tall blond man entered at the same time. The blonde spared not half a heartbeat before ramming his sword through the man seeking to attack Evonne. Then he pulled her into his arms.

Gareth rushed to Rhian. He gathered her into his arms and held her tight against him. His chest shook with the heaviness of his breathing.

He lifted his hand from her back and gasped. "Dear Lord, are you whole?"

Without waiting for an answer he spun her around in his arms and tore her gown from her shoulder. "You are bleeding."

She glanced over her shoulder and nearly fainted at the look on his face. Never had she seen anyone as worried or frightened as he appeared now. "Gareth, I am fine."

"You are not fine!" His roar drew the attention of everyone in the chamber.

Aelthed came forward with Melwyn fast on his heels. Rhian blinked. "Melwyn?"

He lifted his chin in obvious defiance of Aelthed's previous orders. "Nothing could keep me from my assigned duty to the Faucons." He hitched his thumb toward the older man. "Not even this one here."

"Yes. Yes." Aelthed waved off the captain's comments and reached for Rhian. "Let me see."

"I am fine."

Again, Gareth disagreed, "You are not." He lifted his hand in front of her face. "This is your blood."

"It is just a little scratch, that is all."

Aelthed snorted. "I knew your father would not see to your education. You cannot even tell the difference between little and big." He nodded toward the bed. "Get her over there."

Evonne tore herself from her protector's arms and raced to Rhian's side. "What did he do? Oh, my word! Rhian, do as you are told."

"You are making far too much of this."

"Stop it. Give me that." Gareth yanked the book from her arms and handed it to Evonne. He then pulled Rhian over his shoulder and carried her unceremoniously to the bed. Instead of placing her on the bed, he sat down and drew her onto his lap.

Aelthed paused. "Milord, I do not think this is appropriate."

"That is truly too bad. But since I am not moving, you might want to quit thinking and do whatever needs to be done." Gareth's voice brooked no argument.

Melwyn stepped alongside the bed, his sword still in his hand. "And you might want to be quick about it, before the lady bleeds to death."

Evonne stood next to Melwyn. "Yes, please, before my bedchamber becomes a fighting arena."

Rhian shook as Aelthed went to work on her shoulder and back. She shook more from fear of the unknown than pain.

Gareth placed his lips against her forehead, ordering, "Look at me."

She lifted her head, bit her lower lip to quell the sudden trembling and stared into his eyes.

"Tell me truthfully, Princess, are you whole?"

"Yes, I am fine, truly."

He searched her face and seemed satisfied with her answer. "What was he after? The dragon?"

"No. The dragons were keys to a chest. He wanted the book that was inside."

"Dragons?"

While Evonne crossed the room to retrieve the pendants, Rhian explained. "Yes, there are two. One amethyst, one sapphire."

"And I suppose they, too, are identical?"

Evonne answered as she dangled them before Gareth. "Yes. As identical as we are." She held one in each hand and asked, "Which do you want, Rhian?"

"The one that was given to me. The amethyst."

Her sister reached out and took Gareth's hand. She placed the amethyst dragon in his palm. "Keep this safe for her."

He nodded and closed his hand over the dragon. "It still does not explain why this book is so important."

Evonne motioned toward Aelthed. "He can tell you better than I."

Aelthed continued fussing with her shoulder and back while he explained, "I was never positive the book actually existed. I'd only heard rumors of it. Many years ago, when Mirabilus was first…inhabited, the people broke into two groups. One worked for the good of the land. The other sought only the power to control all people and things in existence."

He turned away to glance at the body still on the floor. Aelthed sighed, then turned back to Rhian. "Ironically, the people seeking good became powerful and rich. They recorded their hopes and lessons in a book." He reached out and tapped the book in Evonne's arms. "The evil group were convinced that the book held the secrets that would give them the power."

Gareth looked at the tome Evonne held. "Does it?"

"Nay," Aelthed laughed. "You would shrink away in horror from the secrets it does hold." He lowered his voice as if imparting great knowledge. "Magic. Potions. Spells."

Melwyn's snort broke the seriousness of the moment.

"Regardless of what the book truly contains, it is what people think it contains that matters." Aelthed nodded his headed toward the body. "For example, my brother there believed it would give him the ability to control the world."

"He claimed to be our uncle." Evonne's forehead furrowed in confusion. "I did not know you and Mother had a brother."

"And you were not to know. He chose evil over good and was outcast from Mirabilus years before your birth."

Gareth asked, "The men who died at Browan and on the trail?"

"With your description of them, I would guess they were his sons. They wanted what Evonne and Rhian possess. Rule over Mirabilus. But it would never happen without having the book."

"Why is that?"

"Only the women in our family have a right to rule and it would take the secrets in that book to change that right."

"And what happens if there is a generation without daughters?"

Aelthed laughed. "That has not occurred in over six hundred years."

Gareth frowned before asking, "Why only the women?"

"Now there is an easy question to answer. Because women do not seek war as the first answer."

Melwyn walked away. Gareth's eyebrows disappeared beneath his hair. "Obviously Mirabilus has never welcomed the Empress Matilda onto their shores."

"I will not discuss the current politics with you, milord. I will only tell you that in over six hundred years our people have not died in battle. Our lands have not burned."

"Cease." Gareth raised one hand. "We will agree to disagree and leave it there."

From across the chamber, Melwyn asked, "What about their choice of weapon?" He picked up the sickle and brought it over to Aelthed.

"Inventive. A sickle is a Druid's sword. Hawthorne represents judgement. And I am certain that the wounds caused by this weapon were more frightening than the damage a sword would leave."

Nobody disagreed with him.

Melwyn tossed the weapon into the fire, then asked, "What about the other men who conspired with this one here?"

"Bah." Aelthed made a dismissing sound. "They will slink away like the dogs they are and will bother us no further."

"You sound certain about that."

Aelthed shrugged. "I am certain."

The man who'd entered the chamber earlier with Gareth approached. "Milady Evonne, if you no longer require me, I will return below stairs."

Evonne drew him forward. "Come, meet my sister." She laughed. "However, the circumstances are a little out of the ordinary."

He looked at her in amazement. "That is something new?"

Rhian watched as a look passed between them. It was a look that spoke of their love louder than any words.

Evonne turned to Rhian. "Rhian, may I present Lord Braedon." She turned back to him. "Lord Braedon, my sister, Lady Rhian, and her escort, Gareth of Faucon."

Braedon bowed. "I am honored to make your acquaintance, milady."

"And I am honored that you came to our rescue so quickly. Thank you."

He nodded, then looked toward Gareth. "Faucon? Comte Faucon?"

Melwyn snickered. Gareth shook his head. "No, that is my older brother, Rhys."

"My mistake. I share in the debt of gratitude Mirabilus owes to you for bringing Rhian here safely." He touched Evonne's arm. "I beg your leave." When she softly granted it, he ordered the guards to remove the body and he left the chamber.

"This might sting," Aelthed warned.

Rhian jumped when he shoved what had to be a needle through the flesh on her back.

The older man paused and touched her shoulder. "I am sorry, but you must hold still."

Gareth drew one hand up the back of her head; he slid the other across her side to rest on her lower back and pulled her hard against his chest. With his lips against the side of her head he promised, "It will be over soon. Hold on to me."

He lifted his head briefly and ordered, "Be done with this, Aelthed."

Rhian buried her face in his chest. She refused to scream. Instead, she bit her lip and dug her fingers into Gareth's back. He flinched once, then managed to ignore whatever pain she inflicted on his flesh.

Thankfully, he'd been correct. Aelthed finished quickly. "Very good, milady. I am done." He rummaged around in the pouch hanging from his belt, pulled out a small packet of powder and handed it to Evonne. "Mix this in wine and see that she drinks it all." He then took his leave.

Gareth relaxed his hold on Rhian and she leaned away from his chest. Sweat dripped down her face and plastered her dress to her skin. He wiped the moisture from her eyes and brushed the hair from her face. "You need to rest."

"Do not go."

Evonne leaned forward. "You do need to rest a bit. I will help you off with your gown and make you comfortable. I promise you, he will be within calling distance."

Gareth brushed a kiss on her forehead before lifting her from his lap. "I will be near. Sleep."

After he left the chamber, Evonne set the book down and helped her remove her gown. She then did as Aelthed suggested and mixed the powder in some wine and stood there while Rhian drank the full goblet before stretching out on the bed.

Rhian lay on her stomach and watched Evonne cross the room to pick up the book again. "What will you do with it?"

Evonne carried it over to the fire and tossed it in the flames. "If it is so valuable that evil men will kill to possess it, then it needs to be gone from this world."

"What do you think was really in it?"

Her sister shrugged. "I do not doubt that it contained recipes and instructions for the black arts."

Rhian agreed with her decision to turn the pages into ashes. "Can I ask a question?"

Evonne sat on the edge of the bed. "Certainly you can."

"Who is Braedon?"

Evonne closed her eyes. Her smile fell from her lips. She tipped her head and stared at Rhian, then softly answered, "He is the captain of our guard. The protector of our people. And, he is your betrothed."

Chapter Eighteen

Rhian awoke with her face lying on a damp pillow. She knew the moisture there was from the tears she'd shed after Evonne had left the chamber.

Things were all mixed up. It was wrong. Evonne should be the one to marry Braedon, not her. How did this insanity happen?

Loud shouts filtered through the door to the chamber. "Now. There is no reason this ceremony cannot take place this very night."

Rhian's stomach rolled. Surely they weren't discussing her wedding?

"I say you are wrong. But who am I to decide? Let me explain it to her." Evonne's voice overrode the other ones.

Her sister entered the chamber. Six men followed her inside. "Rhian, are you awake?"

"Yes." With an effort, she pushed herself up to a sitting position. "What is happening?"

"These are the elders of Mirabilus." Evonne pointed toward Aelthed and five older men. "They insisted upon your marriage this very night." At Rhian's gasp, she quickly added, "I tried to convince them that under the circumstances of you being wounded, not knowing Braedon and not having been here even a day yet, that perhaps a little time should pass before letting fate run its course."

Rhian grimaced. "And were you successful?"

"No." Evonne curled her lip at the men and sharply stuck her hand up in the air in a gesture of displeasure, before quickly lowering it. "However they have agreed to a dream quest."

"A what?" Rhian's voice rose.

Gareth stormed into the chamber. "What is happening here?"

Evonne closed her eyes and rubbed her temples. She then asked the newcomer, "Have you seen Lord Braedon?"

Gareth swung around. "He was right behind me."

Evonne marched to the door, stuck her head out into the hallway and ordered, "Get in here."

A contrite Braedon followed her in. "I was not certain you required my presence."

The glare Evonne shot him made Rhian laugh. The two of them, Evonne and Braedon, really did suit each other. They already acted like husband and wife. Her laugh stopped abruptly. The thought that he was to be *her* husband took any humor out of the situation.

Evonne moved to the center of the room, at the foot of Rhian's bed. Evonne lifted her hand and waved the men to her. "Come, gather round." Once the eight men stood before her, she explained, "Rhian is going to have a dream quest tonight."

"A what?" Gareth interrupted.

Evonne turned and rolled her eyes at Rhian, then jerked her head toward Gareth.

Rhian sighed. "Gareth, have patience. That is what she is going to explain."

Evonne continued. "It seems the *wise* men of Mirabilus—" sarcasm dripped from her voice "—have decided that Rhian and Braedon should wed this very night."

Both men, Braedon and Gareth, reared back as if struck.

Gareth opened his mouth to say something, then closed it when the words would not come.

Braedon wasn't as smart. "Tonight? Why tonight? What necessitates such hasty measures?"

"Silence!" Evonne's shout stopped his frantic questions. "Perhaps a quest for answers will give us a hint as to when, and if, this marriage should take place."

To placate the skeptical elders, Evonne asked, "Did not one of the ancients use her powers of dream questing to save our people?"

Rhian's skin crawled at the thought of participating in some pagan ritual. The hairs on the back of her neck stood on end.

One of the elders shook his head, his long white beard swung back and forth across his chest as he addressed Evonne. "But she used the dreams not for herself."

"Would it not be easier to quest after your own fate than another's?"

"Who will interpret these dreams?" Another elder queried, causing the rest to nod in agreement with his question.

"Who better qualified than I?"

Five of the older men laughed at Evonne's answer. Only Aelthed retained a serious air. When the room finally quieted, he offered, "I will assist her."

"You do not trust my skills?" Evonne's voice rose.

"I trust both of you individually." Aelthed's smile held a hint of irony. "But together? Nay. In my brief time with Rhian, I have realized that you and she are too much alike. There is no telling what plot you could cook between you."

The other five men murmured in agreement with Aelthed's suggestion. While Evonne did not appear to take the intrusion to heart, she did not argue with the elders.

Rhian held no such respect for these men—nor for the method of determining her fate. "Is anyone going to ask my opinion?"

Eight voices chimed in unison, "No."

Only Gareth withheld a negative response. Instead, he asked, "What would you suggest, Rhian?"

"It matters not what she suggests." Aelthed stepped forward, his long robe flapping about his ankles. He spoke directly to Rhian, "What you desire is no longer your choice. This is now your home and you have a responsibility to your family and to your people."

He gave Rhian a few moments to digest those facts, then said, "Your young man will not rescue you. Nor will his captain. To do so will brand them outlaws and traitors to their crown."

Rhian sought Gareth's denial to the man's statements. Instead, he ignored her silent plea, staring straight ahead so she could not connect her gaze with his own.

She gripped the bedcovers tightly between her fingers, hoping the action would keep her from screaming at him.

The elder with the white beard stepped forward. "We will permit this ceremony to take place only if Aelthed is present from this moment on until its conclusion." The man pinned Evonne with an unmistakable look of stern warning. "You two sisters will not be left unattended until all is decided."

Evonne paused long enough to glance at Braedon before facing the elders. "Agreed."

Rhian's scream toyed with her throat. She swallowed hard to keep it at bay. A feat made all the more hard as Gareth followed the rest of the men out of the chamber.

Only she, Evonne and Aelthed remained. The old man crossed the chamber, lowered his bony frame onto a stool by the fire before he broke the deafening silence in the room. "Be about it, Evonne. The longer you wait, the more nervous she becomes."

He had that much correct. Rhian's stomach rolled, her head throbbed, her heart beat so quickly and hard that breathing was becoming more and more difficult. She wanted nothing more than to throw herself across the bed and have a good cry before donning a sword and slaying the lot of them.

After what seemed an eternity, Evonne finally moved from her spot at the end of the bed. Rhian could not help feeling sympathy, nay more like empathy for her sister. Not only did Evonne stand to lose the man she obviously loved, but she would lose him to her own sister. Rhian not only understood her sister's pain, she felt it.

Her stomach clenched at the mere thought of marrying Braedon. Thankfully, it was empty; otherwise she'd be rushing for a chamber pot.

She curled her fingers into a fist. Hurt was not the only emotion making her ill. She could not go through with this ceremony. She'd not been raised on Mirabilus. How could they expect her to calmly accept some devil's ritual as the harbinger of her fate?

Rhian narrowed her eyes and watched Evonne kneel before an overly ornate chest. Encrusted with enough jewels to fund an army, the golden chest shimmered in the glow from the candlelight.

Evonne chanted half-heard words that Rhian could not understand before opening the chest and removing two leather pouches, which she set aside. She reached back into the box and with both hands, lifted out an unadorned goblet that appeared oddly plain compared to the chest.

In an attempt to escape this unholy ceremony, Rhian scooted to the edge of the bed and swung her feet over the edge.

"He will die." Aelthed's voice stopped her before her feet touched the floor.

The man did not even have the grace to look at her as he spoke. He kept his face turned to the flickering fire as he tossed herbs onto the now growing flames. "Lord Braedon will kill Faucon if you do not arrive at the hut." Another handful of herbs sizzled onto the fire.

Rhian drew in a steadying breath, certain the man only sought to frighten her. "He would not dare."

"Sir Melwyn has already been removed from the keep. Your Faucon is under guard and Braedon will not hesitate to do all in his power to protect Mirabilus."

"Faucon is no threat to your home."

"He is a threat to your fate. That is a threat to the kingdom." Aelthed pointed toward the window. "See for yourself."

Rhian raced from the bed and leaned her head out of the opening. She could easily see down into the center of the bailey. Six men and Braedon surrounded Gareth with their swords drawn. It would have been impossible for Gareth to fight his way free, for he was bound to a post with his arms tied behind him.

Melwyn was nowhere to be seen. Rhian searched the area for the captain and finally spotted him. Another six armed men were leading the captain out of Mirabilus. Melwyn's hands were tied before him and the men led him across the open field toward the forest like a tethered dog.

She swung around from the window. "Release them. Immediately. You have no cause to treat them in this manner."

Both Aelthed and Evonne ignored her. They were too involved with consecrating the vile goblet to be concerned by her demands.

Rhian rushed for the door and jerked it open only to find her way barred by armed guards.

Again, she shouted at Aelthed and Evonne, "You cannot do this. You have no right to hold me prisoner. I thought this was my home, not my cell."

Aelthed stood up and both of them turned to face her. Evonne held out the goblet. Steam rose from the contents.

Rhian backed away. The guards restrained her. Each grasped one of her arms and hauled her toward Aelthed and Evonne.

She stared at her sister, whispering, "Do not do this. For the love of our parents, do not do this."

Evonne lifted the goblet toward Rhian, ignoring her plea. "Drink. It will soon be over."

The scent of honey-wine wafted to her nose. It carried with it the pungent aroma of unfamiliar herbs. Rhian shook her head. "I cannot." She jerked backward, seeking to pull away from her captors. But her strength was nothing in their hands. They simply pulled her back into position.

Again she pleaded, "Evonne, do not do this unholy act. Let us grasp our fate in our own hands, not let some vile demon ritual decide what is best."

Aelthed nodded to the guards. One man dragged his foot across her ankles sending her to her knees. The other grasped the back of her hair, pulling her head back. *They would force the brew on her? Hysterical laughter threatened to bubble up from her throat.*

Evonne leaned forward, then hesitated. She stood back and shook her head. "I cannot."

Rhian's moment of hope was shattered when Aelthed took the goblet from Evonne's shaking hand and forced the rim to Rhian's lips.

She refused to open her mouth. The guard not holding her head back wrapped his hand beneath her chin, squeezed his fingers on either side of her cheeks, forcing her teeth and lips apart.

Between them, they poured the sickly sweet liquid into her mouth, holding her head back so it ran down her throat.

When the goblet was empty, they released her, letting her fall to the floor. Sick to her stomach and frightened beyond reason, Rhian curled into a ball.

With a hearty curse, Evonne sat down beside her and drew Rhian into her arms. She held her, rocking back and forth, crooning, "Shh, hush. You will not be harmed. All will be well, Rhian. I promise it will be well."

Gareth fought the restraints around his arms. "You heathen bastards, are you such cowards?"

Lord Braedon laughed at his outrage. "Cowards?" He tapped his sword to the bindings. "I prefer to call it a strategic move."

"Not fighting is a coward's way."

"Look around you, Faucon. Not fighting is what keeps you alive."

Between those surrounding him and those going about their duties in just this courtyard, there were enough men to conquer a small country. A fact not lost on Gareth.

Only a blind man would fail to see the riches Rhian stood to gain by remaining here. Mirabilus was more castle than keep. Solidly built of stone with double curtain walls, it would withstand any siege. Surrounded by fertile fields and a game-laden forest, none would ever go hungry. Water flowed into the many wells, ensuring the inhabitants would never suffer thirst.

It was a secure home. Food. Safety. Wealth. Family. Title. Even if he was permitted, what did he have to offer her? Would any sane woman give it all up for love?

If he truly cared about Rhian, he would take Aelthed's advice and leave her be. Did he love her that much? Weary from the assault on his heart and mind, Gareth asked, "What did you do with my man?"

"Sir Melwyn is hale and hearty. Angry as a wet bee, but whole." Lord Braedon relented. "He is on the beach awaiting your arrival with your other men."

"How long will they be required to wait?"

Braedon nodded toward the party leaving the keep. "I will release you as soon as Rhian is secured within the hut."

It hurt to look upon her and know he would never again hold her in his arms, never have the opportunity to tell her what he felt. But he could not look away.

Something was wrong. Her steps faltered. She needed help to stay upright.

The muscles in Gareth's arms and chest strained with his effort to tear the bindings from his wrists. "What have they done to her?"

"Did you think they would simply order her to lie down, go to sleep and dream? She has been prepared for her ordeal."

Gareth swore. "Let her go. I will leave."

"It would not matter. The quest has been approved and will take place regardless of what you do."

"What will happen? Will this harm her?"

Braedon studied him. "You love this woman."

It was not a question, so Gareth did not supply an answer.

"No. She will not be harmed." Braedon placed a hand on his shoulder. "The herbs only help her to relax. They will permit her to sleep deeper, to dream more vividly and if all goes well, to talk in her sleep."

"And then?"

Braedon tightened his fingers on Gareth's shoulder. "And then, my friend, she will marry."

Gareth swallowed past the thickness in his throat. "You?"

The man was slow to answer. Finally, he removed his hand and said, "I will not lie to you. Yes."

"So this is nothing more than a game to placate the women?"

Braedon nodded his head in answer.

In the light of the setting sun, Gareth watched them lead Rhian away until he could see her no more. "You will care for her, not hurt her and never break her heart." To make himself clear, he warned, "I will know in my soul if you do and I will kill you."

Braedon looked up at him. "She is Evonne's sister. I could never bring her harm."

The way the man said Evonne's name made Gareth pause. There was more emotion, more feeling put into that one name than into the promise for Rhian. "You care for Evonne a great deal."

"Yes."

"Then what are we doing? Release me. There is no need for this."

"I know my duty to Mirabilus." Braedon smiled sadly. "I am sorry. This has been decreed since Rhian's birth. As the oldest twin, it is she I must marry. I cannot forsake the duty or the honor at stake."

Gareth knew all about duty and honor. He lived his whole life for the sake of duty and honor. He was only here out of duty and because of honor.

He bowed his head. For honor, he would walk away from here.

Braedon slipped a knife through the bindings around Gareth's wrists. "Go. I bid you safe journey."

As Gareth walked toward the gates, Braedon called out, "I will care for her. I will honor my vows. She will always be safe, Faucon. Always."

Braedon's words echoed in Gareth's head as he walked across the clearing toward the forest. They gave him little comfort. He feared they would give Rhian even less.

Maybe, if Braedon were kind and patient with her, she would come to care deeply for her husband. And maybe, someday, she would forget the escort who'd brought her to her home.

Is that what he wanted? No. He never wanted her to forget him. But it would serve her better to do so.

Gareth rubbed the throbbing between his eyes. He needed to leave this place before he went mad.

"Milord?" Melwyn met him at the edge of the forest. The captain took one look at him and swore curses that would turn a drunkard's head around.

Gareth agreed with each and every one of them. After Melwyn had finally spent himself of swear words, they headed toward the beach. He didn't want to leave, but neither could he stay.

They joined the others along the shoreline. Gareth stared across the stormy water in amazement. How could a channel kick up this much anger?

Raging waves crashed against the beach at his feet. The pounding echoed the torment in his heart and mind. It served only to make losing Rhian worse. It was as if the ocean's water raged with him at his loss.

Unable to cross the channel tonight, Gareth turned to the men. "Make camp." He motioned to Melwyn and ordered, "Find me enough wine or ale to forget I am here."

"It will not help."

Gareth gripped his sword. "I did not ask for your advice."

Rhian gazed about the windowless hut. In the dim light from the single candle she could make out little. But it was obvious that the hut was poor compared to any other abode on Mirabilus. Poor and old.

Built of mud and straw, with nothing but a dirt floor and a small door. She patted the ground beneath her. At least they'd seen fit to provide her with a blanket to sleep on.

She laughed. Why she thought it was funny, she knew not. The idea that she'd fall asleep in this hovel and dream of her fate simply amused her.

Without Gareth, her future would seem like a hovel. Poor, old and lonely.

She choked back a cry.

"Rhian." Evonne's voice seemed to come from far away, yet her sister stood right before her.

Rhian reached up twice and finally grasped her hand. "What is happening to me?"

Evonne stroked her hair. "All is well. You are tired from the drink. Do not fight it, rest. Sleep. I will be right here with you."

"I don't want to sleep."

Evonne stretched out on the makeshift pallet and pulled Rhian down next to her. "Yes, you do." She rubbed Rhian's back and shoulders. "Just close your eyes and sleep."

Unable to ignore the gentle bidding, Rhian let her eyelids flutter closed. A noise across the room made her open them quickly. Someone sat in the shadows against the wall. She tried to sit up. "Who is that?"

"Shh." Evonne pulled her back down onto the blanket. "It is just Aelthed. He will guard us while we rest. Come, Rhian."

Unable to find the strength to argue, Rhian again closed her eyes. She found the blanket surprisingly comfortable and warm.

Soon, Evonne left her side. But Rhian found herself without the energy to care, or the voice to call her back. She simply wanted to fall into the warm cocoon that beckoned her from the dark.

There, she could be alone with her memories and her pain. She was not foolish enough to think she'd be permitted to marry anyone except Lord Braedon. This kingdom was far too rich, far too powerful to permit feelings to get in the way of duty.

The only moments she would ever spend with Gareth would be in her dreams. Rhian felt a tear slip out of the corner of her eyes and down the side of her face, but she couldn't move her hand to wipe it away.

Whatever they had forced her to drink had destroyed her willpower. Every emotion, every thought came alive. And all of them were filled with hopeless hurt.

At this moment she hated Evonne. She hated Aelthed and all from Mirabilus. Her sister claimed to care for her, yet she forced this pain on her.

Rhian choked on her tears. She had been able to hold this storm back, until now. She would never forgive Evonne for this. Never.

"Rhian, let it go. The pain will ease if you sleep. Remember. Dream of love. Let it go."

Her mind swirled with so many thoughts and feelings that she wasn't certain who had spoken to her.

"Dream."

The one word command was lost in the sound of rumbling thunder. She laughed softly. A storm would be the perfect backdrop to the torment inside her head and heart.

Rhian heard the rain beat on the roof of the hut. The wind howled. Thunder shook the building as she drifted off into sleep.

From inside his tent, Gareth stared out the flap and watched the storm build.

He lifted the full goblet to his lips and put it down empty. The ale nearly choked him as it coursed down his throat. He'd lost count a few mouthfuls earlier. His head throbbed, but he remained as sober as if he'd not taken a drop. Even the strong drink was against him.

All he had asked of this night was a chance to sleep a dreamless sleep and to forget for just a while.

It was not to be.

He closed the flap to his tent, then threw himself onto his pallet.

Gareth rolled over on his back and stared up into the blackness of the night. He wanted to forget, but could not. Rhian's face danced before him. The night's breeze carried the softness of her lips against his.

He suddenly feared the dreams sleep would bring. But he could no longer fight off the urge to close his eyes and give himself up to the night.

He heard the rain beat against his tent. The wind howled. Thunder shook the ground beneath him as he gave up his fight and drifted off into sleep.

Chapter Nineteen

Rhian knew she was dreaming. She knew, because she saw the dream take place. While she felt and heard everything that happened, she also watched. The overwhelming lightness spinning in her head terrified her a little, but the dream swept her away until she no longer feared anything.

Gareth reached for her, whispering, "Come here." His callused hands moved slowly against the soft flesh of her back.

"Rhian." Warm and gentle, his breath fell across her ear before his lips found the side of her neck.

Rhian slipped her arms around him, pressing tightly against the hardness of his chest.

How she had longed for this moment. She craved his touch like a man in the desert craves water. He was the nourishment that gave her life.

His touch set her body to tremble. His kiss melted her heart.

He stroked every hill and hollow with his fingertips,

finding the places that made her shiver with need. He slipped out of her embrace to inflame that growing need with the warm caress of his mouth, ceasing his insistent teasing only when she curled her toes and cried out his name.

"You will drive me out of my mind." She gasped past the rapid pounding of her heart.

Gareth rested his cheek on her stomach. Smiling at her, he asked, "Will that be such a bad thing if I promise to travel the road at your side?"

She could do nothing but shake her head. They could go mad together and at this moment she would not mind.

He turned his face away and her breath hitched.

Rhian's face burned with embarrassment as she watched the tableau unfolding before her. His hands were dark against her thighs. His long fingers stroked, memorizing her flesh, until they disappeared between her legs. The blackness of his hair was vivid against the paleness of her stomach. He slid his head lower, covering her curls with his own.

The Rhian on the bed moaned and parted her legs. The one watching gasped and closed her eyes at the fire between her own thighs.

Both merged into one, crying his name out together, "Gareth."

A hand shook her shoulder. "Rhian. Wake up. Come on. Wake up."

"I told you it was too much of the brew." Evonne admonished Aelthed.

"Nay. She will be fine. I have an antidote that will work as soon as she drinks it."

"Rhian!" Evonne nearly shouted in her ear.

Rhian opened her eyes. Dream or no dream, she was on fire. Her body silently screamed for release from head to toe. She took a deep shaking breath and crossed her legs, fighting to stop the ceaseless throbbing.

"Evonne, sister or no, I will strangle you if you ever do anything like this again." Her words came out in breathless pants.

Evonne laughed. "There is a cure for what ails you, but you need to listen to Aelthed first."

Rhian sat up on the makeshift bed. Aelthed handed her a goblet, which she eyed carefully, then looked up at him.

He assured her, "It is safe. It will dispel the effects of the dream drink."

She swallowed the contents in one large gulp and tossed the vessel at him. Soon, her head cleared, her heart ceased its uneven pounding. But her blood still raced hot through her limbs.

Certain she could now form coherent thoughts and words, Rhian asked, "Well? What is the decision? What secrets has this godforsaken ritual imparted?"

Aelthed paced the small hut and scratched his head. "Against my better judgement, I find that I disagree with the elders. We need to go against the original decree."

Evonne's eyes lit up with what Rhian could only describe as hope and joy.

She, on the other hand, was not quite as fast to assume the best. "What are you saying, in plain words, Aelthed?"

"I am saying that Braedon is not the husband for you. He is, however, the prince for Mirabilus and must marry one of the daughters."

"That does not exactly present a problem, now does it? There are two of us. And I am certain it would not require a great deal of coaxing for one to marry the man."

"Yes, but—"

Evonne stepped in front of him, making him stop the infernal pacing. "But what?"

Aelthed crossed his arms in front of his chest, slipping his hands inside his wide sleeve and shrugged. "I was not certain you would be willing."

Both women stared openmouthed at him.

He took a step away. "It was a jest, ladies."

Rhian found her voice first. "An excellent time for a jest, is it not?" She marched toward him. "Evonne will marry your prince. I will marry Gareth of Faucon, if he will still have me and if I can find him."

"He is still here."

She raced toward the door of the hut.

Aelthed and Evonne shouted as one, "Wait!"

Rhian turned back to them, her earlier passion now turning to a raging impatience. She tapped her foot on the dirt floor. "Could you be quick about this?"

Evonne rushed forward, obviously as anxious as she. "I just wanted to tell you that I would be honored if you would attend my marriage on the morrow. It will give us a little more time to talk." She pulled Rhian into her arms. "To let us find a way to span the years gone by and make certain the ones ahead do not pass in the same manner."

Rhian hugged her in return. "I would like that, my sister. I would like that very much." She pulled away and pushed Evonne toward the door. "Go. I think perhaps Braedon is waiting for the worst. He will enjoy this surprise."

After Evonne raced down the path toward the keep, Rhian waited for Aelthed to have his say. It mattered not what he said. She would not remain here. Her future, her fate was with Gareth.

"Child. I regret the need for your ordeal, but at least now, we are all certain which path each of you needs to follow."

"I was certain of my path before you saw fit to drug me."

He shook his head. "You have your ways, we have ours. And here our ways will rule."

"What do you wish me to say, Uncle? That I forgive you? Fine, I do. May I now go?"

"I do not require forgiveness when no sin was committed. No, you may not go. You will be taken to your man as befits a princess of Mirabilus." He shouted for men to attend to them.

"This could take all night." Aelthed's snort only served to increase her impatience. "If he leaves before I get there…"

"He will not leave. He cannot. The storm will not let him." Aelthed peered out the door at the still-rumbling night sky. "I am fairly certain it will not cease until you reach the shore."

Rhian looked up at the sky and frowned. "How can you conclude that?"

He laughed softly and placed his arm about her shoulders. "There is much you do not know about your family. Perhaps one day, when you are more open to things you cannot touch or see, you will begin to understand."

"Perhaps."

He led her out into the rain. "For now, however, we need discuss a suitable dowry to send to King Stephen. I am certain it will go far to ease his mind about the marriage I see ahead."

"You would do that for me?"

"I do nothing." Aelthed laughed. "Child, it is your gold."

"Ah."

Guards fell into step behind them. Aelthed sent one back for two goblets and multiple skins of wine.

"I do not think any wine will be required the rest of this night." The thought of taking even a sip made Rhian's stomach turn.

"It is not for you. It is for Faucon's captain. I need smooth what I am certain are his ruffled feathers."

"Melwyn will enjoy that."

"I am sure he will. And then perhaps he can help me devise a plan to keep your young man from incurring King Stephen's wrath."

Rhian snickered. "That is easy. Gold in Stephen's coffers will make him forget that Gareth did not follow orders exactly, and did not return quite as timely as expected."

Aelthed nodded. "That will be arranged."

Once inside the dense forest, the rain fell through the thick leaves as little more than a drizzle. A few of the men carried torches to light their way, making the trip easy and quick.

When the group stepped out of the forest onto the beach they were met by drawn swords.

Melwyn called for Faucon's men to hold their weapons. His eyes widened when Rhian moved forward. A smile broke his scowl and he nodded toward the larger tent in the center of the camp.

Rhian paused a moment and turned to Aelthed. The old man smiled at her. She raised up on her tiptoes and placed a kiss on his cheek. "Thank you, Uncle. I will see you on the morn."

She spun away and raced toward the tent. The sound of loud snores drifted through the flap, making it easy to slip in unnoticed. Once inside, the still-lit brazier provided enough light for Rhian to see. She peeled off her wet clothing, dropping it on the floor as she silently crossed to Gareth's pallet.

Rhian stared down at the sleeping man. One arm lay at his side, the other over his head. She'd gazed upon him once, back at Browan, when she'd marveled at his size. Then, later, in the darkness of the cave, she'd memorized every ripple of muscle, each jagged scar with her fingertips.

She drew her hungry gaze down his chest. His damp skin glistened in the fire's light. The memory of their night in the cave had not disappointed her. He was still a sight to behold. Her fingertips had remembered his form correctly.

She knew the hair on his chest, softened to a line that ran down his hard stomach and for now, disappeared beneath his braies.

As quietly as possible she dropped to her knees alongside of him. The man was trained for battle. If she touched him, would he awaken? Rhian closed her eyes and offered a quick prayer that he would not.

Gingerly, she reached out and easily loosened the ties that held up his only piece of clothing. While his snoring had ceased, he had not moved. His breathing had not changed.

She kept her gaze on his face and placed her hand on his stomach. A soft smile curved his lips and he leaned into her touch. But his eyelids did not flicker and his muscles did not move even a hairbreadth.

The smell of ale drifted past her nose. She winged an eyebrow. Was it possible that he dreamed in his drunken slumber? There was one way to find out.

Rhian slid her hand lower, beyond the fabric of his braies. He was hot and hard beneath her touch. The mere act of stroking the soft flesh encasing his erection set her afire. She longed to take him deep inside her, to feed the hunger that still pulsed in her veins.

Before she could lose her nerve, she inched the fabric low enough to free him. Her breath came in quick raspy pants. Her mouth was dry with the effort of trying to remain quiet.

Rhian straddled him, wondering briefly if she could do this alone. Before she made up her mind, his hands were on her hips.

She was flat on her back with him staring down at her before so much as a gasp could leave her lips. She'd forgotten how quickly he moved.

"What do you think you are doing?"

She traced his lips with her fingertip. "Is it not obvious?"

"Yes, it is. And perhaps you can explain what made you think sneaking about in this manner would be welcome."

"I apologize, *milord*." The title rolled off her tongue like a curse. "I meant not to offend you."

One day she would drive him mad. Gareth clenched

and unclenched his jaw. "It is your tone of voice that offends me. Not you."

The wind roared around the tent, slapping the fabric against the ropes.

"I am sorry. I only meant—"

"To what? Give me what I have already refused to take from you?"

She turned her head, seeking to hide her face.

He wanted to strangle her. "For the love of God, Rhian." He wanted to kiss her until time stood still. "Mere hours ago you were being given to another." Did she not understand what she was doing to him? "No matter the depth of my love for you, I cannot take what belongs to him."

Lightning ripped across the sky, filling the tent with an eerie glow.

"Evonne will marry Braedon on the morrow."

The loud beating of his heart in his ears ceased. He shook his head at the deafening silence. "What?"

"I said that Evonne—" she mumbled into his chest.

"Look at me," he said, reaching out to lift her gaze to his. He saw the truth in her eyes.

"Evonne will marry Braedon on the morrow."

"How did that happen?"

"He did not appear in my dreams."

Gareth resisted the urge to roll his eyes. He truly didn't care if it was some foolish ritual that freed her from her betrothal.

"And why did you come here?"

She frowned. "To find you."

"For what purpose?"

Rhian trailed a finger down his chest. "Well, I

thought perhaps... That maybe we could..." She stopped. He silently watched her face flush. She closed her eyes and admitted, "I am on fire, Gareth. I need your touch."

"Is it the drink, Rhian?" For some reason he could not name, that one question bothered him.

A long paused filled the tent with silence until she answered, "Yes."

"Would any man suffice?"

Another bolt from the sky lit the tent; ensuing thunder shook the ground beneath them.

Rhian looked up at him. Holding his searching stare she shook her head. "No. Only you."

His sigh of relief whispered into the night. He rolled onto his back and pulled her across his chest, holding her tightly within his arms. Her soft breasts flattened into the hardness of his chest. She twined her legs about his.

Gareth knew they would not escape this night with anything less than all. But honor dogged his mind. He twisted his fingers in her hair and brought her lips to his.

She leaned into his kiss, her need matching his desire. She drew her legs up, once again straddling him. Her fingers stroked his chest and arms.

He slid his fingers out of her hair and ran his hands down her back, whispering, "Come here."

Rhian leaned forward eagerly. Surely the emotions racing through her came from Gareth's touch and not from any drug. The emotions racing through her came from Gareth's touch. This was so much better than what she'd dreamed. Every caress came alive tenfold.

The friction of his callused hands stroking the length

of her spine made her breath hitch in her throat. His steady touch conveyed more than need, more than lust.

"Rhian." His whisper fell across her ear. The warmth and gentleness full of the same wonder filling her own heart.

She pressed tighter against the hardness of his chest. Once she had craved him; now Rhian knew that she needed him to fill the empty place in her life. This man made her whole. She hungered not only for his touch, his kiss, but for the love and safety he offered.

The warm caress of his lips against her neck made her gasp, "You will drive me to insanity." While it would be a nice sort of mindless state, it was not what she wanted, not what her body needed. She moved her lips against him. "Gareth, please."

His deep chuckle caught her off guard and he easily maneuvered her beneath him. "We have all the time in the world, love."

She parted her legs. He kissed her nose. Rhian curled her arms about his neck, but Gareth inched lower, escaping her grasp.

His cheek burned against her stomach. He paused to glance up at her, capturing her fevered gaze with his own. "If insanity is where I take you, the journey will not be made alone."

He trailed the lines of her stomach with searing hot kisses. Her flesh jumped at the touch.

Rhian's cheeks flamed as he settled between her legs. Through a fog of chaos, she knew she should be embarrassed, knew she should cry hold to his far-too-intimate exploration.

Perhaps she would…tomorrow.

The power of the storm still raging beyond the safety of the tent could in no way compare to the power of his touch.

His stroking fingers memorized her flesh, holding her spellbound.

Gareth knew she was ready for him. He could have taken her with little preparation the moment she'd entered his tent. But he wanted more than just her body.

He wanted her to need him with the same crushing desire consuming him. It was imperative that she know the depth of his feelings for her.

While he could not find the words to express himself, perhaps he could find the touch that would say all he needed to say.

Her flesh was smooth beneath his fingers and wherever he stroked, wherever he kissed, it quivered beneath his caress. Gently parting the soft curls, he waited a heartbeat for her to cry hold.

The sudden silence inside his tent told him of her hesitation. Before she could make up her mind, Gareth stroked the hot pulsing flesh with his tongue.

She tensed for one heartbeat before giving herself up to his kiss. Gareth's pounding heart urged him on. She was hot and he easily slid one finger beyond the thin barrier they would soon break through together.

Her breath caught before she moaned and tightened her muscles around the intrusion. Rhian trembled and hardened beneath his teasing tongue.

She arched her back and laced her fingers through his hair. "Gareth, please."

Her raspy plea contained all he'd wanted to hear— the crushing need that matched his own. Eager to fill that need, Gareth stretched up the length of her body, wrapped his arms around her and rolled her atop.

Rhian sat above him, breathless, determined to fill the ache he'd created. She straddled his hips. Stroking his chest and arms with shaking hands, she forced herself not to claw at his skin.

He pulled her head down for a kiss that promised something she could not yet decipher, but was willing to accept. Gareth shifted his hips beneath her and whispered, "At your will, my love."

She was more than ready for him. She had raced beyond fire many heartbeats ago. One more touch of his lips, one more stroke of his fingers would make her shatter into a myriad tiny fragments.

She brushed her breasts across his chest, drawing a low moan from his throat.

He slid one hand between her thighs, stroking, teasing her until she could again barely breathe. "Gareth, please." She begged him to end the torment.

Rhian gasped when the hot tip of his erection slid past the opening to her womb. She'd expected blinding pain. That's what she'd been told. Not this little twinge that soon changed to throbbing need.

She'd not expected the overwhelming desire to envelop his hardness fully within her. Nor had she expected the exquisite sensation of soft wet folds sheathing hot pulsing flesh.

She set the pace, fast or slow, hard or gentle, until she could stand the sweet torture no longer. Near frantic to fulfill this ever-mounting tension, she clawed at his chest. "Gareth, I don't know—"

He took control, pulling her against him, his hands

to her hips and held her in place while he brought them both the release their bodies needed.

She collapsed, sprawling across his chest, clinging to him like a vine gone wild in an unkempt garden.

When their breathing slowed and their hearts beat in a steady even rhythm, Gareth kissed the end of her nose. "Satisfied?"

She moved against him. "I am not certain. Could we try again?"

"My God, what have I done? Created a monster?"

She could not hold back her laughter at the mock horror in his voice.

"No monster, my love. But you have committed a grievous crime." She kissed the spot over his beating heart. "You have gravely wounded me." She flicked her tongue across his hardened nipple, tasting the sweat from their bodies. "You have ruined me." She moved her hips in slow lazy circles. "Completely." Then flexed her legs and moved ever so slowly up, then down. "Utterly."

Before a full giggle could escape her parted lips, he once again had her flat on her back and leaned over her.

His lips hovered near hers. "You were saying?"

Rhian wound her arms around his neck. "You need make an honest woman of me quickly, Faucon. I am a princess, not to be toyed with and then set aside."

He reached down and stroked a line from her knee, up the soft flesh on the inside of her thigh. "Hmm. I fear my mind is a muddle. Tell me again who you are."

She tightened her legs, clasping his hand between them. "I am Rhian of Gervaise, Princess of Mirabilus, soon to be Mistress of…um, what?"

"Browan."

"Egad, by all the saints above. Browan? It will require much work to make that keep a home."

Gareth lowered his head, teasing her neck with soft
kisses and gentle nips. "I am certain you are up to the task."

Rhian moaned. "Browan it is then. Soon to be Mistress of Browan."

"Tell me, soon to be Mistress of Browan, do you
have any plans for the morrow?" He pulled her arms
from around his neck and held them over her head with
one hand.

"None that I think of at the moment. What do you
have in mind?"

"Perhaps there is a clergy of some sort here who can
marry us before we get too carried away."

Rhian sighed. "I rather enjoy being carried away."

He released her, sat up on the pallet and pulled her
into his arms.

The storm outside raged with a final crash of thunder.

She leaned against his chest, suddenly serious. "I
had truly feared that you might withdraw your offer. I
was not certain—"

He lowered his head and cut off her words with a
kiss that drew a moan from her throat and set her blood
racing.

When their hearts beat as one, he broke their kiss and
pressed his lips briefly to her forehead. "Ah, my love,
had I not already vowed to carry you in my heart always? To honor you as my wife for all time?

"My offer would have stood forever." He lifted her
hand and placed it over his heart. "I could do nothing
else. All I have is yours. My heart. My soul. My love."

Rhian felt his heart beat true, strong and steady

against her palm and knew that her days of loss were at an end. "I love you, Gareth of Faucon."

"And I love you, Rhian of Gervaise."

* * * * *

THE STEEPWOOD

Scandals

Regency drama, intrigue, mischief...
and marriage

VOLUME FIVE

Counterfeit Earl by Anne Herries

Scarred after his experiences in the Peninsular War,
Captain Jack Denning feels unable to love. But caught
in a compromising situation with excitement-seeking
Olivia, a proposal is the only option!

N

The Captain's Return by Elizabeth Bailey

Captain Henry Colton is stunned to find his lost love
living as a widow. Given the way they had parted, in
anger, could he now expect Annabel to let him
back into her life?

On sale 2nd March 2007

Available at WHSmith, Tesco, ASDA,
and all good bookshops

M&B

A young woman disappears.
A husband is suspected of murder.
Stirring times for all the neighbourhood in

THE STEEPWOOD
Scandals

Volume 5 – March 2007
Counterfeit Earl by Anne Herries
The Captain's Return by Elizabeth Bailey

Volume 6 – April 2007
The Guardian's Dilemma by Gail Whitiker
Lord Exmouth's Intentions by Anne Ashley

Volume 7 – May 2007
Mr Rushford's Honour by Meg Alexander
An Unlikely Suitor by Nicola Cornick

Volume 8 – June 2007
An Inescapable Match by Sylvia Andrew
The Missing Marchioness by Paula Marshall

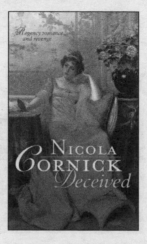

FREE

2 BOOKS AND A SURPRISE GIFT!

We would like to take this opportunity to thank you for reading this Mills & Boon® book by offering you the chance to take TWO more specially selected titles from the Historical Romance™ series absolutely FREE! We're also making this offer to introduce you to the benefits of the Mills & Boon® Reader Service™—

- ★ **FREE home delivery**
- ★ **FREE gifts and competitions**
- ★ **FREE monthly Newsletter**
- ★ **Books available before they're in the shops**
- ★ **Exclusive Reader Service offers**

Accepting these FREE books and gift places you under no obligation to buy; you may cancel at any time, even after receiving your free shipment. Simply complete your details below and return the entire page to the address below. You don't even need a stamp!

YES! Please send me 2 free Historical Romance books and a surprise gift. I understand that unless you hear from me, I will receive 4 superb new titles every month for just £3.69 each, postage and packing free. I am under no obligation to purchase any books and may cancel my subscription at any time. The free books and gift will be mine to keep in any case.

H7ZEE

Ms/Mrs/Miss/Mr...Initials ....

BLOCK CAPITALS PLEASE

Surname ....

Address ....

....

....Postcode ....

Send this whole page to:

The Reader Service, FREEPOST CN81, Croydon, CR9 3WZ